THE BATTLE OF ALL THE AGES

THE BATTLE OF ALL THE AGES

J D Davies

The Fifth Journal of Matthew Quinton

First published in 2014 by Old Street Publishing Ltd,
Yowlestone House, Tiverton, Devon EX16 8LN

www.oldstreetpublishing.co.uk

ISBN 978 1 908699 69 5

10 9 8 7 6 5 4 3 2 1

A CIP catalogue record for this title is available from the British Library.

Printed and bound in Great Britain

Typeset by Martin Worthington

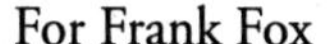

For Frank Fox

As some brave admiral, in former war,
Deprived of force, but pressed with courage still,
Two rival fleets appearing from afar,
Crawls to the top of an adjacent hill;

From whence (with thoughts full of concern) he views
The wise and daring conduct of the fight,
And each bold action to his mind renews,
His present glory, and his past delight;

From his fierce eyes, flashes of rage he throws,
As from black clouds when lightning breaks away,
Transported, thinks himself amidst his foes,
And absent yet enjoys the bloody day;

So when my days of impotence approach,
And I'm by pox and wine's unlucky chance,
Driven from the pleasing billows of debauch,
On the dull shore of lazy temperance,

My pains at last some respite shall afford,
Whilst I behold the battles you maintain,
When fleets of glasses sail about the board,
From whose broadsides volleys of wit shall reign.

John Wilmot, Earl of Rochester
(who fought during the Four Days' Battle of 1666),
extract from *The Disabled Debauchee* (c. 1680)

Prologue

'A four days' fight, young Ned,' I said. 'Well over one-hundred and fifty ships. *Four days*, I tell you. The world had never seen its like before, and perhaps it never will again.'

The keen-eyed, long-nosed young man sitting before me nodded gravely and murmured a response. I did not catch all of what he said; my hearing is as keen as it was those sixty and more years ago, when my ears were subjected to that thunderous bombardment of so many hours' duration, but these days I find that men speak so much more softly than once they did.

Unwilling to ask my youthful Cornish guest to repeat himself, I embarked upon the speech I had addressed to a hundred and more young officers like him over the years.

'I knew them all, of course. All of those who commanded under our flag, back then in the early years of good King Charles's reign: Prince Rupert, aye, and the Duke of Albemarle, too, General Monck that was, the very man who brought the king and monarchy itself back to these isles. And the rest of them, England's famous paladins of the sea. Myngs, Holmes, Spragge – legends all. My dear friend Will Berkeley. Let me tell you, young Ned, there was never a surer friend to a man than poor Will, nor one whose reputation was more unjustly maligned –'

I noticed that the lad seated opposite me in my oak-panelled, tome-strewn library was saying something. I was about to damn his impertinence for interrupting me, but the faculties sometimes play tricks on one: he had not raised his voice, but suddenly I was hearing his words as clearly as if my dear Cornelia were whispering in my ear upon the pillow once again.

'- But, sir, what was it truly that brought about the division of our fleet, and brought us to such a terrible condition that the Dutch could outnumber us so dreadfully?'

He was sharp indeed, this lad who was some sort of connection of the grandson of one of my old Cornish following during those halcyon days after the restoration of King Charles the Second, an age now as remote to most young blades of Ned's age as that of Noah seems to me. He had passed the examination for lieutenant a year or two before, but like so many of his vintage he still had no commission: and that was the simple truth which had brought him to my door, in the almost certainly vain hope that an ancient man's intercession might lead to his promotion.

'Ah, the mystery of why our fleet was divided in the year 1666,' I said, very slowly, as though I was hearing of the calamity for the first time. 'Why Rupert and his ships were sent west to meet a threat that proved an illusion, leaving the rest of us to be pounded very nearly to Hell by the great De Ruyter and all his proud Dutchmen.' I studied the young man's clean, eager face. Like every single one of his generation, he had never experienced a fleet battle; had never even experienced the smallest fight at sea. Could he really conceive of the noise, and the smell, and the slaughter, that I lived through during those four days so very long ago? 'All those good men dead, and for a falsehood –'

My words drifted away, for my mind was no longer in the library with the young man. It was flown far away, to the distant but still well-remembered land that was the first day of June, 1666, amid the chain-shot, the blood and the death. I fancied I held a sword in my hand again as my command exchanged broadsides with Dutchman after Dutchman…

My guest was mouthing something – asking if I was well, or some such youthful nonsense, not realising that no man who has lived almost four score years and ten is truly well. But his concerned mumbling recalled me unwillingly to time and place.

'The cause of the division of the fleet. Well now, Ned, that's a question indeed. Was it heinous conspiracy and treachery or pure accident? I pondered it at the time, of course, as did all of England. But it has not greatly occupied my thoughts since –'

Even as I uttered the words, I knew they were a lie, and prayed that my voice did not betray my duplicity. For the question of the true cause of the division of the fleet, and thus of the terrible battle that sprang from it, had occupied my thoughts very much. It occupied them in those fleeting moments during the four days of Hell we endured in the North Sea when we were not entirely concerned with destroying the Dutch, or preventing them destroying us: *Why? In the name of God, why has this disaster happened? Where are Prince Rupert's ships? Why are all these good men dying?* It occupied them in the days immediately after the battle, when I did rather more than ponder the possibility that our fleet's predicament might be attributable to conspiracy: unless fighting for one's life against the dark power of implacable enemies may be termed 'pondering'. It occupied them on many occasions thereafter, even after I learned the perverse and astonishing truths of the matter.

I looked across at my young guest, and considered telling him the truth; even the truth which I had dared not admit to myself for all these years. But would he believe it? And in any case, what good would it do him, so very long afterwards?

'No, young Ned,' I said, 'It is a history as dead as Julius Caesar. We are fortunate enough to live in an age of prolonged peace, and if you ever hoist your flag, I do not think the lessons of what we endured in the year Sixty-Six will be of much use to you.' He said something, but I did not hear it. 'For what it is worth, I will write on your behalf to the First Lord of the Admiralty, My Lord Torrington. But I fear my recommendation carries little weight these days, when the navy is full of the creatures of our Hanoverian dynasty's royal mistresses and those of our esteemed Prime Minister.' The lad looked at me dumbfounded, for in these lessened times, to criticise either our German monarch or his chosen instrument, Sir Robert Walpole, is akin to farting in the face of a nun. 'No, Ned, I fear it is your abilities, and they alone, that will decide your fate. Your abilities and the goddess of fortune, of course. For all we know, at this very moment a commission made out to you might be sitting upon a desk in the Admiralty, consigning you to be lieutenant of some pestilential sloop in the Caribbee and thus perhaps to fester in an unmarked grave in the Barbadoes within six months.' I essayed a smile, although God knows what the effect of it was upon a young beholder studying the creasing of cracked lips in my ancient, wrinkled face. 'Or else, of course,' I said, 'you may prosper. Perhaps glory, promotion, even a peerage and a landed estate, await you in the years that I will never live to see. Perhaps one day, as it roams the Elysian Fields, my shade will be able to look down and raise an invisible glass of nectar to toast the inestimable victories of Admiral Lord Hawke.'

Part One

THE FOUR DAYS' BATTLE

Chapter One

THE FIRST DAY: FRIDAY, 1 JUNE 1666:
11 AM to 12.30 PM

First paint me George and Rupert, rattling far
Within one box, like the two dice of war,
And let the terror of their linked name
Fly through the air like chain shot, tearing fame.
Jove in one cloud did scarcely ever wrap
Lightning so fierce, but never such a clap!
United Generals! Sure the only spell
Wherewith United Provinces to quell.
Alas, e'en they, though shell'd in treble oak,
Will prove an addle egg with double yolk.

Andrew Marvell, *Third Advice to a Painter* (1666)

'Eighty-one. Eighty-two. Eighty-three. Eighty-four. Eighty-five. Eighty-six.' Lieutenant Christopher Farrell lowered his telescope and turned to look directly at me. 'They outnumber us by thirty, Sir Matthew.'

The horizon to the east-south-east was filled with hulls and sails. The metal-grey sea was rough, whipped up by a strong, warm, blustery south-westerly breeze; Kit Farrell had seemed to take an eternity to count the number of ships opposing us, for the distant vessels kept vanishing behind the swell. Even so, I could still make out the colours flying from the enemy's ensign staffs and topmasts. The Dutch colours.

'For a fleet that's supposed still to be in harbour, they seem quite remarkably seaborne,' I said sarcastically. 'God bless our spies in Holland, who are paid so well for their invaluable intelligence.'

'Forgive the ignorance of a landsman, Sir Matthew,' said the youth at my side, in a tone at once haughty and irreverent, 'but if the enemy outnumbers our fleet so heavily, why are we advancing toward it? Why are we not withdrawing discreetly into the safety of the Thames? Why are we, if I may be so bold as to venture the word, *attacking*?'

'Because, My Lord,' I began, 'His Grace –'

'Because,' interrupted Phineas Musk, the barrel-shaped, bald creature who served nominally as my clerk, 'His Grace the Duke of Albemarle, that was General Monck, that was the man who restored the King, that is our beloved general-at-sea. His Grace thinks as highly of the Dutch as he does of a dog-turd on the sole of his shoe. If he was out alone in a row-boat against the fleet yonder, he'd still consider the odds to be in his favour. My Lord.'

I scowled at Musk; such sentiments ought not to be expressed loudly upon the quarterdeck, where various mates and topmen could hear them. But Musk, an ancient retainer of the Quinton family, had somehow acquired the sort of licence that kings once gave their court jesters. He spoke the brutal truths that most men preferred to dissemble, and seemed perfectly impervious to any reprimand. Besides, he was entirely correct. At the council-of-war two days previously, I myself had heard the obese old Duke of Albemarle's contemptuous dismissal of our Dutch enemy, uttered in his broad Devon brogue: 'A land of atheistical cheese-mongers wallowing in bog-mud, gentlemen. Cowards to a man. One good English broadside and they'll run for home, shitting themselves in fright.' The Duke's confidence seemed not to have been shaken a jot by the loss of nearly a third of his fleet, despatched west under his joint general-at-sea, Prince Rupert of the Rhine, to intercept the French fleet that was reported to be coming up the Channel to join its Dutch allies, or else perhaps to stop the French invading Ireland, or Wales, or the Isle of Wight. No man seemed entirely certain what the French were meant to be doing, which was ominous. The prince had been recalled, but God knew where he was, or how long it would take his ships to return.

'Ah yes,' said my young companion, 'His Grace. Never was the ducal address of honour so inappropriate. Was there ever such an ungraceful Duke in England as poor, fat old Georgie Monck?'

I frowned. There were men within earshot, and it did not do for them to hear their betters denigrating those who were better still. But I could say nothing. The lad was an Earl, and I was merely the brother and heir to an Earl. He was also given a quite remarkable degree of licence by the King, and, it was said, an even more remarkable degree of it by virtually every woman in London, from bawds to baronesses. By many of the men, too, allegedly; and, as some would have it, even by some of the animals. It was no surprise that his eyes were already old and tired, with bags beneath them that bore witness to far too many debauches. His shirt was open to the waist: to emulate the seamen, he claimed, though few of them were so underdressed in such a strong breeze, and none wore shirts of the finest silk. I suspected that the young man's display of his bare chest might have been prompted by other, and rather baser, considerations. For this was John Wilmot, the young Earl of Rochester, come to sea as a volunteer on my ship, so that he could demonstrate his bravery to – well, it was not entirely clear which of his recent *amours* of any gender or species he was meant to be demonstrating it to. His father and my brother, the enigmatic Earl of Ravensden, had been friends and allies in exile, forever plotting to overthrow Cromwell and restore King Charles to his throne, and this connection proved sufficient to place the poetically-inclined young Earl aboard my ship. In a moment of weakness, I even agreed that My Lord could bring with him his pet monkey, an astonishingly evil creature that now gazed at me malevolently from its favoured perch in the mizzen shrouds.

'Your orders, Sir Matthew?' said Lieutenant Farrell, although he knew full well what my orders were going to be. We seemed to have known each other for an eternity, although in truth it was less than five years since the life of Captain Matthew Quinton, heir to an earldom, had been saved by the stocky, illiterate young Wapping tar Kit Farrell. We made a bargain, that day when the *Happy Restoration* was wrecked off Kinsale: I taught Kit how to read and write, and in return, he taught me the way of the sea.

'We will clear for action, Mister Farrell.'

All around us, trumpets were blowing and drums beating as our consorts in the White Squadron began to do the same, pulling down the partitions below decks to create unobstructed spaces for the guns. Our fleet was forming into line of battle, but with no regard for any formal order. We were in a desperate hurry to be at the Dutch, and ships fell in wherever they could. Those flying the ensign of the Red Squadron, which should have been in the centre, intermingled with we of the White, which should have formed the vanguard of the fleet.

Kit moved stiffly to the rail and barked the necessary orders. Only a few months earlier, during my previous commission, both he and Phineas Musk had taken bad wounds in a sea-fight with a great Danish man-of-war. By rights, both should have been ashore, regaining their strength; but only death itself would have prevented my two mismatched companions from standing alongside Captain Sir Matthew Quinton on the quarterdeck as we sailed into battle. Kit needed the pay, and the prospect of glory and promotion that battle presented; Musk seemed to regard himself as the unlikely guardian angel of the entire Quinton family. Even so, the two men, one old, the other young, were moving about the heeling deck rather more slowly and delicately than usual. In truth, they resembled a pair of ducks, waddling inelegantly upon a steeply sloping river bank.

Our own trumpets sounded, and the drums beat out a steady rhythm. Officers' whistles sounded their shrill commands. Canvas fights were slung across the decks: protective nets, these, to offer the men some rudimentary concealment against enemy fire. From below came the unmistakeable sound of partitions being taken down, sea chests being thrown into the hold, and gunports being opened. The ship was being made ready for her first battle.

The prospect had an enervating effect upon the crew. Even if many were privately terrified, fatalistic or prayerful, all joined lustily in song after song: the hoary old favourites of the English seaman since time immemorial. From laments for loves left ashore to obscene denunciations of the Dutch, the men went through them all, and with a substantial leavening of Cornishmen, this was a crew that could sing better than any in the fleet. I even found myself joining in.

'They eat up our fish, without reason or laws, but now they are going to pay for the sauce!'

Lord Rochester clapped enthusiastically, leering as he did so at Denton, the young servant-lad who was attending me.

Suddenly, there came a shout from the ship's waist: 'God bless Sir Matthew and his mighty prick!'

That brought a cheer and some laughter. I saw the eyes of those on the quarterdeck fix upon me, waiting to see my reaction. Kit, standing closest to me, was particularly pensive, no doubt concerned at his proximity to an explosion from a captain outraged by such insolence. The sly, obnoxious Lancelot Parks, resplendent in his yellow uniform as Captain of the new-fangled Marine detachment that we carried, stared at me eagerly, awaiting my word to despatch one of his men to deal with the miscreant who had taken the name of the ship and its captain in vain. But Phineas Musk merely sniggered, while Lord Rochester grinned, he being especially partial to jests about cocks and cunnies. My command, the *Royal Sceptre*, was new, one of the big Third Rates that had emerged from the royal dockyards within the last couple of summers. But the more irreverent members of my company – that is to say, very nearly all of them – had promptly rechristened her 'the king's prick'. Knowing our sovereign lord rather better than the lowest grommet or swabber, I wondered whether the very same mischievous thought had actually been in His Majesty's mind when he christened her. It would not have surprised me, and that thought shaped my response to the insolent shout from forward.

I strode to the quarterdeck rail, gripping it tightly as the ship heeled hard to larboard in the strong wind.

'Well, then, my brave lads!' I shouted. 'Let's show the Dutch butterboxes what a great English prick can do! Let's thrust it and thrust it again until we've truly pricked the Hollanders' pride!'

I offered up a silent prayer of thanks that my Dutch wife Cornelia was not within earshot. I would have suffered mightily for such a tirade against her country of birth; moreover, there was every likelihood that her twin brother Cornelis commanded one of the ships that we were fast closing. But my little speech served its purpose. My crew, many of whom were stout-hearted Cornishmen who had served with me since my second commission, cheered me lustily, waving their fists in the air. But as I smiled, laughed and waved with them, I could not but think upon the odds that we faced, and the two strange circumstances that had brought us to this pass. Why had we received no word of the Dutch being at sea? Above all, why had Prince Rupert and the rest of our fleet been detached, and where in the name of God were they?

* * *

But we were not the only fleet with questions to answer. As we began to fall down toward the Dutch, the enemy's ships came into view ever more clearly. Until then, the strength of the breeze and the choppy waters had concealed a startling fact about our opponents: they were at anchor. Many of them still had their sails furled. Even now, over four hours after the fleets had first sighted each other, only the squadron nearest to us appeared to be getting under way. The sight of their sails filling with the breeze had fooled both Kit Farrell and myself: the bulk of the fleet behind them was immobile. Moreover, many of their ships were far off to the north-east, and would only be able to come into action against us with great difficulty. If the Duke of Albemarle was being unwarrantably bold, then his adversary, the much-vaunted Lieutenant-Admiral Michiel De Ruyter, seemed to be almost suicidally complacent.

'Well, Lieutenant,' I said to Kit, 'what do you make of it?'

My friend and I had our telescopes fixed upon the enemy. I could make out the distinctive ensigns of the five Dutch admiralties: there, the three-barred Prince banner of the Maas and Friesland; there, the nine-barred Triple Prince of Amsterdam and the North Quarter of Holland; there, the Vlissingen ewer jack of Zeeland, where I had lived in exile before the King's restoration and had acquired a wife. And, just as plainly, I could make out the anchor cables that secured the mighty fleet of the United Provinces to the bottom of the North Sea.

'They cannot have expected us to fight today,' Kit said. 'With the strength of the wind, and our weakness in numbers, it would be a reasonable conclusion to draw. De Ruyter will probably have expected us to retire into the Thames. That would have been the strategy of any prudent admiral.'

The *Royal Sceptre* heeled even further to larboard. The same was true of the rest of the fleet. We were a glorious sight, bearing down upon the enemy in what was still a rudimentary, incomplete line of battle. Sails filled, flapped and roared in the strong breeze. Spray broke over our bows and those of our fellows as we rode the heavy sea. Yet magnificent as the spectacle was, it betrayed our weakness. We were fewer in number, as Kit Farrell said, but that was not all.

'Nor will De Ruyter expect us to engage when hamstrung,' I said.

I went to the larboard rail and looked down. The sea was swelling and breaking above the lower deck gunports, which were closed against the treacherous waters. The same was true of every one of our consorts.

The eager Rochester joined me.

'Hamstrung, Sir Matthew? How are we hamstrung?'

'We will be engaging the Dutch to larboard, My Lord – that is, fighting them from this side of the ship. Yet the wind is making us heel – that is, pushing us over – so far in that direction that we cannot use our lower deck guns. Our demi-cannon – that is, our heaviest guns, firing thirty-two pounds balls – are on that deck. Whereas the same wind will lift all the Dutch batteries well clear of the water.'

The young man seemed perplexed by this; as, indeed, the young Matthew Quinton had once been. 'How can this be, Sir Matthew?'

'It is our English fashion to cram as many heavy guns as possible into every conceivable space on the ship, My Lord, especially low down. So when we are able to lie side by side against the Dutch in a light sea, we have the advantage and can batter their hulls to hell and back. They carry lighter guns, and fewer of them, mounted higher in their hulls. But our ships sit much deeper in the water than theirs, so in a sea like this, we dare not open the lower ports.'

Just then, we heard cheering from the ships that were close to us. I looked astern, and saw a very familiar ship bearing down rapidly, all sail set as she overtook the entire van. She was a fine spectacle: the *Swiftsure*, old but still mighty, mounting seventy-two great cannon. A large white flag streamed from her foretopmast. My own men ran to the ship's rail, shouting and waving. Her quarterdeck drew parallel to ours, and I was barely three-hundred yards from her captain, whose familiar long-nosed face broke into a broad grin. He raised his feathered hat, and I replied in kind.

'Leave some of the Dutch for the rest of us, Will!' I cried through my voice trumpet.

'Best put on more sail then, Matt, or else De Ruyter himself will be my prisoner before noon!'

I laughed. It was good to see Will in high spirits again; or, to give him his proper due, Sir William Berkeley, Vice-Admiral of the White and as such my divisional commander, one of my oldest and dearest friends. I had a painful recollection of a drunken evening in a Holborn tavern, some weeks earlier, when Will, far gone in his cups, bemoaned the whispers and barbs that had come his way since the previous summer. His conduct during the Battle of Lowestoft, our crushing victory over the Dutch, had been singled out for criticism: 'Children in the street taunt me for cowardice, Matt,' he slurred, 'and I cannot bear that. In the next fight, I will do whatever it takes to restore my reputation. Whatever it takes.'

Although it was a warm June morning, the thought chilled me. I stopped laughing, drew my sword, and brought it up grimly in the traditional warrior's salute. Will, too, became serious. He nodded slowly, then drew his own blade and returned the salute. A moment later and he was out of sight, obscured by the *Swiftsure*'s stern rail and her huge ensign. But something about the *Swiftsure*'s course struck me as strange. The same thought evidently occurred to Kit Farrell, who came up by my side.

'He's luffing up to windward. Why in God's name is he doing that?'

Will Berkeley's course was taking his ship steadily toward the south-west, closer and closer to the wind: in other words, further away from the Dutch fleet he had seemed so intent on attacking but a few minutes earlier. It was exactly the opposite course to one which a man weighed down by charges of cowardice should have been following.

'No signal,' I said. 'None that I have seen, at any rate – either from him to us, or from the Duke to him. But we have to follow him, Kit. We are his second in the division. Whatever is in Will's mind, we have no choice.'

'Oh for the honour of the navy, for the honour of the Quintons,' said Musk sarcastically.

I gave my command to Philemon Hardy, the thin, grey-haired ship's master, who greeted it with open-mouthed astonishment. Nevertheless, he was too good an officer to question his captain's order. Men scuttled aloft to adjust the sails, which strained noisily against the wind. Orders went to the helmsman to bring the whipstaff over. The *Royal Sceptre*, and the other half-dozen ships of the Vice-Admiral of the White's division, began to fall into the wake of their flagship, moving steadily away from the main body of the fleet. Away from the Dutch.

'This is wrong, Sir Matthew,' said Kit, emphatically. 'He has no cause to do this –'

'Perhaps he is thinking of the Lowestoft fight, last year, when we of the Red stood to windward, waiting and watching to see where we could attack to best effect.' I levelled my telescope on the quarterdeck of the *Swiftsure*, but could obtain no clear sight of Will Berkeley. 'But in that battle, we had equal numbers. Now, we only stand a chance of winning if every ship attacks immediately –'

A gun boomed out. We were too far from the enemy for the engagement to have begun; thus I knew at once what it was. Albemarle had fired off a recall order. He was commanding Will to close up again with the main body of the fleet: to take up his rightful station in the van of the fleet, a station which, by implication, he had deserted. There could not have been a more humiliating, or a more public, reproof.

'God in Heaven,' I said, 'what effect will this have on Will? The aspersions of cowardice from last year already haunt him like angry ghosts, and now the Duke dishonours him before the entire fleet.'

Kit and Musk said nothing. They knew, as I did, that George Monck, Duke of Albemarle, hated gentleman captains. Like many about the court, the duke resented Will Berkeley's rapid rise from lieutenant to admiral in five years, promotion that had been due entirely to his family's influence with the King. Albemarle would relish any opportunity to humble the proud young man, and Will's inexplicable manoeuvre, executed for God alone knew what reason, had given him the perfect excuse to do so.

But as I gave the orders that would bring the *Royal Sceptre* back into the line of battle, close to the very front of the fleet, I knew that Albemarle's hatred was not confined to Will Berkeley alone. I had seen his eyes on me at councils-of-war, and I knew what was in his thoughts. I was almost exactly the same age as my friend. I, too, had risen rapidly to high command and a knighthood, at least in part because my brother was close to the King. I, too, had not been able to tell one end of a ship from another barely five years before. Thus I knew that in the eyes of the Duke of Albemarle, our general-at-sea and supreme commander, I was nothing but another worthless gentleman captain. He did not hate Will Berkeley alone: he hated me, too.

* * *

For the next hour or more, I was concerned only with my own ship. I went below, ducking low even on the main gun deck, moving among my crew. They were busy making ready for battle. Great guns were being polished, the cartridges and shot being made ready. Hogsheads of water and soaked blankets were being moved into position, ready to subdue any fires that broke out. Some of the men who could write were making wills, or writing letters to loved ones; those who could not were importuning those who could to write such things for them. Some were murmuring prayers or psalms.

I stopped from time to time to talk to individual gun crews. I knew most of these men well: I respected them, and I flattered myself that they respected me. Many of them were Cornish, originally part of the crew of the frigate *Jupiter*, whose command I had inherited in strange circumstances some years before. In due course, they became my own following – volunteers who, for some unfathomable reason, preferred to serve under me rather than any other captain.

'Durdatha whye, Jowan!'

'Dew boz geno, Syr Mathi!'

Thus I exchanged some of the only Cornish words I knew with John Treninnick, a shambling, bent creature whom one could have mistaken for a cripple. But his condition was caused by many years of labouring in the confined seams of the tin mines; in truth, Treninnick was one of the strongest men and nimblest seamen that a captain could wish to have in his crew. Alongside him stood his messmates, the minute John Tremar and the vast George Polzeath. Dozens of Cornishmen with names profoundly alien to an English ear thronged the deck: Trezise the cooper, Trevaskis the armourer, Carkeek, Hobba, Gummo, Penaluna, and all the rest of them. I had acquired some even more exotic followers during my previous commissions: the likes of Ali Reis, a Moorish renegade, Julian Carvell, a runaway Virginian slave now serving as my coxswain, and Macferran, a fiery-haired young Scots fisherman. These were men I would trust with my life, proven fighters who formed the backbone of a ship's company that was otherwise largely unknown to me: many of the new recruits were pressed men, chiefly Londoners and northerners, and although most of them seemed to be experienced hands, I had no notion of how they might perform under fire. Several of them eyed me suspiciously, and it occurred to me in that moment that they were thinking exactly the same thing about me. A gentleman captain, no more than five years at sea and only just twenty-six years of age: so just how would this jumped up young royal favourite, Sir Matthew Quinton, behave himself in battle?

But there was an even more troubling element to the composition of my crew. I encountered it on the lower gun deck, where the ports remained firmly closed against the choppy waters beyond. The dimly lit space could easily have been taken for a bastion of a fortress under siege.

It contained five dozen soldiers, uniformed in yellow tunic-coats, busily engaged in the tasks that consume soldiers before any battle: filling bandoliers, sharpening swords and pikes, cleaning muskets.

Lancelot Parks stepped in front of me and bowed his head in salute. His young Ensign, a keen and bright-eyed lad named Lovell, stood slightly behind him and did the same.

'Your men are ready for the fray, Captain Parks?'

'Ready to write a glorious first chapter in our regiment's history, Sir Matthew!'

'Let us hope so, Captain. Let us hope so.'

We exchanged a few more words, but then I beat a hasty retreat. I found Parks almost unbearable: he had about him the eagerness and arrogance that only those who have not experienced battle can possess, and it seemed to me that his example was likely to ruin the prospects of young Lovell. But as I made my way back up the ladders toward the quarterdeck, I knew that I had other, more personal reasons for turning my back on the Marines of the Lord Admiral's Regiment. Once, I had wanted nothing more than to be an officer of the King's army; indeed, that was what I had been, albeit briefly, albeit only in the tiny Royalist army-in-exile. Now, though, I looked upon soldiers as all sailors did, namely, as creatures with the intelligence, grace and usefulness of crabs. This new Marine regiment, as yet largely untried in battle, was a case in point. Worse, our governors had decided in their wisdom that these sea-soldiers should replace a significant number of sailors in the larger ships of the fleet. Unsurprisingly, those who knew how to reef and haul resented the fact that they had to put in extra watches to make up for the presence of so many ignorant landsmen. The lower deck lawyers who somehow fetch up in every crew exploited this by promoting the notion that the soldiers were aboard ship, not to fight the Dutch more effectively, but to cow and bully the seamen. Thus there had already been several fights on the *Sceptre*, many more on some of the other ships of the fleet. I prayed that when it came to close quarters fighting with the Dutch, our men would remember exactly who it was they were meant to be killing.

I returned to the quarterdeck. Now, at last, there was evidently activity in the Dutch ranks. But it was not a form of activity that I had anticipated.

Kellett, the bravest and most able of my young servants, handed me my telescope. I joined Kit Farrell and Rochester at the larboard rail. The latter had acquired a telescope of his own, presumably from one of the master's mates, but he might as well have been looking through it from the wrong end.

'They are fleeing, by God!' he cried. His tone was at once exultant and disappointed: he could see his hopes of impressing countless young ladies (or lads) of the court with tales of martial valour vanishing upon the wind.

I studied the Dutch fleet. 'Whatever they are doing, My Lord,' I said, 'they are most certainly not fleeing. That is not the Dutch way. But it remains to be seen just what they *are* doing.'

The furthest divisions of the Dutch fleet, off toward the south-east, were still entirely immobile. Among them was a ship flying, at both her mainmast head and ensign staff, the tricolour of the United Provinces of the Netherlands. It could only be the flagship of the admiral commanding the Dutch fleet. Yet the famed De Ruyter seemed asleep, as though there was no English fleet advancing toward him at all.

The same could not be said of the nearer squadrons. As I watched through my telescope, I saw three ships cut their anchor cables in their haste to be under way. At the heart of this more active cohort was another great ship flying a Dutch tricolour from the main.

'Tromp is in a mighty hurry,' I said. 'Perhaps he seeks to avenge his father.'

Cornelis Tromp, Admiral of Amsterdam, was the son of the great Maarten Tromp, who had been killed by Cromwell's fleet during the first war between ourselves and the Dutch; a fleet commanded by the same man whose flag now flew from the *Royal Charles*, General George Monck, the Duke of Albemarle.

'Not only a hurry, Sir Matthew,' said Kit Farrell, who was studying the motion of the Dutch ships intently. 'He is forming a line of battle.'

'By God, so he is,' I said. 'They have learned their lesson at last.'

'A line of battle, Sir Matthew? What is that, pray?'

I turned sharply toward Rochester, but just in time, I remembered that not too many years before, the young Matthew Quinton would have asked just such a question. Thus I answered patiently, like a teacher addressing a particularly backward pupil. In truth, the noble lord's monkey, perched on the ship's rail close to me and leaning forward with seeming attentiveness, gave the appearance of the more promising student.

'During the first war between ourselves and the Dutch, My Lord, back in Cromwell's time, we adopted a new tactic, the line of battle – having all our ships follow each other, in a great single line. This allowed us to bring to bear, and make best use of, the massive weight of shot from our broadsides. The Dutch, though, preferred their old method of charging head-on, aiming to close and board.' Rochester nodded, although his pained expression reminded me of a schoolboy trying to conjugate particularly complex Latin verbs. 'The results were devastating, and to our advantage. During both the late war and the first battle of this one, the Lowestoft fight last year, the sheer power of our broadsides shattered the smaller Dutch ships and drove them from the sea.'

In truth, it had not been quite so simple; but I doubted whether the noble Lord could cope with such niceties as the myriad factors that could affect a fleet's rate of fire. As it was, he seemed satisfied with my explanation. But as we watched Tromp's ships fall into line ahead, one after the other, it was clear that a new game was afoot. An unknown game, where both fleets fought in line, not just one. A game in which the Duke of Albemarle's confidence might prove misplaced.

Both fleets were now moving south-east, away from the coast of England and toward that of Flanders, but on converging courses. Very soon, we would be within range. I called my officers together, received their reports, and despatched them to their stations with words of encouragement. On the whole, they were a good body of men: a new ship like the *Royal Sceptre* was a plum post, and there was always ferocious competition for such offices. Hardy, the master, was a younger brother of Trinity House, a veteran seaman who had commanded merchantmen in the Levant and Virginia trades. Richardson, the carpenter, had been a shipwright in the royal dockyard at Portsmouth. He knew his business, but was a silent, sullen man who grew animated only when attempting to explain his unfathomable conviction that he knew how to build a four-decked ship. Burdett, the gunner, was an old Parliament-man who had served in the New Model Army's siege train; although this made him anathema to some of the Cornish, who were Cavaliers to a man, he clearly knew his business and seemed a quiet, discreet man. Urquhart, the boatswain, was a Scotsman bred up in the king's navy, learning the ropes in the great Ship Money fleets. He seemed able enough, although I regretted that his appointment meant I was unable to secure the office for Martin Lanherne, the valiant Cornishman who had been with me since my second command. Rather than serve under another, Lanherne had returned to his native county to serve in the press gangs; I pitied any unsuspecting young Cornishman who encountered him on a quiet country lane.

As on any ship, the complement of warrant officers was completed by a purser (Stride, a fawning Irishman appointed through the influence of the Duke of Ormonde), a surgeon (Rowan, an elderly man who seemed positively to relish the feel and sound of a blade sawing through bone), a cook (Prentice, who had lost a leg in the Gabbard fight), and a chaplain. The latter was a strongly built, dark haired man of middle years clad in a simple cassock. He emerged from below, looked about the deck and over towards the Dutch fleet, then picked up a musket from a stand upon the deck and aimed it toward the fast-approaching Tromp.

'So is it a good day for killing Dutchmen, Sir Matthew?' he asked in his familiar Shropshire accent.

'If God wills it, Francis. As I expect you will tell us shortly.'

The Reverend Francis Gale smiled, strode up to the quarterdeck, called the men in the waist to gather before him, and launched into the prayer before battle prescribed in the Book of Common Prayer.

> *'Oh most powerful and glorious Lord God, the Lord of Hosts, that rulest and commandest all things; thou sittest in the throne judging right, and therefore we make our address to thy Divine Majesty in this our necessity, that thou wouldst take the cause into thine own hand, and judge between us and our enemy –'*

Francis Gale was now the respected vicar of Ravensden, but when I first encountered him, he was the sottish chaplain of my second command, the frigate *Jupiter*, tormented by the brutal killing of the love of his life during Cromwell's attack on Drogheda. Francis attained peace of mind in those same bloody hours of battle when I discovered my vocation as a seaman. We became fast friends, and, at my behest, my brother, the Earl, subsequently presented him to the living. But Francis Gale was not a man to be long content with the comforts of a country parish. He served with me in two of my subsequent commands, proving equally adept at exorcising evil spirits and wielding a cutlass against the enemies of Old England. I was somewhat surprised that the Earl and the Dowager Countess had consented to yet another leave of absence to enable Francis to serve with me at sea, but Charles explained all before I left London to join my command.

'I am content,' said the Earl of Ravensden, 'and more importantly, so is our mother. She has been in transports of delight since that troublesome tinker Bunyan was thrown back into Bedford gaol, and commends Francis for his part in the arrest. The dissenters of the Hundred are much discouraged, and skulk behind their hedgerows. So I think that in this present moment, mother would grant the Reverend Gale anything he asked, even her hand in marriage.'

I laughed, for Francis's flattery of the venerable Dowager Countess of Ravensden was entirely shameless. In turn, she, for whom the word virago might have been coined, was known to blush and simper in his presence like the most innocent of virgins.

'Stir up thy strength, oh Lord, and come and help us; for thou givest not away the battle to the strong, but canst save by many or by few. Oh let not our sins now cry against us for vengeance –'

'The bloody flag!'

The cry came from the lookout at the maintop. I ran to the stern rail, snatched my telescope from Kellett, and focused on the vast, unmistakeable shape of the flagship *Royal Charles*, some ten or twelve places behind us in the line, spray cascading over her huge bows as she breasted the waves. There, at her foretop, flew an enormous plain red flag.

The bloody flag.

The signal for every ship to fall upon the enemy and fight to the death.

Chapter Two

THE FIRST DAY: 1 JUNE 1666: 12.30 PM to 6 PM

Monck yet prevents him ere the navies meet
And charges in, himself alone a fleet,
And with so quick and frequent motion wound
His murd'ring sides about, the ship seem'd round,
And the exchanges of his circles tire
Like whirling hoops show'd of triumphal fire.
Single he does at their whole navy aim,
And shoots them through a porcupine of flame.
Andrew Marvell, *Third Advice to a Painter* (1666)

'Ready, Mister Burdett!' I raised my sword. 'On my command – wait – wait –' I brought the sword down.'*As each gun bears, give fire!*'

The larboard broadside of the *Royal Sceptre* fired in anger for the first time. The deck shuddered as the culverins down on the upper deck fired and recoiled. Likewise, the short demi-culverin cuts on the quarterdeck belched flame and recoiled across the deck until held by the tackle. I felt the familiar kick in the chest and stomach, heard the roar that sometimes deafened those unaccustomed to it. The crews immediately set to, scouring and cooling the gun barrels before ramming home the ladles bearing the powder charges, then the wadding, then the great round balls themselves. Although the wind blew most of the smoke away, enough of it swirled back over the deck to fill my nostrils with the now-familiar acrid stench. I stole a glance at the Earl of Rochester, for I knew this was his first experience of war. His open mouth and streaming eyes made it plain that his battle virginity had been well and truly deflowered. As if to echo the emotions of its master, his monkey let out an unearthly shriek and disappeared below decks.

I squinted through the smoke, trying to make out the extent of the damage, if any, to our opposite number, a fifty-gunner of the Amsterdam admiralty. Burdett came onto the quarterdeck to report, but before he could speak, the flames of our opponent's broadside spat defiance from her gunports. I heard the whoosh and whistle of chain- and bar-shot, but it was well above me. I looked up and saw three or four holes in the main course, one or two in the fore.

Burdett saluted. 'Reckon we put half a dozen balls into her hull, Sir Matthew. But most fell well short. Difficult to get the aim right in this heavy a sea. Same for them, of course, which is why they've fired so high.'

'Very well, Mister Burdett. Do your best, once we have reloaded.'

'If only we could use the demi-cannon on the lower deck, Sir Matthew. Then, it would be a different matter.'

Francis Gale, standing nearby and cradling a musket incongruously against his cassock, nodded. 'I shall pray for a calm sea, Master Gunner.'

'Amen to that, Reverend.'

With that, Burdett returned to oversee the reloading of the guns on the upper deck.

'Why is it that we fire low and the Dutch fire high, Sir Matthew?' Rochester asked.

'It is not a universal rule that they do this and we do that, My Lord,' I said, 'but in general, our ships have more guns than theirs: Dutch ships must be smaller than ours to navigate the shoals off their coast, and their harbours are shallow. And theirs are often lighter built than ours, with less heavy scantlings.' I saw the mist cloud his eyes once again. 'The dimensions of the frames and the beams,' I said. Still the mist swirled. 'The thickness of the wood.' At last, some sort of understanding seemed to dawn. 'So usually, but not always, we fire into their hulls from a distance, hoping to kill their guncrews and break their spirit –'

As if to illustrate my point, our second broadside fired, Burdett now having my authority to fire at his own discretion. A shot struck the Amsterdammer in the very middle of the hull, next to one of the gunports. A jagged gap appeared, as if the wood was merely paper that had been punched through, and even across several hundred yards of open water, the screams of men on the gun deck were clearly audible. The Amsterdammer fired off her response almost at once. Rochester ducked, but for a second time, almost all of her shot passed well above our heads.

'We fire into the hulls from a distance, hoping to cripple the ship that way,' I said. 'They fire for our masts and rigging, hoping to disable us, allowing them to close and board. But with the sea as it is, My Lord, it is devilishly difficult for either of us to make our shot strike where we wish it to. The only blessing is that we have the wind, which means we determine the range – the only way the Dutchman, yonder, can carry out his preferred tactic of boarding us is to come up into the wind, and that we will not let him do.'

Rochester's expression was troubled, and I realised that I would have to explain to him what having the wind meant, and what the weather gage was. Yet again. Having already explained it to him at least five times, both before and after the fleet's sailing from the Thames. Fortunately he seemed to realise that this was a question it was probably better not to ask, and with some thankfulness I moved away to the starboard rail, to see how the rest of the battle fared.

At first sight, all seemed well; indeed, better than well, given the odds we faced, and that remained the case for much of the afternoon. The two fleets were sailing south-east, parallel to each other, each fleet in its line of battle. We were sailing close-hauled with the weather gage, being closer to the south-westerly wind than the Dutch. Many of the Dutch ships were still out of action, well to the north. All along the line, ships were cannonading each other. As was so often the case in battle, the rival commanders had sought each other out: thus the Duke of Albemarle in the *Royal Charles* came up with De Ruyter, who was under way at last in his flagship, the proud new *Seven Provinces*, and the two mighty ships were trading broadsides. Ahead of us, Will Berkeley was particularly hotly engaged against Tromp's flagship, the *Hollandia*.

'It seems auspicious enough,' said Francis at one point in the middle of the afternoon. And so it did. As yet, we had no casualties at all aboard the proud King's Prick, and precious little damage, other than a few broken shrouds and torn sails. The fleet, too, was more than holding its own.

But I had an uneasy feeling, and as we looked out from the quarterdeck of the *Royal Sceptre*, I could sense that Kit Farrell and the other veteran seamen shared it. With the exception of the flagships, most ships – ourselves included – were exchanging no more than one or two broadsides with each Dutch ship that came up parallel with us, and we were exchanging them at a distance, causing little damage and receiving little in return. Albemarle's orders were to ensure that the Dutch could not get near enough to board, but that, in turn, meant that we were not near enough for our broadsides to devastate the enemy, especially as we were not engaged with any one of them for long enough. With the odds against us as they were, the only way in which we could hope to win was by overwhelming Tromp's and De

Ruyter's squadrons very quickly, before the unengaged Dutch ships to the north could come into action. But with the firing as desultory as it was, and with the sea still too heavy for us to open our lowest ports and thus deploy our heaviest guns, it was simply impossible for us to strike a decisive blow. I still waved my sword and pointed it at the enemy to encourage the men, but with every successive broadside, I could feel both my enthusiasm and my vigour declining. Soon, a half-hearted stab in the general direction of our next opponent was the best I could manage. And as time passed, I could see more and more mastheads closing from the north. The unengaged Dutch ships were coming into the line. Soon – very soon – their advantage in numbers would begin to tell.

Yet still Mars, the God of War, seemed to favour the outnumbered English. During a lull when we were not engaged, I took a little bread, cheese and wine, and reflected upon the example of my ancestor, the first Earl of Ravensden, who had fought valiantly alongside Henry the Fifth at Agincourt. There, the odds were infinitely worse, but somehow the outnumbered English cut down the flower of French chivalry. I said as much to Musk, who seemed to think that the act of bringing me the wine entitled him to partake liberally of it.

'All well and good, Sir Matthew, but your noble ancestor and King Hal were on land. Good, firm place, the land. You know what you're doing on the land, not like this damnable concoction of water, wind and tide that's called an ocean. A hundred things can go amiss in a battle on land and not affect the outcome. Here, though, the slightest shift in the wind, or the snapping of a rope, and all can be turned topsy-turvy in the blink of an eye. '

Proof of Musk's philosophy came almost at once. Rochester and some of the younger, more fetching mates and midshipmen were at the stern rail, pointing excitedly towards the rear of the Dutch line, away to larboard. I went over and joined them, and saw at once that a great ship was on fire. With the wind so strong, the flames took hold in no time at all. The hull burned from end to end. The sails blazed. Flames licked their way up the masts and along the yards. Great orange tongues of fire stretched out eastward, carried upon the wind. Even we on the *Royal Sceptre*, so far away, could feel the heat from the conflagration. The ships closer to the blazing wreck dared not approach her, so intense was the fire. Consequently, the crew was doomed. Through my telescope I could see the tiny shapes of men, some on fire, some turned black, leaping into the sea. It is one of the most paradoxical but most universal truths that the majority of sailors cannot swim; and even those of the Dutch crew who could, stood no chance of reaching safety in such a heavy sea.

'The poor bastards,' said Musk. 'Not even the greasiest Dutch butterbox whoremaster deserves to die like that.'

'Amen to that, Musk,' I said.

The hulk blazed for the best part of an hour before the flames reached her powder room and she blew up, vast pieces of her planking flying into the air like paper blown by a breeze. By then I had more urgent matters to occupy me, but as Francis Gale said a prayer for the men of the burning wreck, one thought above all consumed me. The blazing ship flew the flag of the Zeeland Admiralty. Thus I prayed that she was not the command of my brother-in-law, Captain Cornelis van der Eide. Cornelis was a stolid, humourless man, but he was brave, a fine sailor, and above all, he was my wife's brother; and I did not relish the prospect of telling Cornelia that her twin had perished, not by suffering the noble death-wound in the heat of battle that all seamen of honour dream of, but by drowning or being burned alive, the fates that all seamen dread.

* * *

For the next half-hour or so, we were engaged with a stubborn opponent that carried some fifty guns and flew the flags of the North Quarter Admiralty. The wind had now abated a little, and although we still could not open the lower deck gunports, Burdett and his gun crews were able to maintain a more accurate fire. So could our enemy, of course, but this captain had a different intent. He evidently fancied himself a hero, and luffed up to bring his ship's bows toward us three or four times, as if intending to come as close as he could into the wind to grapple and board us. But although we had less freeboard, we were still significantly higher out of the water than our opponent, and that gave us the advantage in small arms fire. Parks's Marines swarmed to the larboard rail of the forecastle and into the tops, sending down a hail of musket fire onto the Dutchman's deck and toward her gunports, trying to deter the gun crews on her lower decks. Much as I resented the presence of these new-fangled sea-soldiers, and disliked Parks himself, I could only admire the accuracy and speed of their fire. A very few of the Sceptres were useful with a musket – Macferran, up in the maintop with a dozen or so of the Marines, had been a prodigious poacher in Argyll, and could hit a deer or a man a quarter-mile away with the right weapon – but most seamen preferred the likes of the cutlass and the half pike, for which as yet there were no opportunities. But we were close enough to hurl *grenados*, and the men in the waist, martialled by Kit Farrell and Boatswain Uruqhart, were throwing them at the Dutchman with loud shouts and deprecations.

'This one's for my brother that you killed at Guinea!'

'For God, King Charles and Mevagissey!'

'Stick this up De Ruyter's arse!'

The quarterdeck was a little more refined, but equally warlike. Francis Gale had tucked his cassock beneath a breastplate and was firing his musket with some skill. Musk preferred pistols; there was a persistent rumour within the Quinton family to the effect that he had been a highwayman in his young days, and he was certainly proficient with the road-thief's weapon of choice. Above all, Musk was a fine judge of distance, invariably sensing the moment when the two ships moved too far apart to be within range of each other. Meanwhile, Lord

Rochester had discovered *grenados* with unconcealed delight, and was cheerfully lobbing them toward the Dutchman. But the noble Earl was hopelessly unco-ordinated. Musk and I both glanced at him in trepidation, fearful that he would release a shell at the wrong moment, or send it in entirely the wrong direction. The possibility of the entire quarterdeck of the *Royal Sceptre*, including the heir to Ravensden, being obliterated by a disastrous mis-throw from the over-eager young libertine, seemed rather more immediate than the prospect of any serious damage being inflicted by our Dutch opponent.

For my part, I maintained a steady fire with my pistols, reloaded and returned me with brisk efficiency by Kellett and my other young servants, Coleby, Smart and Denton. But the more I fired, the more I doubted the point of doing so. The sea might have been a little quieter, but it was still difficult to steady oneself upon the deck and almost impossible to take an accurate aim – even when we were within range at all, which was only for a few minutes at a time. All the while, though, our culverins and demi-culverins kept up their fire on the smaller North Quarter ship, and the effect on the latter was becoming apparent. Her rate of fire, both from her great guns and from the muskets on her deck and in her tops, started to fall away.

A shout from the lookout at the maintop – a great, deep noise, then the sound of rope and canvas tearing apart…

I ran to the other side of the quarterdeck, taking my telescope from Kellett.

'What is it, Sir Matthew?' Rochester demanded.

'Look yonder, My Lord. There, in the Dutch line. Two of them have collided! Great God – one of them is Tromp himself!'

It was an astonishing sight: two mighty men-of-war locked together, their rigging entangled, the bow of the one wedged onto the bow of the other. Even as we watched, the mainmast of Tromp's flagship *Hollandia* came down, taking her tricolour command flag with it. Yet again, good fortune seemed to be carrying the battle the way of the

English – or as Musk had put it, turning everything topsy-turvy in the blink of an eye. Collision is always a real possibility in a sea-fight, for ships are often sailing very close to each other; and the Dutch were unaccustomed to the line-of-battle, where each ship was meant to keep station only a very short distance from those ahead or astern of it, to give an enemy no room to break through gaps in the line. But the collision of the two great ships – Tromp's *Hollandia* and the *Leifde*, as we later learned – meant that they were falling away to leeward, helplessly entangled. Thus there was not just a gap in the Dutch line, but a huge, gaping, tempting passageway. An empty avenue of sea presented itself, stretching away to the irresistible target at the end of it, exposed and unable to manoeuvre. The *Hollandia*. The great Admiral Tromp himself.

'The Vice-Admiral, Sir Matthew,' said Kit, pointing ahead and slightly to larboard.

The *Swiftsure*, with the white command flag streaming from her foretop, was adjusting sail and beginning to fall down with the wind, making for the gap and the crippled *Hollandia*. Will Berkeley was intent on redeeming himself in the eyes of Albemarle, the fleet and the kingdom. Will was sailing to seize or destroy Tromp.

* * *

'Your orders, Sir Matthew?' asked Hardy, the *Royal Sceptre*'s master.

I said nothing, instead scanning as much of the battle as I could see with my telescope. Will's opportunity was obvious, but so too was the terrible risk he was taking. He had to get up to Tromp before the Dutch could bring down enough reinforcements to seal the gap in the line. With far fewer ships at his disposal, Albemarle could not similarly reinforce Will, even if he was so inclined. The general was still heavily engaged against De Ruyter, and now there was a new threat. Through the smoke and the great melee of masts, sails and hulls, I caught glimpses of our Blue Squadron, in the Rear. But now there were Dutch flags to the *west* of the Blue – in other words, to windward. The Dutch rear divisions, strengthened by the ships that had been out of action to the north, but which were now coming into action almost by the minute, had broken through the Blue and gained the weather gage. If Albemarle was going to redeploy his ships in the centre to reinforce anywhere, it would have to be there. And that meant Will Berkeley's charge at Tromp, unsupported, was likely to be suicidal.

'Your orders, Sir Matthew?' Hardy repeated, with a more obvious note of urgency in his voice.

My *Royal Sceptre* was the *Swiftsure*'s second. Under the fleet's orders, and by naval tradition from time immemorial, the second supported the flagship of its division. Will Berkeley was one of my dearest and best friends. Every bone in my body, every feeling in my heart, every last shred of my sense of honour, screamed out the order to go to his aid. But my head knew full well that without further reinforcement, following in Will Berkeley's wake was simply insane. We and the remaining ships of Will's Vice-Admiral's division were too few on our own. If we sailed after our flagship, unsupported – and as the senior captain remaining, I would have to give that order – there was a strong likelihood that we would be overwhelmed. Dozens, perhaps hundreds, of the men aboard the King's Prick and the other ships of our division would be slaughtered. And given the existing disparity in numbers between the fleets, the loss of the six remaining ships of the Vice-Admiral's division of the White Squadron would almost certainly lose us the battle. No other ships of our fleet showed the slightest sign of sailing to support the *Swiftsure* or her division. A bitter thought struck me: even if there was no threat from the north, would Albemarle sail in any case to support two young gentlemen captains – representatives of a breed he detested? Even as the thought came to me, I saw the *Royal Charles* begin to turn into the wind and break out the blue flag at the mizzen peak, the signal for the rest of the fleet to follow in his wake. To follow west-north-west: towards the Blue Squadron, away from the *Swiftsure* and ourselves.

As I stood alone – desperately alone – at the larboard rail of the quarterdeck, I could see the gap in the Dutch line beginning to close. Slowly but surely, the enemy fleet was swallowing the *Swiftsure*. Will Berkeley was sailing to his fate, whatever that was to be.

'Your orders, Sir Matthew?' demanded Hardy, for a third time.

I could barely speak the words I had to speak, such was the unutterable guilt, grief and sense of dishonour that coursed through me.

'We tack to follow the general,' I said.

Chapter Three

THE FIRST DAY: 1 JUNE 1666:
6PM to 8PM

Born each other by in a distant line,
The Sea-built Forts in a dreadful order move;
So vast the noise, as if not Fleets did join,
But lands unfixt, and floating Nations strove.

John Dryden, *Annus Mirabilis: the Year of Wonders, 1666* (1667)

A naval battle is like a prize fight. The protagonists pummel each other mercilessly for hour upon end, but there are moments in the fight when both draw apart, and the action pauses. No word has been spoken, no order given. There is an unspoken understanding that now, for this hour, the two sides will simply stop fighting. In a prize fight, the two men will regain their breath, have their wounds dressed, and get their doxy to wipe the sweat from their bodies. In a sea-fight, the fleets make haste to repair their damage. Carpenter's crews scuttle aloft to repair or replace yardarms, sails are repaired or new ones hoisted, shattered sheets and shrouds are spliced or replaced, blood is washed from the decks, bodies are hastily slung over the side. Boats scurry between the flagships, bearing the admirals' messages to each other. Officers and men greedily eat and drink whatever victuals can be brought to hand. Such it was that first evening, between about six and seven.

I sat upon the carriage of one of the quarterdeck demi-culverins, chewing on a leg of cold chicken and drinking pungent Essex beer. I had abandoned my breastplate; what little protection and honour it afforded were as nothing to the joy of feeling a relatively cool breeze on one's chest. Musk, feeling the effects of his old wound, had lain down on the deck without ceremony, and was wheezing like an ancient bull. I could see Francis Gale walking among the men in the ship's waist, giving a word here, saying a prayer there. Shortly I would join him, to encourage the men and to examine the condition of the wounded: miraculously, as yet we had no deaths among our company. Kit Farrell was below, overseeing repairs on the gundeck. With my other officers occupied, and the Dutch a distant but menacing presence away to the east, I had time to contemplate what had passed. The last sounds of gunfire had died away in the south-east: the gunfire of the *Swiftsure*, out of sight amidst the vast wooden fortress of the Dutch fleet. The poor, doomed *Swiftsure* – and there was still a part of me that cursed myself for not defying Albemarle and ordering the *Sceptre* to sail to her assistance. I tried to mollify my guilt by telling myself that if Will had been fortunate, perhaps he had surrendered in time, or been taken alive. Knowing Will Berkeley, though, the former was unlikely: as he had told me countless times, the Berkeleys could trace their descent even before the Norman Conquest, and no Berkeley had ever surrendered. And I had a strange feeling. Perhaps it was the exhaustion and light-headedness brought on by battle; perhaps it was the beer swilling in my largely empty stomach. But somehow, I knew for certain that I had seen my friend for the last time.

The Earl of Rochester sat by me. He was silent, staring blankly out to sea, sipping occasionally from a pewter tankard filled to the brim with Rhenish wine.

'Well, My Lord,' I said, 'is battle as you expected it to be?'

'It is hell,' he said, his voice husky from screaming obscenities at the Dutch. 'Hell.'

There was a strangeness about him, especially about his stare, that worried me. I had seen men made mad by battle, and did not think the King would forgive me if I brought one of his favourite court wits back from sea as a Bedlam-man.

'There are yachts and ketches bound up the river with despatches,' I said. 'We could easily secure a place for you aboard one of them.'

Rochester smiled, but it was an older, grimmer smile than I had ever seen on his face.

'You mistake me, Sir Matthew,' he said. 'Our bishops and preachers, those mewing killjoy be-cassocked turds, never teach us that is possible for a man to enjoy Hell. The sound of the guns and the smell of the powder – the ships upon the swell – the sight of dying Dutchmen – I have never felt such, such – *excitement.* I thought I had reached the height of ecstasy inside a tight young pageboy, but that was nothing next to this. I may even write a poem, if I can find the words to describe it all.'

There are many different kinds of madness, of course, and this, too, was a kind I had seen before. Indeed, it was a kind that had tempted me, many times, very nearly drawing me into its seductive clutches. As it would again, all too often. It is a particularly dangerous kind of insanity. For although wars and battles have to be fought, to enjoy them is akin to carving deep cuts into one's own flesh for pleasure, or deliberately sleeping with whores whom one knows to be pox-ridden: as, indeed, was Lord Rochester's particular penchant, even more so than buggering his pages.

Still heavy-hearted over the fate of Will Berkeley and the *Swiftsure*, and unwilling to confront Rochester' troubling battle-crazedness, I stood up and moved to the captain's inviolate domain, the starboard side of the quarterdeck. As I did so, I heard a cry from the maintop.

I levelled my telescope on the *Royal Charles*. She was clearly getting under way again, and I knew her intention. That had come in a message from the flagship, delivered by a smack barely half an hour earlier. There was to be no forming of the line of battle. We were going to sail directly against the Dutch in an all-out attack: and for whatever reason, Albemarle had decided that the *Royal Sceptre* and her despised gentleman captain would lead the *Royal Charles* into battle. We were to be the flagship's second, and the vanguard of the fleet.

* * *

'Now, Sir Matthew?' asked Burdett.

'Now, Master Gunner,' I said.

The wind had fallen away. I gripped the starboard rail, peered over the ship's side, and saw the lower deck gunports swing open. The muzzles of the vast demi-cannon pushed out. At long last, the sea was calm enough for our proud English ships to bring their main armaments to bear. Only just, admittedly: we had barely four feet of freeboard between the lower battery and the sea. But now, if God willed it, the King's Prick and the rest of our fleet would finally give the Dutch an almighty reckoning.

We were sailing south-east, with most of the Dutch fleet to windward – that is, to the west – of us, they sailing north-west. De Ruyter, Tromp, Evertsen and their captains obviously had the same intent that we did. This was no time for refined tactics, or rarefied theory: this was a charge, pure and simple, the two mighty fleets going at each other like armoured knights in the lists.

A large two-decker of the Zeeland Admiralty came at us first. She was a fine sight, her beakhead and bowsprit rising and falling with the gentle swell, her great sails set, her ensigns streaming out toward the north-east. And she was well commanded, her captain not deigning to waste powder in futile shots from her bow guns. But as we came parallel with each other, albeit on opposite courses, his broadside blazed away. Flames spurted from muzzles, smoke billowed through the gunports as the great cannon recoiled. Our own gun crews retaliated immediately, Burdett's gun captains on the lower deck unleashing all their frustration at being impotent for so long. I stood at the starboard rail, sword in hand, screaming encouragement, and watching as our balls hit the Dutchman low, shattering timber around and below her lower battery. Lighter built and with lighter ordnance, she sat higher in the water than we did. Consequently, her own shot played havoc with our upper works. The main sail, a new one hoisted barely an hour earlier, was in shreds by the third broadside. The canvas fights, rigged to give some protection to those on the upper deck, were in tatters. Parks's Marines exchanged volley after volley of musket fire with their counterparts on the deck and in the tops of the Dutch ship, Ensign Lovell in particular always seeming to be in the thick of things. For all my scepticism about the usefulness of these new-fangled sea-soldiers, I had to admit that they seemed to be proving their worth.

Suddenly a great ball struck amidships, shattering the ship's rail, ripping one of the starboard culverins from its carriage and upending it. The great gun flipped over as easily as a feather in a breeze. The huge iron weapon fell onto three living members of the gun crew and the bloodied remains of another three, already killed by the shot. Kit Farrell ran from his station in the forecastle, hastily ordering a half-dozen men to assist him. By chance, Lancelot Parks was close to the carnage, but he seemed rooted to the deck, staring at what lay before him. With no thought for my dignity, I ran forward, clearing the elaborately carved quarterdeck stair in a single leap. I knelt and put my shoulder to the gun. The barrel was still hot from its last firing, but my discomfort was nought alongside that of the men trapped underneath.

'Jesus! Oh, merciful Jesus!'

The screams came from Hollister, a keen lad of Essex whom I had rated an able seaman just the day before. But he was trapped directly beneath the First Reinforce, the heaviest part of the gun, which lay directly across his waist. His pelvis, guts and manhood would all have been crushed beyond repair under the great weight. Kit Farrell and I looked at each other. I nodded. Kit drew his flintlock pistol and blew Hollister's brains out.

I turned and saw Lancelot Parks's face. The captain of Marines had turned very pale, and the stink about him suggested that he had soiled himself. He rocked backward and forward, then vomited profusely onto the deck. Some of his men, including young Lovell, witnessed the spectacle, and glanced knowingly at each other.

The other two survivors of the gun crew would live, despite being spattered in the blood, gore and flesh of their fallen comrades, for they were closer to the muzzle. Wethered, a stout man, clearly had both legs shattered, but still he smiled.

'Sure way to a cook's place now, Sir Matthew,' he said. 'Promotion. More pay.'

As the cannon roared all around us, I clasped his hand. 'You shall have my recommendation for it, Wethered. You may count on it.'

Proudfoot, the other, was an idle, cheating rogue of a pressed Londoner whom I had ordered to be flogged at the Nore. Fate had decreed that his name would now haunt him for ever: his left foot lay beneath the muzzle, and would have to be taken off by the surgeon's saw that very hour. I had no words for him. His twisted expression, bitter tears and anguished prayers proved that he was all too aware of the clear proof of God's intervention in human affairs that he, and his name, now represented.

I returned to the quarterdeck. The Zeelander was past us now, putting on more sail to seek out new and easier targets further back in our fleet. But there was a new threat: not directly to ourselves but to the flagship, the *Royal Charles*, barely three-hundred yards astern of us. Bearing down on her starboard side was a huge new Dutchman, flying the flag of the lieutenant-admiral of the Maas Admiralty.

'The *Eendracht*,' said Hardy. 'Aert van Nes. One of their best seamen and hardest fighters. He and the Lord Duke are made for each other.'

'*Eendracht*?' said Lord Rochester. 'Did she not blow up in the Lowestoft fight, last year? Are the Dutch bringing ghost ships against us now?'

'The old *Eendracht* certainly blew up,' I said. 'I witnessed it.'

A vast fireball – a great hull, torn apart – the body parts of human beings, raining down out of the sky…

'Their new ship of the name,' said Hardy. 'Seventy-six guns. My brother commands the packet boat to Rotterdam, and saw her being built there.'

'Very well,' I said. 'We are the Duke's second, Mister Hardy. Time, I think, for us to second him. We will tack into the Dutchman's wake, thus coming across his stern and raking him, then cannonading him on his larboard beam while the *Royal Charles* bombards him from starboard.'

'A difficult manoeuvre, Sir Matthew. We will be turning into the path of the Dutch fleet –'

'I am aware of that, Mister Hardy. But if we do it swiftly enough, and if our ships support us, we can give this *Eendracht* the same fate as her predecessor.'

The orders were given, men raced aloft to adjust sail, the helm was put about, and the great bows of the King's Prick began to turn into the wind.

* * *

'Damn him,' I said.

'He's too good a seaman to play into your hands, Sir Matthew,' said Kit Farrell, almost approvingly.

The *Eendracht* was stymying our intended manoeuvre by coming round to starboard. The wind was now directly behind her, so she could manoeuvre easily, whereas we were still swinging clumsily through onto our new tack. Worse still, van Nes's course seemed to be aimed at putting him in the ideal position to attempt on the *Royal Charles* the very tactic I had hoped to use against him, namely raking the enemy ship – firing into her fragile and poorly defended stern, thus devastating the entire length of the cleared decks. But in turn, John Kempthorne, Albemarle's flag captain, was one of the very best English seamen of those days, an old Levant Company skipper and a staunch Cavalier. Kempthorne saw van Nes's stratagem at once and nudged the huge bows of the *Royal Charles* around too, closer to the wind. Thus there was a strange moment when our three great ships formed a vast and almost perfect triangle of wood upon the sea, each trying to gain an advantage upon the other. All three broadsides blazed away at once, the waves of fire rippling from bow to stern on each ship.

'Advice, gentlemen!' I cried.

'Bring her between the *Royal Charles* and van Nes,' said Hardy. 'We are more manoeuvrable than the flagship. And it is your shortest and quickest course to bring us back into action, Sir Matthew. Van Nes is unlikely to refuse the fight, for he will still be determined to get through us to get at the Duke.'

'But the Duke will not thank us for denying him a duel with the *Eendracht*,' said Kit. 'And the *Royal Charles* has a much heavier broadside than ours – we should not disable it by interposing ourselves between the flagship and the Dutchman.'

'Then what would you advise, Mister Farrell?'

'Take her to windward of the Dutchman, Sir Matthew. To the north-west. Then van Nes will lie between the *Royal Charles* and ourselves. We will have him between us, as a nut in a nutcracker.'

'Madness, Sir Matthew!' cried Hardy. 'We would have most of the Dutch fleet to windward of us, bearing down – and the ships in their van would prevent us getting back to our own line –'

'Wait,' I said. My eyes were trained on the *Eendracht*. 'Her course has changed slightly. The angle has sharpened.'

'No,' said Kit, 'he can't be thinking – it's never been done –'

'Which gives it an element of surprise,' I said. 'Look, the Dutchmen are starting to mass in the forecastle. There's no doubt about it. He's going to attempt to secure to the starboard quarter, right at the stern, and board there.'

The *Eendracht* was an astonishing sight as she edged closer and closer to the elaborately gilded stern of the *Royal Charles*. The Dutch had always favoured boarding as a tactic, but the conventional wisdom was to attempt to board *forward*, grappling onto the multitude of cables and ropes in the bows. To attempt to board at the stern, in the highest part of the ship and with precious little to secure to, was unheard of – but if it came off, the enemy could strike directly at the head and heart of the British fleet. At the Duke of Albemarle himself.

'He has made our decision for us,' I said. 'We must divert him from attacking the flagship – and we can now only do that by forcing him to fight both sides of his ship at once. Mister Hardy, if you please, a course to bring us onto the larboard quarter of the *Eendracht*.'

We were very close to the wind, the edges of our sails flapping ominously. But slowly and surely, the *Royal Sceptre* began to make her way north-by-west, heading for the windward quarter of the huge Dutch ship. But one thing puzzled all of us on the quarterdeck.

'The *Royal Charles* has stopped firing,' said Kit.

The difference between the two great antagonists was marked. The *Eendracht*, edging ever nearer to her target, was firing at will, pouring shot upon shot into the vast wooden sides of our flagship. But the *Royal Charles* was silent. It was as though she was waiting – but for what? Albemarle had been a soldier long before he was an admiral: did he actually relish the prospect of hand to hand combat? If so, was he going to allow the Dutch to board?

Too late, I realised the answer. Too late, because our course and speed meant that we were bound to be in the path of…

Over forty spouts of flame issued simultaneously from the starboard battery of the *Royal Charles*. The very sea itself seemed to shake. The flagship appeared to move sidewise, driven by the recoils of her massive cannon-of-seven firing forty-two pound balls. A monstrous cloud of gunsmoke belched from her ports and rolled back over the hull, momentarily hiding the great ship from view. I caught a glimpse of the *Eendracht*, her planking and rigging torn asunder by the titanic broadside, falling away astern of the flagship, all thought of boarding gone. But I had no time to consider the fate of the Dutch. I felt the impact of large cannon-shot well forward, and heard screams from the forecastle. Smoke obscured my view, but I knew we had been hit.

I ran forward with Kit, leaving Hardy to con the ship. We reached the foot of the forecastle, by the ship's bell, and looked upon carnage. A man's severed arm skated past my feet on a stream of blood. I looked up – foresail shredded, foreyard hanging at a wild angle, foretopmast felled, standing rigging largely gone. Kit had run up onto the forecastle itself, and now shouted a report back to me.

'Bowsprit's splintered, Sir Matthew, and the beakhead's a wreck! Two men dead, another four injured!'

Men were already rushing forward to do what they could. One of them was Carvell, who nodded a grim salute. 'Thought the flagship was meant to be on our side, sir,' he said, before going to try and secure a severed shroud.

I became aware of Phineas Musk by my side. 'So has General Monck repented of his decision to restore the king, then? Has he rejoined his old colours and restarted the civil war?'

'Their aim would have been obscured,' I said, albeit without much conviction, 'the gun crews on the *Royal Charles*. There'd have been smoke from the *Eendracht*'s firing, and from our own, firing at the Dutch. Friend firing upon friend is always a risk in a sea battle, Musk.'

'That's the thing since the king came back, though,' said Musk. 'So many of the people we now call our friends look damnably like the ones we used to call our enemies.'

Richardson, the carpenter, and Urquhart, the boatswain, stepped before me, saluted, and delivered their reports. But I did not need to hear them: it was already obvious that we could not continue to fight. We would have to fall away from the warring fleets, make good our damage, and then see if we could make our way back, all the while hoping that the Dutch did not change course and swallow us up. Or, worse, that De Ruyter did not spot our vulnerability and send in fire-ships to finish us off. But there was no choice. The shattered *Royal Sceptre* withdrew from the battle.

THE FIRST DAY: SATURDAY, 2 JUNE 1666: 8pm to Midnight

The night comes on, we eager to pursue
The combat still, and they asham'd to leave;
Till the last streaks of dying day withdrew,
And doubtful Moon-light did our rage deceive.

Dryden, *Annus Mirabilis*

We laid up to the south-east of the warring fleets. As the evening shadows lengthened, we could still plainly see and hear the continuation of the battle, away to the north-west of us: the blazing and roaring of the great guns, the vast clouds of smoke obscuring the setting sun as the two great navies passed each other again and again. But aboard the *Royal Sceptre*, that mattered very little. We were focused solely on repairing the ship; on getting her into a fit state to rejoin the battle. Richardson's crew sawed and hammered like men possessed. Down in the waist, timbers were hastily fastened into makeshift splints for the fore-yard, then hoisted into position, with John Treninnick leaping about the yard to secure it as if the thought of falling had never entered his head. He had an assistant, too, of a sort: Lord Rochester's monkey evidently looked upon Treninnick as a kindred spirit, if not actually a member of the same species, and went wherever he went. Other men were at work on the beakhead and bowsprit, cutting away the damaged wood and rigging, replacing it with new. I had seen crews effect battle repairs before, but the sheer speed with which it could be done never ceased to amaze me. The English seaman can be a surly and idle brute, but when his survival or his pay depends upon it, no man on Earth can work so hard or so long. Thus, as the very last embers of the sun faded in the west, over behind the invisible shore of England, my officers came to me and assured me that the King's Prick was ready to sail once again.

'Very well, gentlemen,' I said. 'Mister Hardy, we will set a course to rejoin the fleet.'

I looked toward the north-west. It was now too dark to make out the fleets, which could only be in that quarter. Moreover, the sounds of battle had died away with the setting of the sun. Almost certainly, the fleets would have hoved to for the night; there was no prospect of the action resuming before the morning. That being so, I ordered a brief period of rest for the men – a chance for Prentice, our one-legged cook, and his mates, to serve up some bread and cold stew, and for each man to dip his tankard into a barrel of good English beer.

During the respite, Francis Gale came to see me on the quarter-deck.

'It is Captain Parks, Sir Matthew,' he said. 'He worries me. You had better come and see.'

We went down, onto the main gun deck. Men were sitting in their messes, between the cannon, eating their stew and drinking their beer. Some of my old Cornish following, like George Polzeath, stood or saluted as I passed; a few called out greetings. But many were too exhausted to give me any sort of an acknowledgement.

Francis led me down another deck, then down to the surgeon's cock-pit on the orlop. It was a dark, stinking space, lit only by a couple of lanterns slung from the beams. Rowan, our venerable surgeon, grunted what might have been a greeting, then returned to sewing up a gaping wound in the right thigh of Draycott, a burly boatswain's mate. As my eyes grew more accustomed to the darkness, I became aware of a figure sitting on the deck in the corner, slumped against a futtock. It was Lancelot Parks. His eyes were fixed on Draycott's bloody leg. He was mumbling to himself: psalms, prayers, and one name, repeated over and over. Venetia.

'A bad case,' Francis whispered.

'We've both seen it before, Francis. Battle can do this to men.' My friend knew that better than most: the horrors of the siege of Drogheda had driven him to seek solace in a bottle for a decade or more. 'But that does not make it any easier.'

'He refuses to leave the cockpit,' growled Rowan. 'Says he wants to stay in the presence of blood and human corruption. Fucking madman – begging pardon, Sir Matthew.'

Parks seemed not to have heard the surgeon's bitter words. His eyes were closed, and he nodded his head in rhythm with the words he was reciting.

'The Duke will be sending a despatch boat into the Thames in the morning,' I said. 'If we get back to the fleet tonight, we can put him aboard it.'

I went over to the Marine captain, knelt down by his side, and attempted to comfort him. But his eyes did not register me at all. With a heavy heart, I returned to the quarterdeck and summoned Ensign Lovell to inform him of what had happened.

'You are now in acting command of the Marines on this ship, Mister Lovell.'

The boy's face was frozen in shock. 'Y – yes, Sir Matthew –'

'I was an Ensign, and younger than you, when I fought my first battle, Mister Lovell – the first time that I commanded men. You will do well enough, I think.'

'Yes, Sir Matthew.' The boy pulled himself to his full height and stood to attention. 'It will be an honour to command the men, and an honour to serve alongside you.'

I realised that I had misjudged young Lovell. I had taken his hesitancy as proof of trepidation, perhaps even fear, but it was not that at all. The lad was proud, and excited. He would certainly do well enough, and if he lived, he would be a far better officer than Parks had ever been.

Then I gave the order for the ship to get under way.

* * *

'Sail ho! No – sails ho – *many* sails ho – dead ahead!'

I had been dozing, lulled by the lapping of the black waters below and the gentle billowing of the sails above my head. But I was fully awake in an instant, and also fully aware of what the oncoming sails meant. It was the Dutch. On that tack, sailing on that course, it could only be them. We were about to sail right into the heart of the Dutch fleet.

I turned to my officers. I have never seen such a collection of grim faces: but whereas the expressions of the veteran warriors Kit Farrell, Burdett and Francis Gale were determined, those of the youthful Lord Rochester and Ensign Lovell betrayed ill-concealed excitement, Phineas Musk's was as unreadable as ever, and that of Philemon Hardy was anxious beyond measure.

'We cannot outrun them,' said Kit, simply.

'They will surround us in minutes!' cried Hardy. 'The entire Dutch fleet!'

'Then what would you have me do, Mister Hardy?'

'Surrender, Sir Matthew! Surrender now, before we are blown to pieces! We have fought well today – there would be no dishonour in it –'

Hardy was no coward: his advice was no more than common sense. And it was tempting. For the officers, surrender would be comfortable

– at worst roomy quarters in a Dutch castle, at best living on parole in Amsterdam or another city with a full measure of earthly delights. But I thought of my men, and the tales of the hell-hole prisons where ordinary sailors were confined. Prisons full of plague and disease, where the solitary privy was a single hole in the floor to serve two-hundred men or more.

I remembered Will Berkeley's words: *Berkeleys do not surrender.* Nor do Quintons, by Heaven.

'No,' I said. 'God willing, the Dutch will be as surprised to see us as we are to see them. We will attempt to sail straight through their fleet, gentlemen, and fight our way out to the other side. If we die in the attempt, or are forced to surrender after all, then at least we will have attempted it. Mister Farrell! Give orders to summon all hands to their stations! Mister Burdett, prepare to fight both sides of the ship at once! Ensign Lovell, your men to their quarters, if you please! Mister Gale, the prayer before battle!'

'Sailing straight through the Dutch fleet,' said Musk. 'That is what you said, Sir Matthew? I didn't mishear, perchance? The entire fucking Dutch navy, and you propose just to sail straight through it, at night, as easily as if you were punting on the Ouse?'

I glared at him. 'That is exactly what I said, Musk. That is my order. You see fit to take issue with it?'

For once, the old rogue seemed discomfited by the ferocity of my response. 'No, Sir Matthew. Not at all, Sir Matthew. It strikes me that in similar circumstances, your grandfather and father would have given exactly the same order.'

And they were fucking madmen, too. Musk did not have to say the words, but I knew full well that they would be the ones in his mind.

Trumpets were already sounding and drums beating on the Dutch ships approaching us, and as Francis Gale prayed for victory, our own sounded our reply. The off-duty watch emerged from below and joined their brethren at the upper deck guns. Above my head, our ship's vast white ensign flapped eerily in the light of the *Sceptre*'s stern lanterns. And up ahead, I saw more and more huge black shapes looming out of the darkness. One, above all, appeared to be heading directly for us. I could just make out the tricolour command flag flying proudly from the maintop. The ship had to be the *Seven Provinces*, the Dutch flagship. It was De Ruyter himself.

Our starboard battery opened fire, bow to stern, and the *Seven Provinces* replied in kind as she came up alongside us. A sea battle by day is terrible enough, but a sea battle by night is one of the most dreadful spectacles any man can witness. The flames from the cannons' muzzles are more brilliant than in daytime, momentarily lighting the entire scene and forming a vision of hell as fire spouts across the sea. The smoke, merely a grey and foul-smelling inconvenience by day, takes on a new life of its own, swirling into strange and ghostly shapes, as though the wraiths of long-dead sailors are trapped within it. But for a ship's officers, a night action is blindness, pure and simple. Gunners cannot aim, for they cannot judge the roll of the enemy ship. The Marines and seamen with muskets cannot make out their targets. I feel shot strike our hull and masts and tear through our sails and rigging, but how bad is the damage? I cannot tell. A captain can only trust in God and the initiative of his petty officers. So it was that night aboard the *Royal Sceptre* as we battled the great De Ruyter himself.

Unable to see from the quarterdeck, I strode up and down the waist and forecastle, waving my sword toward the enemy and shouting encouragement.

'God be with you, boys! Don't let our fire slacken! Coleby, there – get down to the magazine, see why they're so slow at sending up fresh cartridges! A farm on Ravensden land to the man who kills De Ruyter!'

In the darkness, and with faces blackened with powder and sweat, it was nearly impossible to make out individuals. I must have passed countless men whom I knew well, but failed to recognise or acknowledge them. Even by night, though, the red hair of Macferran, part of the gun crew of one of the starboard culverins, was unmistakeable.

'Hot work, Macferran!'

'Not too hot for a Scotsman, Sir Matthew! This one's for Saint Andrew and the royal House of Stuart!'

The culverin fired and recoiled, Macferran leaping forward to swab the barrel. All around me, men were exhausted. But somehow they fought on, reloading, firing, reloading, firing, each man like an automaton. Boys ran up from below with fresh cartridges and shot. But how much was left?

'Kellett!' My young servant was at my side, eager to be of assistance; and as on previous occasions, rather too evidently enjoying the sights, sounds and feelings of battle. 'To Mister Burdett – my compliments, and I would have his report on the state of the shot, cartridge and powder remaining to us!'

Kellett saluted and ran down to the gunner, who was overseeing the firing of the mighty demi-cannon on the deck below. The *Seven Provinces*' broadside fired again, and the unmistakeable whistle of bar-shot passed not far above my head. The Dutch were firing to disable our masts and rigging, their customary tactic. I looked up, and could just make out huge tears in the mainsail. But it still seemed to be filling, and we were maintaining our course and speed.

'Mister Burdett's compliments, Sir Matthew,' said the breathless Kellett, 'and we have fewer than twenty balls per culverin, a few more for the demi-cannon. Plenty of bar, chain and grape, though. Powder, no more than eighty barrels.'

I returned to the quarterdeck and made some swift, rough calculations in my head. We had already fired five broadsides against the *Seven Provinces*. At this rate, we would run out of powder or shot long before we got past the last Dutch ships. If we ever got that far, of course.

At least our first opponent was very nearly past us. The *Seven Provinces*' starboard quarter came up level with ours, the two quarterdecks directly opposite each other for a brief moment. And then a curious thing happened. The light from our stern lanterns, combined with that from those on the Dutch ship, made it just bright enough to make out the men on the enemy quarterdeck. One of them was a strongly-built bull of a man with a huge black moustachio. He raised his hat, and I brought up my sword to return the gesture. It was my first sight of the living legend that was Michiel Adrianszoon De Ruyter, the Netherlands' greatest admiral.

* * *

'If you seek proof of miracles,' said Francis Gale, 'I think you have it.'

'Miracle?' said Musk. 'With all respect, Reverend, I'll call it a miracle when I'm back in my own bed, safe and unscathed.'

But 'miracle' was one of the few words that came close to describing our apparent good fortune. After our encounter with the *Seven Provinces*, we had sailed unscathed through what must have been most of the Dutch fleet. We saw black shapes away to starboard, and off to larboard, and ahead: but apart from a few desultory shots from long range, we had been barely troubled at all for a half-hour or more. It was as though there was a vast gap in the middle of the Dutch, and we were sailing straight through it.

'They won't know what's happened,' said Kit. 'They'll have seen the firing up ahead, but they won't know what the outcome was. As far as they know, De Ruyter might have captured us, or we might be trying to run. They won't be expecting us to do what we're doing.'

I was not so certain. 'The Dutch are no fools,' I said. 'At least some of the ships passing us must have identified us – and if they have, they'll be using their stern lanterns to signal to the ones behind them.'

'Ships dead ahead!' It was the cry of the lookout in the foretop. 'Ten ships! None behind!'

'The Dutch rear squadron,' I said. 'Get past them, and we are clear.'

I took up my telescope and squinted, trying to make out shapes in the gloom. After a minute or two, I was able to see the dim shapes of sails and hulls. Ten ships, in tight formation. Unlike so many of their fellows, these were clearly not oblivious to our presence, or confused about what might have been happening up ahead. These ships knew exactly who we were, where we were, and what we were trying to do. This was the force that the Dutch intended to stop us. Now, too, I could dimly make out their ensigns.

I attempted to put a brave face on it. 'The Zeeland squadron,' I said. 'It seems I am to shake hands with my brother-in-law.'

I never knew for certain which of the ships that attacked us was the *Adelaar*, the command of Captain Cornelis van der Eide. It was immaterial. For the next half-hour or so, we were bombarded in succession by each of the Zeeland ships. They attacked both sides at once, and as I strode back and forward on the upper deck, it was clear that we could not survive much longer. The men were exhausted. Directly in front of my eyes, Treweek, a fine old Wadebridge seaman who had sailed with me since the *Jupiter*, suddenly clutched his chest and slumped forward over the barrel of the culverin, stone dead. No shot had touched him: his heart had simply given up. The other Cornishmen in the gun-crew muttered the Lord's Prayer in their own tongue: *Agan Tas-ny, us yn neft, Benygys re bo dha Hanow*... Then, without further ceremony, they slung Treweek's warm corpse over the rail.

All the time, my mind calculated the amounts of shot and powder that remained. At our current rate of fire, we would run out at about midnight. There seemed to be a strange appropriateness about that.

'Sir Matthew!' It was Kellett. 'Look! The Dutchman luffing up toward us on the starboard bow – he's flying white flags! Flags of truce!'

It was a large ship – somewhat larger than the *Royal Sceptre*. And at the maintop, it flew the command flag of the Lieutenant-Admiral of Zeeland himself.

A voice bellowed from a speaking trumpet. The voice spoke good English, albeit with a thick accent. 'English captain! You have fought bravely! But your ship is surrounded. You are badly damaged. And I have not yet unleashed the worst on you. You know that. So I give you this final chance, Captain. Surrender now, with honour. I assure you and your men of quarter, and treatment fitting for those who have fought well.'

I sent Kellett for my own speaking-trumpet, and shouted my response across the water. 'My thanks, Admiral Evertsen,' I said in my fairly fluent Dutch, 'but it is not come to that yet. Know that you fight Sir Matthew Quinton and His Majesty's ship the *Royal Sceptre*, and we fight on for the honour of England and our King.'

'My respects, Sir Matthew,' Cornelis Evertsen shouted in Dutch. 'Your good-brother will be sorry to see you perish in such a terrible manner. You will not reconsider?'

'I will not. And pass on my respects to Captain van der Eide.'

I raised my sword. The flags of truce came down on the Zeeland flagship, and she began to sheer away. I dropped my sword again, the signal for Burdett to unleash our starboard broadside against Evertsen. A futile gesture at such a distance and in such darkness, but a token to prove that the *Royal Sceptre* intended to fight on. Then the Dutch ship disappeared into the gloom, and suddenly all was very quiet.

'What did he mean, Sir Matthew?' asked the Earl of Rochester. 'What is the worst he can unleash on us? How will we perish terribly?'

Musk peered out into the darkness, his eyes straining to see into the gloom. Without turning to face Rochester, he said one word: the single word that was in the thoughts of every seaman aboard. The one thing that sailors feared almost as much as the sea itself.

'Fireship.'

* * *

It was on us almost before anyone saw it. A tiny craft, its crew stealthily secured it to our starboard quarter using grappling hooks. Marines and seamen fired their muskets at where they thought the departing crew would be, rowing for dear life away from their deadly charge, but by then, smoke was already billowing from the fireship's hold. It was followed in short order by the first flames, licking across the deck toward the hull of the *Royal Sceptre*.

There was one chance, and one chance only, of saving our ship. I ran down to the main deck, then to the stern, to the space that contained my cabin; or would have contained it, if the partitions had not been taken down when the deck was cleared for action. If I could climb out of a quarter gallery window, and get down onto the deck of the fireship…

but another had had the same thought. Kit Farrell was already at the quarter gallery. All along the deck, men stood by their guns, looking on in fear and astonishment: fear at the knowledge of what lay just a few feet away from them, secured firmly to the ship's side; astonishment at the sight of their two most senior officers disputing which of them should go to an almost certain death by trying to cut the fireship adrift before it could take hold.

'My ship, Mister Farrell!' I shouted. 'My responsibility!'

'Not your only responsibility, Sir Matthew. You have a wife, and you are the heir to an earldom. It does not matter if the poor tarpaulin Kit Farrell dies down there, but it matters greatly if Sir Matthew Quinton does.'

'But your wound, Kit!'

'Better to reopen the wound than for all of us to burn alive, Sir Matthew.'

Musk appeared by my side, having made his way from the quarterdeck at a rather more sedate pace than my own.

'He's right,' the old man said. 'You know full well he's right. And if you argue the toss any longer, the ship'll burn.'

He *was* right. But that did not make it any easier as I watched Kit seize hold of a rope fastened to the carriage of the nearest demi-cannon, haul himself painfully out of the quarter-gallery, and lower himself down the rope into the dense, stinking smoke billowing from the fireship.

I peered out of the window, trying to make out Kit's figure on the deck far below. He had been down there too long – he must have been overcome by the smoke, or burned by the flames that were now melting the paintwork of the quarter-gallery – or else his efforts had reopened the wound he sustained but a few months earlier.

Long moments of silence and dread turned into minutes. Kit had failed, he was dead, and very soon, the rest of us would be so too.

There was a sudden jolt, then the creaking of wood.

'He's done it!' I cried.

Clear water appeared between the fireship and our hull. The blazing wreck began to drift away upon wind and tide, the grappling ropes that secured her to the *Sceptre*'s hull neatly severed. And there, hauling himself up the ship's side on the rope secured to the demi-cannon, was Kit Farrell.

Eager hands pulled him inboard, and we sat him down on the deck to recover his breath. I despatched Denton, my servant, to fetch him a tankard of ale, which he downed in one.

'Hot work, Lieutenant?'

'Smoke too thick – couldn't find the fastenings for the grappling ropes –'

'Take your time, Kit. Get your breath. You saved the ship. Men have been granted commands for less –'

'Sir Matthew!' It was Kellett's voice, from the ladder to the upper deck. 'Another fireship! On the other quarter!'

I ran back to the quarterdeck. There it was, a nearly identical craft, firmly secured to the larboard quarter-gallery.

'Damn them,' said Francis Gale. 'They must have secured when all our attention was on the one to starboard.'

This new threat was even more dangerous than the one Kit had just eliminated. The first fireship had been to leeward, so drifted away as soon as the grapples were cut. But this one was to windward. Even if we had a second hero to equal Kit, it would avail nothing: even if the fireship were cut loose, the wind would continue to push it against our hull. And that same wind would fan the flames more vigorously, as it was already doing. The quarter-gallery was already alight…

I was aware of someone talking behind me, and turned. It was Lancelot Parks. He was standing by the starboard rail, mumbling the same words, over and over. 'Thou, Matthew Quinton, art the Beast. I am the false prophet. Forgive me, Venetia. Thou, Matthew Quinton, art the beast. I am –'

As Francis Gale and I rushed forward to try and take hold of him, he leapt onto the carriage of the nearest demi-culverin. He turned, looked at me, then jumped over the ship's rail. I ran to the side and peered down into the waters, but he was gone. Even if Parks could swim, his breastplate and heavy sword would have dragged him under.

'Revelation Nineteen, Verse Twenty,' said Francis. '*And the beast was taken, and with him the false prophet that wrought miracles before him, with which he deceived them that had received the mark of the beast, and them that worshipped his image. These both were cast alive into a lake of fire burning with brimstone.* Almighty God, we give thee hearty thanks, for that it hath pleased thee to deliver this our brother Lancelot Parks out of the miseries of this sinful world. Amen.'

'Amen.'

I had no time to mourn the captain of Marines. I could hear a clamouring further forward, then shouts.

'The ship's ablaze!'

'God have mercy on our souls!'

I ran to the quarterdeck rail. Many men were massing forward, trying to edge away from the flames that were now spitting all along the larboard quarter, above the level of the quarterdeck. One, then another, then a third and a fourth, all from the London pressed draft, climbed onto the rail and jumped. Some of the sturdier and longer serving men were trying to calm the others – I saw Carvell, Ali Reis and many of the Cornish rushing hither and thither – but more and more men were jumping, convinced they stood a better chance in the water.

'If as many as a quarter of them can swim, I'm the Grand Turk,' said Francis.

'And those who can don't stand a chance of being picked up by a Dutch ship,' I said. 'They won't come near while the fire blazes, in case our magazine blows up. One thing for it, Reverend Gale.'

I drew my sword, and Francis drew his. 'One thing for it indeed, Sir Matthew.'

We both ran forward, straight into the heart of the mob, our swords waving above our heads.

'Sceptres, stand firm!' I cried. As Francis pummelled men in distinctly unclerical fashion, I leapt up onto the steam gratings around the galley chimney. 'Stand firm! We can still save the ship, but only if you return to your stations –' Another man climbed onto the rail and jumped. 'Listen to me, you fuckwits!' I screamed at the top of my voice. 'I will run through the next man who tries to jump! You hear me? This sword, in your gut. Or yours. Or yours.' I pointed the weapon vaguely at faces that seemed particularly terror-stricken. 'I swear it upon the honour of Ravensden!'

My venom seemed to be having an effect. The clamour subsided. Men looked at each other uncertainly. And now my other officers were advancing, in unison – Hardy, Burdett, Urquhart, even Lord Rochester, all armed to the teeth. Rochester's monkey advanced alongside its master, spitting and hissing ferociously. Behind them came Lovell and his Marines, a menacing line of yellow-coated uniforms spread out across the deck, muskets primed and levelled, their new young commander fearless and resolute. But it was one sight above all others that finally turned the tide. Up from below came the familiar, stocky figure of Kit Farrell. In his hand he bore the sword that had severed the grappling ropes of the first fireship.

'Well, Sceptres?' I cried. 'Are you going to dishonour the heroism of Lieutenant Farrell, there, or will he be your example?' No more men moved toward the rail. 'Very good! Mister Hardy, Mister Urquhart – organise chains of men to bring up buckets from the pumps! Mister Carvell, there, to lead the men facing the fire! Lieutenant Farrell – take a party with the firepoles we have, to push the fireship away!'

'Is there still time?' asked Francis.

'God knows,' I said. 'Let us pray that there is –'

God's apparent rejection of our prayers seemed to come immediately. A sudden shaft of flame shot up from the quarterdeck rail and caught the foot of the mizzen sail, which caught light at once. If the fire spread into the running rigging and the other sails came down, the upper deck would be doused in flames from end to end.

'Lower the yard!' cried Kit.

Men ran to the shrouds, and the sail began to come down. But by now it was well alight, and bringing it onto the deck seemed just as likely to spread the flames as if it was left aloft.

Phineas Musk emerged from below, panting heavily. Behind him came my little body of servants, Kellett, Coleby, Denton and Smart. They were carrying what seemed to be bundles of wet rags, which they flung over the blazing sail as it came down to the deck. Clouds of steam rose. The fire was doused.

'Well done, Musk! Well done, boys!' I cried as I approached them. Only when I was immediately by them did I recognise one of the dampened 'rags' as the charred remnants of my best frock coat.

'Only stock of linen we could get our hands on in time,' said Musk. 'Only stock of linen that was all in one place, not scattered throughout the ship.'

'My *wardrobe*, Musk?'

'Think on it this way, Sir Matthew – Lady Quinton will greatly enjoy dressing you in new clothes.'

And so she would. But my ambivalent feelings about Musk's quick thinking were overtaken at once. A ragged cheer broke out from the men along the larboard rail, and at the gunports on the deck below. I ran to the rail, peered over, and saw the fireship falling away from us, carried past our stern by the very wind that had threatened to hold her to our hull. Kit and his men had done their work well: thankfully, the Dutch had secured this second vessel with fewer grapples than the first, relying principally on the wind and tide to keep her tight to our hull.

Without thinking upon my honour or dignity, I, too, joined in the men's cheering at our deliverance. Truly, God was an Englishmen; God was a Sceptre.

Finally, I returned to the quarterdeck. There were no hulls around us in the midnight darkness. I could just make out the distant lights of many stern lanterns: the enemy fleet, moving away to the south-east. The Dutch must have seen the fireships secure to our hull, seen the flames spreading, and assumed, entirely reasonably, that we were doomed.

But we were not. We were safe.

* * *

Fate is a strange business.

I have lived long enough to be able to say that with some authority. Indeed, the very fact that I am alive to say it is proof of the dictum. Why has fate preserved me for so very many years, when it decided that Lancelot Parks should go insane and throw himself into the sea? Why did fate preserve the *Royal Sceptre*, surrounded by the entire Dutch fleet and attacked by two fireships?

But I did not learn the most fateful consequence of that dreadful first day of the battle until many months later, when my dour good-brother Cornelis and I were together for the first time since the war. We were in the austere library of the van der Eide house in the

Zeeland port of Veere, a library that contained precisely one book: an enormous, well-thumbed and copiously annotated edition of the Bible in Dutch. We talked of what we did during that great fight, and of where our ships were in each hour of each day. Naturally, we talked of that first night, and of how the Zeeland squadron had fallen upon the *Royal Sceptre* as we tried to fight our way back to our own fleet. Unknown to either of us, Cornelis's *Adelaar* was one of those that attacked us during the night.

'That was *your* ship?' he said, more than a little incredulous.

I rarely saw Cornelis astonished; Calvinism does not look favourably upon astonishment. But now, he was.

'Yes, indeed. It was a miracle we managed to escape.'

Cornelis shook his head.

'More than a miracle, brother. Do you know what you did?'

'We fought off two fireships –'

'No. You did much more than that. When our flagship, the *Walcheren*, parted from you after Evertsen's offer of quarter, you fired off a random broadside, did you not?'

'We did. No more than a warning shot in the dark, to let Evertsen know that we still had teeth.'

'Oh, you did much more than that, Matthias. You killed him. You killed Evertsen, one of my country's greatest seamen.'

I knew that Admiral Cornelis Evertsen had fallen in the battle, but not when or how. It had been a chance shot as the ships parted by night, no more. Some men will call that the will of God, but I prefer to call it the working of fate. For if that was not fate, what is?

THE SECOND DAY: 2 JUNE 1666

Our little fleet was now ingag'd so far,
That, like the Sword-fish in the Whale, they fought.
The Combat only seem'd a Civil War,
Till through their bowels we our Passage wrought.

Dryden, *Annus Mirabilis*

I know what resurrection feels like: namely, like being raised from the dead.

The preachers will say I should burn in hell for this presumption, but a man nearing his ninetieth year cares not a fart for preachers or their cant. But no man's sleep can ever have been more like death than the three hours I snatched under a tarpaulin on the quarter-deck of the *Royal Sceptre*. It was a dreamless void, from which I was awakened rudely by that most unlikely archangel of rebirth, Phineas Musk.

'Fleet's getting under way,' said Musk. 'Half past five in the morning. Or three bells of the morning watch, as Mister Farrell insists I should call it. You seamen keep cursedly foul hours, and call them cursedly stupid names.'

I was about to damn Musk with every obscenity in my vocabulary for stirring me: my body was demanding another hour or ten of sleep. But a captain has to set an example, so I rose slowly and looked about me.

It was a glorious morning, the rising sun having been up for some forty minutes already. The wind had fallen off even more during the night, so we had a breeze of very nearly ideal strength from the south-west. And all around us, the fleet was re-forming for battle. All pretence at preserving the original order was gone now, and ships fell in where they could. We had finally rejoined the fleet at one in the morning, meaning we were the last ship into the anchorage and thus were on the very edge of it. But now, with the fleet moving off to the south, we were in the van, and duly fell in behind the new leader of the line, the mighty *Prince*, flagship of the Admiral of the White Squadron, Sir George Ayscue. There, away to the south-east, stood the myriad sails and ensigns of the Dutch, under sail toward us on the opposite tack. To the south-west, the sea was empty. There was no sign of Prince Rupert's fleet, returning from its mission to the west. But by the same token, there was no sign of the enemy that he had been sent to intercept: the French, coming to the aid of their allies, the Dutch. A French fleet containing my old friend and shipmate, Roger, Comte d'Andelys, who commanded the powerful new ship-of-the-line *Foudroyant*.

I wiped my eyes. Kellett brought me a jug of breakfast ale and a piece of bread.

'Joy of the morning, Sir Matthew,' said Kit Farrell, who was always unconscionably merry around dawn.

'And joy to you, Lieutenant. We are fit for battle, then?'

'As fit as we can be, Sir Matthew. The carpenter and his men have worked miracles on the larboard quarter-gallery. But –'

A cursory glance around the deck told me what Kit was so reluctant to say aloud. Men were scrambling along the yards, loosing our sails. Others were at the capstan, hauling in the anchor. But unaccustomed faces were at some of the stations, and others had fewer men than they should have done.

'How many?'

'Mister Musk mustered them at two bells, Sir Matthew. Eleven men killed yesterday, another twelve too badly wounded to man their stations. And thirty-four –'

'Thirty-four jumped to their deaths during the fireship attack. So we have lost nearly an eighth of the crew, Kit.' My friend nodded. 'Well, then – let us hope we beat the Dutch today, Lieutenant.'

* * *

I have a good memory for a man of my years. Indeed, it is usually significantly better than the memories of those who are barely a quarter of my age: in these days when almost the whole of England is awash on a sea of gin, even young men seem incapable by dinner of remembering what they had for breakfast. But when it comes to the precise order of events on that second day of the battle, I can chiefly recall only fragments of memories, and they come above all from flashes of the senses, from sight, smell and sound.

The little ships of both fleets – the yachts, galliots and the like – dashing hither and thither between the great hulls, fighting their own vicious miniature battles.

The sea carpeted with fallen masts and sails, interspersed with the bloated bodies of dead men.

The stench of gunsmoke, which hung over the battle like a shroud, the winds too light to disperse it: so thick at times that we could barely identify the nationality of the ship we were firing at, or see our own forecastle from the quarterdeck.

The men at the guns, stripped to the waists, sweat pouring down their bodies as the muzzles got ever hotter. The sun beating down relentlessly, its shafts sometimes piercing the smoke to cast a strange, ghostly light upon our decks.

The roaring of the great guns. The shock of their blast, striking one as hard as a punch in the chest. The sounds of the different types of shot as they sped through the air. The firing of muskets, with the pop of matchlocks contrasting with the sharper sound of the newer flintlocks. The shrill blast of officers' whistles. The cracking of timber as masts, yards and hulls splintered. The screams of men in their death throes, and of the wounded being carried down to the surgeon's cockpit. My own voice, hoarse from shouting orders and exhortations all day long. My swordarm, painful from having the heavy weapon in hand for hours on end.

Pass the Dutch on opposite but parallel courses, fire three or four mighty broadsides, try to break through their line and prevent them breaking through ours, tack, rest and repair in the interval, pass each other again, repeated over and over throughout the day, God knows how many times – even soon after the battle, some men were prepared to swear on their mothers' graves that we and they had passed five times, others said seven, others nine.

At one point, we thought we had won. Tromp and his squadron somehow became detached from the rest of the Dutch fleet and were lying to leeward, in the east, with our Red Squadron pouring down onto them. Fresh Holles, the charming rogue who later became a friend of sorts, once told me of it, as we sat drinking wine in the Southwark George:

'We had them, Matt. I'd taken the *Spiegel* with my *Antelope* – we'd set the *Liefde* on fire – two of their biggest ships, and we were pressing Tromp himself. We'd have won the war there and then, that afternoon, if you and the White had come to our aid. We saw the *Prince* coming up, the rest of you behind her. But did that old woman Ayscue come down to support us? No, he and the rest of you sailed merrily by –'

'Hardly fair, Fresh. There was another Dutch squadron to windward of us. If we'd moved to support you, they'd have split our fleet in two, isolating the Blue.'

'Stuff, Matt Quinton. Stuff, I say. A bold admiral would have been able to overwhelm Tromp before their other ships could move. As it was – well, you know what happened. The great De Ruyter himself smashes through our line and rescues Tromp. Now *he* knows what boldness means, that man. Not that I witnessed it, of course, because that was just after they blew my fucking arm off.'

Holles raised his glass to his lips with his right, and sole remaining, hand.

'You got a knighthood out of it, Sir Frescheville. And old Lely's painting of you and Rob Holmes wouldn't have been as fetching if you still had the other arm.'

'Fetching? You think it's fetching, with Holmes wearing that ludicrous turban? You have damned strange tastes in art, Matt Quinton.'

In one sense, though, Fresh Holles was right. That moment when we could have overwhelmed Tromp before De Ruyter rescued him was a glorious but missed opportunity to secure a decisive victory. For as the afternoon wore on, every inconclusive pass weakened the smaller fleet. Although we had taken on some fresh powder, shot and beer from a victualling hoy before dawn, we were running short of all three once more. But that was not the worst of it.

I sat upon the deck, sweating profusely, breathing hard and drinking a tankard of ale. The afternoon heat was as bad as any I had known in the Mediterranean, or on the west coast of Africa, but this was made worse by the all-pervasive gun smoke, forever clawing away in the throat and the nostrils, making the eyes stream. Down in the waist, men were slumped against gun carriages. Macferran, as stout and fit a man as I ever knew, seemed dazed, not really knowing where he was. On the quarterdeck, Musk was asleep on the deck, curled up against a pile of roundshot. Only Kit seemed fully aware, barking orders hoarsely through his voice trumpet to the helmsman at the whipstaff and those adjusting the yards and sails. We had just come through another tack and were heading north-west again. Off to the north were the Dutch, making their own turn. We had perhaps a half-hour at most before the next pass would begin: before men who had already endured more than any man should be asked to endure would have to do it all yet again. It was the same story throughout the fleet. In truth, we were very nearly not a fleet any longer, but a disordered mass of hulks with a profusion of fallen masts, shredded rigging, torn sails and ensigns. All around us, exhausted crews were erecting jury rigs on men-of-war that had been battered beyond their limits. We had lost ships like the *Swiftsure*, and others were so badly damaged that they had been forced out of the fight. We had a little over forty ships left that were serviceable, and they only barely. England's pride, its Navy Royal, was in ruins.

'God be with you, Sir Matthew,' said Francis Gale, lowering his heavy frame awkwardly onto the deck to sit beside me.

During the passes, Francis was as ferocious as our toughest men, firing his musket repeatedly at our opponents and exhorting backsliders. But during the intervals, he was the shepherd of his flock, moving from gun crew to gun crew and man to man, giving whatever words of comfort he could.

'And with you, Francis,' I croaked.

'Do you wish to pray, Matthew?'

'For victory. For the return of Rupert's ships. For Will Berkeley to be still alive. For deliverance from this hell. To see Cornelia again. For more beer. Those are my prayers, Reverend Gale.'

Francis nodded. 'Not dissimilar to those of nearly every man in your crew. Nor my own, in truth –'

There was a shout from the maintop lookout. I got to my feet, wearily and unsteadily, then walked heavily to the stern rail. Denton brought my telescope, and I looked away to the south-eastern horizon.

'It seems the Dutch have been praying too,' I said to Francis, 'only with rather more efficacy. A dozen sail. Reinforcements. Fresh ships, fresh crews. And no sign of Rupert with our own. We have lost, Francis. We have lost the battle. We have lost the war.'

* * *

The Dutch reinforcements were too far away to participate in the next pass, which took the form of all the others: in this case we were sailing north-west with the weather-gage, the Dutch south-east. The enemy gunfire seemed to have acquired a new ferocity, no doubt born of the Dutchmen's excitement and new-found resolve at seeing fresh ships about to come to their aid. Once again, though, the exhausted gun crews of the *Royal Sceptre* and the other ships of the fleet put up a stout resistance, although our fire was now markedly more ragged than it had been earlier in the day. At one point, we were engaged with a particularly persistent Rotterdammer, which came in closer than the rest. This fellow had many more musketeers in his tops than any other ship we had yet encountered. God alone knows how he fitted them all up there; perhaps the Dutch had recruited a Marine Regiment of dwarves. For some time, though, the enemy kept up a withering rate of fire onto our upper deck. No man could move in the open, and we of the quarterdeck took cover as best we could beneath remnants of the canvas fights, or in the steerage below. The Earl of Rochester alone seemed positively to enjoy the experience. As the musket-balls peppered the deck planking like hailstones, the noble lord laughed hysterically and recited one of his poems:

'I rise at eleven, I dine about two,
I get drunk before seven, and the next thing I do,
I send for my whore, when for fear of a clap,
I spend in her hand, and I spew in her lap –'

His monkey, which seemed to have become accustomed to battle and evidently approved of his master's verse, applauded enthusiastically.

Just then, I saw a movement over by the forecastle. Stride, the ship's purser, peeked out. A corpulent landman from one of the middle counties of Ireland, more accustomed to ledgers than the heat of battle, he could have had no grasp of the danger he was in. A shot struck him in the shoulder and span him round. He fell forward onto the deck, writhing in agony.

The upper deck was a killing ground. Lying out in the open, Stride would surely be hit and killed by more musket-shot. No man dared venture out into the open to retrieve him.

No man except one.

Lord Rochester ran forward, still reciting his poem:

'If by chance I then wake, hot-headed and drunk,
What a coil do I make for the loss of my punk!
I storm, and I roar, and I fall in a rage,
And missing my whore, I bugger my page –'

He sprinted across the deck, head bowed as though guarding his eyes from a sudden rain shower. The Dutch kept up their fire, but the noble lord seemed invulnerable; and as he ran, his monkey shrieked incessantly. Rochester reached Stride, pulled the purser to his feet by his good arm, and dragged him into the shelter of the forecastle.

'Brave,' said Kit Farrell.

'Brave and lucky,' I said.

'Madman,' said Musk. 'And now he'll live to write yet more poems about cocks, cunnies and whoring wenches. Like the world needs poets.'

Our *Royal Sceptre* could still put up a tough enough resistance to see off the Rotterdammer, which finally broke off the engagement. This latest pass completed, we awaited the flagship's orders to tack once again. But this time, no flag broke out in the rigging of the *Royal Charles*. Instead, I spied a galliot racing across the water from the *Royal Charles* to our squadron's own flagship, the *Prince*.

'The Duke's orders to Ayscue, no doubt,' I said to Kit. 'We shall know the upshot soon enough.'

The upshot took the form of orders from our admiral to the captains of several ships, the *Royal Sceptre* included, to repair at once aboard the *Prince*. It was a mighty risk, to summon a council with the Dutch to the south-east, presumably about to tack back toward us to resume the battle, but the *Sceptre*'s longboat duly carried me across the relatively calm sea toward the vast hull of the *Prince*. The great old ship had been England's pride for over half a century, eclipsed in size but not in prestige by the newer *Sovereign* (which still lay in the Medway, so enormous that it had proved impossible to man it). She had received damage – we all had – but wounds that would have disabled or sunk a smaller ship seemed like mere pinpricks on the *Prince*. Her spectacular gilding seemed to glimmer in the sunlight. The *Prince* was a palace afloat: a palace and a fortress, her vast brass cannon-of-seven protruding from the lower deck gunports as the *Sceptre*'s longboat brought me alongside.

Sir George Ayscue, Admiral of the White, stood in the middle of his spacious and lavishly decorated admiral's cabin. A well-dressed, fair-haired man of middle build, distinguished principally by huge bags under his eyes which gave him the look of a bloodhound, Ayscue was something of a curiosity among our admirals: godson to an Archbishop of Canterbury, no less, he had nonetheless thrown in his lot with Parliament and later gone off to command the Swedish Navy. As I entered the cabin, he was talking to the other chosen captains of our squadron, who, being nearer, had got across to the flagship well before me: Terne of the *Triumph*, Clark of the *Gloucester*, Moulton of the *Anne*. The connection between us was immediately obvious. We were the captains of the biggest ships that remained in the White Squadron.

'Ah, Quinton,' said Ayscue brusquely, in his strong Lincolnshire accent. 'Good. Glad to see you alive. Splendid business, your night fight – a miracle you made it through. Your man Farrell is the talk of the fleet, you know.' My fellow captains nodded appreciatively. This meant much to me: they were all veterans of the much-vaunted Commonwealth navy, bred to the sea almost since their births, and I was the only young gentleman captain in the cabin. 'Anyway, gentlemen, to business. The Duke's orders. We are not to tack again – God willing, there are to be no further passes today. The fleet is to hold this course, west by north. It's to be a fighting retreat back to the Thames mouth. The Dutch reinforcements give us no other option, especially with no sign of Prince Rupert and his fleet. We and the strongest ships from the Red and Blue are to form a rearguard, fifteen ships in line abreast, shepherding the others into the river.'

We four captains looked at each other. The same thought was in all our minds, but it was the most senior of us, bluff old Rob Clarke, who articulated it.

'It'll be difficult to bring that off, Sir George. The sands constrain our course, and once they bring their reinforcements into play, the Dutch can bring fifty to bear against our fifteen.'

'And what if the French have slipped past Rupert?' asked Harry Terne, a New Model Army veteran whom Cromwell had sent to sea. 'By dawn, we could have eighty against our fifteen.'

'You're probably the last man among us who believes the French fleet is real, Harry,' said Ayscue, smiling. 'God knows who spread that malicious lie, just as only He knows why our illustrious ministers of state saw fit to believe it. But even without the French, the odds against us are grim enough, as Captain Clarke rightly says.'

Ayscue beckoned forward one of his servants, who filled five fine Venetian glasses with wine. One of the perversities of naval battle is that huge masts fall, mighty hulls are shattered, and men are slaughtered by the dozen, but very often, the most delicate items aboard a ship survive a battering entirely unscathed. Ayscue handed a glass to each of us, then raised his own.

'It has been an honour to fight alongside you, gentlemen,' he said. 'Let us pray that tomorrow brings us good fortune – that it either carries us safe home into the river's mouth, or brings us Prince Rupert's squadron and victory. To the morrow.'

We raised our glasses.

'To the morrow.'

Chapter Six

THE THIRD DAY: SUNDAY, 3 JUNE 1666: DAWN TO 5PM

The long disaster better o'er to veil,
Paint only Jonah three days in the whale,
Then draw the youthful Perseus all in haste
From a sea-beast to free the virgin chaste…
For no less time did conqu'ring Ruyter chaw
Our flying Gen'ral in his spongy jaw.

Marvell, *Third Advice to a Painter*

We had stolen a march on the Dutch. At dawn, we could plainly see the enemy some six miles astern of us. As my good-brother Cornelis told me later, they had not expected us to retreat when we did, so had made their own turn to the north much too late. The winds were very light, but slowly and surely, the shattered English fleet was edging ever nearer to safety.

The morning was a time of rest. Many men had slept for only two or three hours altogether since the battle began, their captain among them. But now, with no cannonading and little wind, hence only infrequent adjustments of sail, we were able to resume a semblance of normal watch-keeping. Thus the off-duty men were able to lay down on the decks and snatch some blessed, refreshing sleep, while the duty watch continued to repair the damage from the previous two days of fighting. Even Rowan, the elderly ship's surgeon, emerged blinking into the open air, having been confined to his cockpit in the darkness of the orlop deck since the battle began. He had succeeded in stitching up Stride's shoulder, and thus had somehow managed to keep the purser alive. Truly, the old man deserved the very long draws he took upon his clay pipe, his eyes closed as he took in the pleasurable tobacco smoke.

They say that a captain and his ship are like lovers, and I can testify to the truth of that. Like a lover lying alongside his beloved in a bed, a captain instinctively senses the rhythm of the other's body. Even in the depths of sleep, a change in the other's breathing, or an attack of night-fear, will wake the lover in an instant. So it was on that third morning of the battle. I was in the very depths of a black, dreamless sleep, but somehow, suddenly I was aware that the *Sceptre* was picking up speed, and beginning to heel a little more to starboard. I woke, got to my feet, and looked about.

'Wind's getting up, Sir Matthew,' said Kit Farrell.

I looked up at the sails and flags, and saw the truth of it. Kit and Philemon Hardy, fine seamen and officers that they were, already had men aloft; as I watched, our white pennant unfurled and caught the strengthening breeze. All along the line abreast of the rearguard, the same thing was happening. But we could not put on too much sail, or else we would overhaul the smaller and, in many cases, badly damaged ships ahead of us. The Dutch had no such concerns. The gap between the fleets was already halved, and was diminishing by the minute.

At noon, Francis Gale conducted a brief Sunday service, after which the crew fell to dinner, one of Prentice the cook's tolerable salt beef stews. Thus nourished both physically and spiritually, the men were ready to return to their guns. It was as well that they were: by two in the afternoon, the Dutch had caught us. The vast demi-cannon stern chasers of the *Prince* and the *Royal Charles* fired, hurling thirty-two-pound balls toward the enemy, thus signalling the beginning of the day's fighting.

A big Zeelander was bearing down on us. I went down to the main deck, where the culverin protruding from the starboard stern port in the space where my cabin usually stood was manned by Polzeath, Tremar, Treninnick and three other Cornishmen, Olver, Dawe and Penhallurick. Burdett was moving from one gun to another, constantly computing angles and distances in his head.

'Ready to give them a hot reception, Master Gunner?'

'Aye, Sir Matthew. We've all the advantage in a chase – more and bigger guns in our sterns than they've got in their bows. And we can put our best gun crews to the task.'

'Very well, then. So, George Polzeath and John Tremar, do you think you can shatter yonder Dutchman's heads, so they have to shit over their ship's rail?'

'Reckon we can, Sir Matthew,' said the minute Tremar. The huge, taciturn Polzeath grunted in agreement.

'On your command, then, Mister Burdett.'

The gun crew went into their accustomed routine, the burly Dawe ramming home the cartridge, Treninnick the wadding, Olver the shot. Polzeath, as gun captain, stood ready, the lighted linstock in his hand.

'Give fire!' cried Burdett.

Both chasers, and those on the upper deck, fired simultaneously. The gun deck filled with smoke, but the Cornishmen were already controlling the recoil, Penhallurick already in position to swab. As the smoke began to clear, I went to the stern windows and looked out at the Dutch ship.

'Well done, lads!' I cried. 'The heads are shattered, and plenty of the beakhead rigging too! Keep up that sort of fire, and they'll soon be turning tail and running for their sea-gates!'

The chaser gun crews cheered, but they and I knew that it was a pyrrhic victory. Destroying one ship's heads was not going to stop the Dutch fleet. Their superiority in numbers was overwhelming. Unless we could get back into the river by the end of the day, they would catch us and destroy us.

Scobey appeared, running along the deck, halting before me and offering a sketchy salute.

'Beg pardon, Sir Matthew. Lieutenant Farrell's compliments, and he thinks you will want to be back on the quarterdeck.'

I went back up onto the upper deck. To either side, the other ships of our rearguard were blazing away with their stern guns. The *Sceptre*'s deck shuddered as our own guns fired again. But the attention of the men on the deck was not fixed on the duel between us and the oncoming Dutch. Every man was looking southward.

One of the yachts on scout duty in the distance had loosed her sails and was firing a gun. Our lookout bawled something, but I could not make out his words. On the ships to windward of us, men could be seen pointing toward the south-west.

Scobey brought me my telescope. Kit, Hardy and I all peered hard into our eyepieces. There were tiny shapes on the horizon. White shapes. Sails. Many of them.

'It's a squadron, all right, if not an entire fleet,' said Kit. 'From the south-west. From the Channel.'

'But which one?' I said.

I squinted even harder, staring at each new hull in turn as it came up over the horizon. Staring at the masts. Trying to make out the mastheads, and an admiral's ensign. If it was the white of the Bourbons, and thus the Duke of Beaufort's French fleet – including my friend Roger d'Andelys and his *Foudroyant* – then we were undoubtedly doomed. They and the Dutch behind us would trap us in a vast pincer. They would wipe out our fleet, leaving England open to invasion and conquest. But on the other hand…

I caught sight of a tiny shape that could only be a flag. I steadied myself and focused intently on it, blotting out everything around me. For some time, perhaps entire minutes, it was invisible, as if the breeze had fallen away or it had become furled around the masthead. Then, at last, the wind caught it, and the colours streamed out.

Red, white and blue.

I lowered my telescope. 'The Union at the main,' I said. 'It's the prince.'

They were already cheering on the windward ships. This set off a vast echo across the waters, each crew joining in as they realised what was happening. Down in the waist of the *Royal Sceptre*, exhausted men roused themselves, went to the ship's side, waved, punched their fists in the air, and screamed with joy. Ali Reis, the Moor, had tears streaming down his cheeks. Macferran danced a jig with Berrington, a foul Londoner who hated anyone that was not an Englishman, but who, in that moment, loved the young Scot like a brother. Lord Rochester, his monkey upon his shoulder, embraced my young servant, Kellett; I prayed that joy at our reinforcement was the only thought in the noble lord's mind. Further astern, though, Philemon Hardy, Kit Farrell and I hugged each other like long-parted sweethearts.

With every moment that passed, the glorious sight became more glorious still. There was the *Dreadnought*, flying at the mizzen the flag of the ferocious Ned Spragge; there, the *Revenge*, bearing one of the proudest, most battle-honoured names that any English man-of-war can possess; there, the tough old *Victory*, commanded by the legend that was Sir Christopher Myngs. Above all, the bow wave surged around the cutwater of the mighty *Royal James*, the flagship, as she ploughed through the sea toward us. Aboard her, no doubt urging his ships forward as once he had urged his cavalry against Cromwell's Ironsides, would be the man I had long held responsible for the death of my father at the Battle of Naseby. The man who, despite that, was now my patron in the navy: the man whom entire swathes of England had once looked upon as the devil incarnate, and one of the most famous warriors in the entire world.

Prince Rupert of the Rhine was charging to our rescue.

* * *

Through the afternoon, we steered west-south-west toward the prince, who was sailing north-north-east to join us as swiftly as possible. The Dutch, realising that they were about to lose the advantage, redoubled their attacks against us, but our stern chasers continued to hold them off. Once we united with the prince's squadron, the question of why our fleet came to be divided in the first place would be forgotten. All the suspicions, all the dark rumours about conspiracies and treachery, would be swept away. All was set fair to turn the tables on the Dutch.

There was one cloud: a cloud which hung above the heads of our ship's master and lieutenant, poring over the chart table next to the whipstaff. Musk informed me of an altercation between them, so a little before two bells of the Last Dog, I went down to see what the matter was. Both men pointed to a chart which was covered in a bewildering pattern of lines. It was as if the great Van Dyck had got drunk and attempted to execute a portrait by holding a pencil in his teeth.

'It's been impossible to keep accurate track of our position, Sir Matthew,' said Kit. 'We and the Dutch have tacked back and forth so many times, always out of sight of land, that no captain or master in the fleet is certain of exactly where we are.'

'Nonsense,' said Hardy. 'I am as certain of our position as any man can be. We are here' – he stabbed at a point on the chart – 'some fifteen leagues north-east of the North Foreland. Well clear of the difficulty that Lieutenant Farrell perceives.'

'That difficulty being, Mister Farrell…?'

'The Galloper, Sir Matthew. Mister Hardy believes that both we and Prince Rupert's fleet are well to the north of it. But what if we are not? What if the Galloper lies between us?'

I stared down at the chart. There it was, clearly marked – the Galloper Sand. The estuary of the Thames and the southern North Sea beyond it is full of huge and dangerous sandbanks, and the Galloper is one of the largest of them all, a giant wall of sand that stretches for miles, almost due east of Harwich.

'The Galloper cannot lie between us,' said Hardy, emphatically. 'Is Captain Kempthorne of the *Royal Charles* wrong? Is Sir Joseph Jordan, who has been sailing these waters for fifty years? Every veteran seaman in the fleet knows where we are! I am a Brother of Trinity House, Mister Farrell, and I tell you –'

Hardy was never able to speak the rest of the sentence. The *Sceptre* stopped abruptly. The great hull shook. The timbers screamed in protest. We were thrown from our feet. My left shoulder slammed against a great timber knee, causing such pain that I could only assume I had broken it. I got up. Kit was on the other side of the steerage and seemed unharmed, merely winded. The helmsman, Teague, was picking himself up. But Philemon Hardy lay still on the floor, a dark pool seeping from the ugly gash in his head.

'His head went straight against the end of the whipstaff, Sir Matthew,' said Teague. 'Smashed his brain open.'

Perhaps it was for the good. Hardy had been a proud man, and he would have found it difficult to bear the humiliation of being so catastrophically wrong. I gave orders for Urquhart, the boatswain and an experienced ship-handler, to succeed immediately as acting master, and for a party to attend to the corpse. The remains of Philemon Hardy would be sewn into a hammock and stored in the hold, in the hope that we might get an opportunity to give him a more dignified farewell than that accorded to so many of the fleet's casualties, who had simply been slung unceremoniously over the side.

Clutching my shoulder and wincing at the pain, I made my way back up to the quarterdeck, followed closely by Kit. I looked quickly to starboard and larboard. The ships most nearly level with us, the

Dunkirk of the Red Squadron and the ancient *Saint George* of the Blue, were similarly aground, as was the flagship, the *Royal Charles*, a little further off to the north-west. Our hull seemed to be at once swaying unnaturally and growling like some vast, indignant beast. And there were the Dutch, closing rapidly. They built their men-of-war smaller than ours, with shallow draughts to enable them to traverse the shoals in their own waters. If we could not get off the sand, they would batter our stranded ships into matchwood.

'The smaller ships ahead of us would have gone over it without even knowing it was there,' said Kit. 'They are not to blame for not warning us.'

'Disaster upon disaster,' I said, pacing my quarterdeck furiously. 'The fleet divided. Rupert sent west. Now this. Well, Francis –' I turned to the *Sceptre*'s chaplain – 'do you have a prayer to get a fleet off a sandbank?'

'The Church always has a prayer, Sir Matthew. A prayer for any and every occasion. I was but now contemplating Acts, Chapter Twenty-Seven, where the Angel of the Lord assured Saint Paul that all those on his ship would be saved –'

'Aye, Reverend,' said the Earl of Rochester, 'but was not Paul's ship wrecked anyway?'

'I had not taken you for a theologian, My Lord,' said Francis.

'One needs to know the Commandments before one can break them, Reverend.'

Francis smiled; he was enough of a realist to know when he had encountered a lost cause, and the Earl of Rochester was most certainly lost to any semblance of the Christian faith. Instead, Francis brought his hands together in supplication, raised his eyes to the heavens, and recited the words of the Book of Common Prayer.

'O most glorious and gracious Lord God, who dwellest in heaven, but beholdest all things below; look down, we beseech thee, and hear us, calling out of the depth of misery, and out of the jaws of this death, which is ready now to swallow us up: save, Lord, or else we perish –'

The sails strained. The ship's timbers groaned. Men looked anxiously over the ship's rail, down towards the waters yellowed by the sand being churned up by our keel. There was one great, final shudder and then the ship surged forward once more. We were free of the Galloper.

Francis turned to Rochester. 'Such, My Lord, is the power of God Almighty.'

'No, Reverend, in all truth. Such is the power of the rising of the tide.'

I took up my telescope and studied the great ships of our rearguard. All of us had scraped the sandbank and got over it, even the large *Royal Charles*.

All except one.

As the rearguard gathered speed again, a gap opened between ourselves and the largest ship of all, still stubbornly stationary upon the sandbank. The huge, ancient *Prince* drew far more water than any other ship in the fleet, and she was stuck fast. The flags still streamed out from her stern and maintop, but the *Prince*, the pride of England, was on her own. And bearing down on her rapidly was the entire Dutch fleet. The enemy now knew exactly where the Galloper was, but in any case, their smaller hulls and shallower draughts meant that they did not need to fear it.

There was nothing any of us could do. The Duke sent back a few frigates in the hope of taking off the crew, but both wind and tide were against them. As I watched through my telescope, Dutch ships surrounded the *Prince*. There could only be one outcome.

'Her flags are coming down,' I said to those around me on the quarterdeck. 'She's surrendered.'

There was an audible groan from the crew of the *Royal Sceptre* and the ships nearest to us. The *Prince* symbolised England in a way that no other individual ship did, not even the larger *Sovereign*. More immediately, she mounted a hundred superb brass guns, and together with those lost with the *Swiftsure* on the first day, the loss to our fleet's gunpower was catastrophic. Ayscue, too, was one of our best admirals, and no English sea-officer of his rank had ever surrendered; indeed, to this day, no other has. But worse was to come. The *Prince* floated off at high tide, but the Dutch seemed unable to do anything with her – Cornelis later told me that they found her rudder too badly shattered, and in any case she was too vast to negotiate the shallow channels of the Dutch coast – and at about three bells of the Last Dog, flames ignited on the upper deck of the great ship. Within a couple of hours, she was alight from stem to stern. At midnight, as I watched from the stern rail of the *Sceptre*, she blew up.

* * *

During the evening, while the *Prince* burned astern of us, the joint admirals – now reunited – summoned a Council of War of the flagmen and senior captains aboard the *Royal James*. I was barely dressed for the part; my best frock coat, which had somehow survived Musk's improvised fire-dousing during the fireship attack, would not fit over my heavily bandaged shoulder. Rowan, the surgeon, had inspected it, causing me more agony than a sword-wound as he prodded into my flesh, but eventually pronounced it to be badly bruised, not broken. So I was in a fit, if under-dressed, condition to be rowed across to the Prince's flagship. Kit Farrell accompanied me; the generals-at-sea had sent for him specifically. But in the first instance, he remained outside Prince Rupert's great cabin while the rest of us clapped old friends on the back and toasted the reuniting of the fleet. Then we set to the serious business of the council, namely thrashing out the new dispositions.

'My ships to form the new van,' said the Prince in his strong German accent. 'They are undamaged, fresh for battle. Kit Myngs to lead with his division. The very approach of the terror of the Spanish Main will have De Ruyter scuttling back to his harbours.'

We laughed – and God knows, we needed humour, with the blazing *Prince* in plain sight through the windows of the *Royal James*. Sir Christopher Myngs nodded in acknowledgement. He was a modest man, despite the fame attached to his name: a small, florid Norfolk man with slightly receding hair. His appearance and manner belied his quite astonishing reputation. For years on end, Myngs had wreaked havoc on the Spaniards of the Caribbee, raiding their ports and pillaging their huge treasure ships. I am told that to this day, mothers on Cuba who wish to bring their children to obedience threaten them with Myngs' ghost coming back to terrorise them. An admiral who loved nothing more than to take part in the seamen's deck-games, and hated nothing more than hanging them, it was no surprise that Kit Myngs was beloved throughout the fleet.

'Very well,' said Albemarle. 'Now, the question of a successor to poor Ayscue in command of his squadron.'

My ears pricked up; whoever received the vacant flag would be my immediate commanding officer. Somewhere deep inside me, a small devilish voice spoke up: *why not me*? But I dismissed it immediately. I did not have the seniority for a squadron command, although a division, say as Rear-Admiral of the Blue, might be a different matter. In truth, though, I knew I had no prospect of such a promotion as long as the Duke of Albemarle was in sole, or even only joint, command of the fleet; for even if Prince Rupert, my new patron in the navy, advanced my case, he would hardly prevail against Albemarle's bitter opposition to gentleman captains. The bad grace with which the Duke accepted the King's appointment of Will Berkeley as Vice-Admiral of the White had been palpable enough, and poor Will's fate would surely have confirmed Albemarle in his prejudice.

'The Duke and I have conferred privately,' said the Prince, 'and have decided that by virtue of his great merit, and his gallantry in this battle, the flag should go to Sir Robert Holmes.'

I looked across the table. Sir Thomas Allin, Rupert's flag captain on the *Royal James*, a dour old Suffolk Cavalier with vast eyebrows, a haughty demeanour and an unhealthy obsession with the protocols of saluting, looked even more thunderously discontented than was his wont. He was undoubtedly much senior to the new recipient of the flag, and had cause to be angry. But as I shifted my gaze from him to my new admiral, I had equal cause to be well content. I nodded in deference to Sir Robert Holmes, who grinned back at me. We were old friends, having fought together on the African coast. Indeed, Holmes's depredations there had been one of the principal causes of the war. I dreaded to think just how much my head would ache after Robin Holmes and I found an opportunity to celebrate his elevation.

'Now, the chief command of the fleet,' said Albemarle. 'The original instructions from His Majesty the King and His Royal Highness the Duke of York appointed us as joint admirals, flying one flag, in the same ship –'

'But in the circumstances,' Rupert interrupted, 'we have decided it is fittest that we remain in our respective flagships, each flying the Union at the main. That way, I can exercise better command over the van during tomorrow's battle.'

There was an awkward moment or two of utter silence. The men around the table looked at each other, unsure what to say. The Duke of Albemarle's face was a mask; even a kingmaker dared not publicly contradict the son of a king. Was it truly his will that the command should be divided, or was it solely the will of Prince Rupert? But whatever its origin, the decision had clearly been made, and there would be no going back. An English fleet would go into battle with two equal heads in two different ships. The potential for confusion at best, disaster at worst, was obvious to every man in that cabin, but none of us uttered a word. Instead, the meeting resumed its ordinary course, with the talk turning to the precise ordering of each division.

As we left the great cabin an hour or so later, my new admiral took me aside. I offered him joy of his promotion, but that was not what concerned Holmes.

'So what do you make of it, Matt? Rupert to remain in this ship, the Duke in the *Charles*?'

I was careful in my answer; although I counted Rob Holmes as a friend, I did not entirely trust him. I do not think I ever found any man who did.

'His Highness is never happy at being under others, or equal to any,' I said. 'You know that better than any man, Rob – you've served him longer than any of us.'

I recalled a visit I had paid to the prince in his rooms at Whitehall Palace, not long after he and Albemarle were commissioned as joint admirals. Rupert was a most scientific prince, ever tinkering with machines and mixing chemicals. He had transformed a large chamber into a laboratory, much to the dismay of the palace functionaries, who were convinced he would blow them all to kingdom come at any moment.

'A dual command,' said Rupert, pouring a foul-smelling liquid into a jar, where it reacted with the contents to produce a noxious green cloud. 'Monstrous. Unworkable. My cousins the King and Duke of York have been swayed by Albemarle and Penn and Sandwich, all Cromwell's generals-at-sea. "Oh," they say, "look how we triumphed over the Dutch with our commanders in double or even triple harness, all in the same ship!" Madness, Quinton, nought but madness. Englishmen do not like a double-headed monster leading them. I am minded to resign my commission. Let them send out George Monck on his own and see how the fat old turncoat fares. Yes, I am certain I will resign. Now, tell me of your uncle Tristram's experiment with feeding mercury to a monkey –'

I uttered some flattering words to mollify the prince, but I do not now entirely recall them. In short, though, it was no surprise to me that Rupert was delighted beyond measure when the fleet was divided and he was given his own independent command, sailing off to the west to intercept the French fleet that was believed to be approaching England's fair shore. None of us could know what that decision would presage. No, none of us could know.

'Aye, true, the prince isn't a man who likes constraint,' said Holmes, whose assessment of Rupert's opinions was rather more explicit when he was in his cups. 'But then, neither is Albemarle. He was just as keen for the fleet to be divided in the first place, if not keener. Still, whatever we think of it won't make one jot of difference – the course is set, and let us pray there's a safe haven at the end of it. But you'll come with me over to the *Defiance*, to toast the hoisting of my flag, Matt? There's no risk of a night engagement, and I'm mightily thirsty.'

'Sorry, Rob. The Prince and Duke have requested me to attend them privately, with my lieutenant.'

That lieutenant was pacing the quarterdeck of the *Royal James*, discussing God knows what with Hart of the *Rainbow*. I summoned him below, and together we went into the great cabin.

'Your Highness, your Grace,' I said, 'I have the honour to present and name Lieutenant Christopher Farrell.'

'Lieutenant,' said Rupert appreciatively. 'I have returned from my westerly cruise to find your name a byword in the fleet. A byword for initiative, and for valour.'

'I – I merely did my duty, Your Highness,' said Kit, who was ever tongue-tied in the presence of the great.

'Would that every man in the fleet saw such heroism as his duty,' said Albemarle, growling in his broad Devon brogue. 'Thus it is only right and proper that your example should be amply rewarded, Lieutenant, so that others will be encouraged to follow you. Especially as you are a true seaman, a good staunch Wapping tar. The sort of man that the navy of England needs, in truth.'

Albemarle glanced at me knowingly, then turned, looking instinctively for his secretary: but he did not find him, for Sir William Clarke's leg had been shot off during the flagship's brush with the *Eendracht* on the first day. He was somewhere below decks at that very moment, dying in agony. Instead, Prince Rupert nodded to his own amanuensis, who handed him a familiar-looking sealed vellum document.

'You testify to the good qualities of this man, Sir Matthew, beyond the gallantry he displayed in saving the *Royal Sceptre*?' Prince Rupert's question, couched in his familiar, strong German accent, was accompanied by a rare smile. 'You recommend him without hesitation?'

'I do, Your Highness. Without hesitation.'

'Very well, then. Mister Farrell – ' Rupert handed the document to Kit, who was swaying slightly on his feet – 'we, Rupert, Prince Palatine of the Rhine, Duke of Cumberland, and George, Duke of Albemarle, joint admirals of His Majesty's fleet, hereby appoint and commission you to command His Majesty's ship the *Black Prince*, the post being vacant upon the death in battle of Captain Walter Jackson. May your command of her be victorious and prosperous.'

The *Black Prince*, of Holmes's old division in the Red Squadron: a fine, nimble Fourth Rate frigate of forty-six guns, sister ship to the *Wessex* that I had commanded in the Mediterranean some three years earlier. Far better than my first command in the navy – and my second, come to that. It was a dizzying elevation indeed. Kit opened the seal and stared blankly at the words on the vellum. I knew him well enough to know what he would be thinking: that he, who had been but an illiterate master's mate so very recently, now commanded a mighty royal warship. He could read the words that made him so, too, thanks to the bargain he and I had made with each other in Kinsale fort so few years before. He was a king's captain now, and that rank alone conferred upon him the status of a gentleman. In both our profession and in society, he was very nearly my equal. Truly, Kit Farrell had gone up in the world, and I was not a little proud of the part I had played in his rise. How proud his widowed mother would be, too. Perhaps there would even be limitless free beer for her customers at the Slaughtered Lamb in Wapping.

I grinned, extended my hand, and spoke the words I had longed to utter since that fateful day when the young Kit had saved my life.

'I give you joy of your command, Captain Farrell,' I said.

'Aye, joy,' growled Albemarle. 'Let us trust it is indeed joy for us all tomorrow. For tomorrow, gentlemen, we attack.'

Chapter Seven

THE FOURTH DAY: MONDAY, 4 JUNE 1666: 4 AM TO 4 PM

Thus reinforc'd, against the adverse Fleet,
Still doubling ours, brave Rupert leads the way;
With the first blushes of the Morn they meet,
And bring night back upon the new-born day.

His presence soon blows up the Kindling fight.
And his loud guns speak thick like angry men;
It seem'd as Slaughter had been breath'd all night,
And Death new pointe his dull Dart agen.

Dryden, *Annus Mirabilis*

The fourth day: cloudy and misty.

At dawn, a delegation approached the quarterdeck. There were twenty or so men, some of them among my oldest and closest followers – the likes of Tremar, Polzeath and Macferran. They seemed unlikely mutineers, and I could not think of anything they might have concerns about: the victuals were no more foul than usual, the decks were mostly scrubbed clean of the blood of their shipmates from the previous days, and we seemed in no greater danger of being slaughtered by the Dutch than we had been at any stage in the battle. So it was with some puzzlement that I stood at the head of the quarterdeck stair, looking down gravely.

It was the tiny Tremar who stepped forward, his Monmouth cap clutched respectfully in his hands.

'Begging pardon, Sir Matthew,' he said, 'but there's something that mightily concerns us all.'

The rest of them nodded vigorously and murmured assent.

'Speak, then, Tremar. You know me for a fair man, I trust – a captain who will always listen to his crew's concerns.'

'That you are, Sir Matthew. Well, sir, it's this. We're all pleased beyond measure that Lieutenant – that is, Captain Farrell, has got his command, sir. Couldn't be happier, in truth.'

I tried to remain impassive, but I had half-expected this. Kit Farrell was immensely popular on the lower deck: there were bound to be men who wished to follow him into his new command. But for them to include these, men whom I had counted as unfailingly loyal to me – very nearly as friends, indeed…

'Well, then, John Tremar. If Captain Farrell has sufficient men to exchange for you, I am sure we could accomplish it before we engage the Dutch again –'

'No, Sir Matthew. You mistake us, sir. No man seeks to go to the *Black Prince* – we are Sceptres, and until this battle ends, we live and die with you aboard the King's Prick. But now Mister Farrell has gone to his new ship, we have no lieutenant. And that troubles us, Sir Matthew.'

It troubled me, too, if truth be told, and had done ever since I left the *Royal Charles* the previous evening with the newly-minted Captain Farrell. Rupert and Albemarle had not seen fit to commission a new lieutenant to the *Sceptre*, which left me with an immense gap among the officers who were qualified to stand watches. The ship's master, Urquhart, was new to that role, and I could hardly elevate him to acting lieutenant within a day. If Martin Lanherne had been with us, I would not have hesitated in appointing him. But he was far away in Cornwall, press-ganging men into the King's navy. I had briefly considered making Ensign Lovell into an acting lieutenant. Although he knew nothing of the sea, he was a brave lad who would have amply filled one of a ship's lieutenants' most important roles, namely encouraging the men by his brave example: or, as a cynic like Fresh Holles or Lord Rochester might have put it, by standing out in the open and being shot at. But that would have left the Marine detachment without an officer, and having lost their captain, Parks, in such dire circumstances, that was a risk I dared not take.

'My thanks to you and the men, Tremar, but I see no means of giving us a new lieutenant before we engage again.'

'That's what we were thinking about, Sir Matthew. And we reckoned there was one among us whose undaunted courage under fire amply qualifies him to be our lieutenant.'

Musk? I thought. *He would be the oldest, fattest lieutenant in the navy, but perhaps there was some merit in the notion* – but then I saw some of the men looking toward Lord Rochester. *Great God, no. Rochester for lieutenant of a man-of-war's crew? It would be like placing a satyr in charge of a convent.*

'Aye, Sir Matthew. We all think that our new lieutenant should be Lord Rochester's monkey.'

For a moment, every single one of the men standing in front of me, and Rochester himself, remained stone-faced and silent. Then the noble earl burst out laughing, followed by the delegation. Even George Polzeath, ever the most serious of men, had tears streaming down his cheeks. I looked around in confusion, but then I, too, began to laugh. Indeed, I doubled up with laughter, only for that to trigger a wave of pain from my damaged shoulder.

'A noble jest, My Lord,' I said to Rochester, who was laughing so much that he had to cling on to the ship's rail to steady himself.

'A jest, Sir Matthew? How can it be so, when we have found you a lieutenant?'

The beast in question was sitting upon a demi-culverin, looking suspiciously at a cabbage that one of the master's mates had given it. I went toward it, and it hissed.

'So be it, then, noble monkey!' I cried, now enjoying the jest as much as any of the rest. 'By the powers vested in me by His Highness Prince Rupert and His Grace the Duke of Albemarle, I, Sir Matthew Quinton, do name you – My Lord Rochester, just what is this officer's name?'

Rochester grinned.

'Sir Matthew,' he said, 'even aboard a man-of-war, I think that the name I call this noble monkey would be too obscene for public consumption.'

'So be it, My Lord. I do name you lieutenant of His Majesty's ship the *Royal Sceptre* for the remainder of this expedition. Do your duty well, Lieutenant Monkey!'

The beast hissed even more malevolently.

* * *

When we found the Dutch, away to the south-east, they had the weather gage. At first, the fourth day of the battle seemed set to be a repeat of the second: a series of inconclusive passes, the two fleets arrayed in their long lines, firing at each other from a distance. Late in the morning, though, I saw Myngs's *Victory*, leading our line, suddenly tack and make directly for the Dutch, followed by the ships nearest him. They cut sharply across the wake of the rearmost ships in the Dutch line, Admiral Tromp's Amsterdammers, the *Victory* sailing very nearly under the stern of the last Dutch ship.

'He's going for the weather gage!' I cried.

It was a glorious but heart-stopping sight. The *Victory*, first built back in the days of the first King James, but newly rebuilt at vast expense into a formidable titan of the oceans, charged directly at the enemy, her starboard broadside blazing away. It was obvious what Myngs was trying to do: get round the Dutch line, get to windward of them, and gain the advantage of the wind. But it was obvious to the enemy, too, and they were determined to stop him. The Dutch line edged further and further to the west, the van tacking and racing south-east to cut off the English attack.

'God be with you, Kit Myngs,' I prayed.

We were tacking and closing the enemy too. The two vast lines of ships smashed into each other, each seeking to break through the other. Rupert's ships, ahead of us, hammered at the Dutch, the mighty *Royal James* blazing away on both sides of her hull. From our position, a good half-mile or so behind, we could see fireships igniting. But sails, hulls and gunsmoke obscured our vision: it was impossible to see whether the fireships had any effect or not.

'The *Black Prince* will be in there somewhere,' I said to Francis Gale. 'Let us pray that fortune favours Captain Farrell.'

'He has always struck me as a young man with an ample measure of good fortune,' said the *Royal Sceptre*'s chaplain.

'Sir Matthew!' It was Johnson, one of the master's mates. 'The flagship is hoisting a signal!'

I had no need to peer through my telescope; the *Royal Charles* was dead ahead of us, no more than three-hundred yards away. And the flag she was hoisting was a very familiar one.

'The blue at the mizzen. We are to follow in her wake. She's starting her turn, gentlemen. We're going to follow the *Royal James*, and cut straight through the Dutch fleet.'

This would take us into the very heart of the storm. Within minutes, a sixty-gunner of the Maas Admiralty came up on our larboard quarter, and we began to trade broadsides. The *Sceptre*'s quarterdeck demi-culverins fired, recoiled, were reloaded. Boys ran up from below with fresh cartridge and shot. Young Lovell's Marines, and their counterparts on the Dutchman, exchanged musket fire. Musk raised a pistol as though he had no care in the world and were merely discharging it to scare birds off a corn field, then fired it at the Dutchman's quarterdeck. Denton loaded my own pistol, handed it to me, and I, too, gave fire, revelling in the familiar thrill of the blast and the recoil. Rochester took up a *grenado* and pulled back his right arm, ready to throw it. But Lieutenant Monkey leapt forward, snatched the little bomb from his grip, jumped onto the larboard rail, and flung it at the Dutch ship. The *grenado* burst on the quarterdeck. It blew the left arm off the nearest Dutchman, who grabbed at the bleeding stump in shock and agony, tottered to the ship's side, and fell into the sea. The monkey turned toward us with an expression on its face that could have been construed as a broad grin. Then the 'lieutenant' of the *Royal Sceptre* shat copiously over the deck.

'I trust you approve the gallantry of your new lieutenant, Sir Matthew!' laughed Rochester.

'Alas, My Lord, I shall have to reduce him back to the ranks again for breaking the order against relieving oneself on deck!'

A new threat – a great hull appeared through the gunsmoke, to starboard. An Amsterdammer, by her ensigns. We would have to fight both sides of the ship at once. Burdett already had men running to the starboard guns. A minute or two later, they opened up on our new opponent.

'She's coming in close!' shouted Urquhart. 'Any closer, and our yards will touch!'

'Marines, to starboard!' cried Lovell from the other side of the quarterdeck. 'Fire at will!'

Our volley was met by an identical response from the Dutch Marines. Orchard, the senior master's mate, was standing between Urquhart and myself. Suddenly the right side of his skull blew away, and he fell to the deck, groaning and writhing, clutching the remnants of his head. The piece of bone and hair struck my face, bloodying my forehead. Then our demi-cannon thundered on the gundeck below. The *Sceptre* shook, but it was as nothing to the effect on the Amsterdammer. Her hull shuddered as huge timbers shattered and spiralled into the air. The Dutch ship seemed to physically move across the water, such was the force of the blow. She sheered away, and I saw clear water ahead, both the *Royal Charles* and ourselves moving into it to follow Prince Rupert's ships. We were through the Dutch line. We had the weather gage.

For the moment, we were unengaged. I slumped against a gun carriage and began to settle my breathing. I saw young Scobey and Denton emerge from below, carrying jugs of ale for the quarterdeck. There was a shot, the whistling sound of a ball crossing the water, a parting shot from the stern chaser of the Amsterdammer. Denton's right arm was torn off at the shoulder a moment before the ball shattered Scobey's chest, driving him back hard onto the stock of a demi-culverin. I ran to him at once, but the loyal young lad was already dead. Denton lived, but his blood was pouring from the terrible wound in his side.

'Tell,' he whispered, 'tell my mother –'

A steam of blood from his mouth put paid to Denton's last words. Kellett, his close friend, came up from below at that moment. The lad's face turned white, and he spewed over the deck.

Francis came across, and began reciting the prayers for the dead. As he did so, I looked upon the remains of my two young servants, and damned the world. All those hopes, all those ambitions, snuffed out by a chance shot. Two brave young lives that would be forgotten amongst the greater carnage of this titanic battle.

There was no time for mourning. Urquhart was pointing astern, and I turned my telescope toward what was happening behind us.

'The Zeelanders,' I said. 'They're going to try to break back through our line!'

We had got through the Dutch by pouring through a gap in their line of battle and getting to windward of them. Now the Zeeland squadron was going to attempt to do exactly the same to us. One of them was sailing directly for the gap of a cable and a half or so between ourselves and the *Antelope*, directly astern.

'Hold your position, Fresh,' I murmured, 'for God's sake, hold your position!'

The two broadsides of the Zeelander spat out simultaneously, to be met by an immediate response from the *Sceptre* and Fresh Holles's command.

'Wish we weren't relying on that man,' said Musk, who had no time for Holles. 'What's it that your Mister Pepys calls him? A wind-fucker? Seems like fair comment to me.'

The Zeelander came on, still aiming for the non-existent gap. If he attempted to force the passage, he would be devastated by our stern chasers and rammed by the *Antelope*, which would have no sea-room to do anything else. Again our broadsides roared. We were within pistol-shot of the enemy's beakhead now, and all of us on the quarter-deck, along with Lovell's Marines, were blazing away. Still the *Antelope* held her position. But…

'Damnation! Look there, Musk! Fresh Holles has kept station with us, but by doing so, he's pulled away from the *Ruby*, Will Jennens's ship! Will's foremast's nearly gone, by God – he can't keep his position – and both *Antelope* and *Ruby* are only Fourth Rates, and the Dutch can see that –'

Four Zeeland ships, one of them Vice-Admiral Banckert's flagship, all of them bigger than our two Fourths, were sailing directly for the widening gap between the *Antelope* and the *Ruby*. Our own adversary, seeing the easier course and that the addition of his own strength would tip the scales decisively in favour of the Dutch, fell away and altered course toward the stern of the *Antelope*. But the change of course turned the quarterdeck of the Zeelander toward us, and as we unleashed one last broadside against her, I spied her captain through my telescope. I could not see his face, but his build was all too familiar.

'It seems we have traded fire with my good-brother, Musk,' I said.

'He's still alive, then? Damn. Thought I'd heard the last of his sanctimonious Dutch prating. Still, I suppose Lady Quinton will be happy that her twin's still got his head on his shoulders.'

But I had no time to contemplate my brush with Captain Cornelis van der Eide, my brother-in-law. The Zeeland ships were pouring through the gap astern of the *Antelope*, and it was apparent at once that our fleet's position was desperate. The Blue Squadron was now isolated, caught on the wrong side of the Dutch. Meanwhile the *Victory* and her seconds, all battle-scarred and badly damaged, were falling further and further away to leeward, very nearly out of sight as I peered through my telescope.

I only learned the fate of Sir Christopher Myngs much later, from his lieutenant John Narbrough. The *Victory* had become embroiled in an almighty duel with a huge Dutch flagship, and early in the engagement, Myngs's face was shattered by a musket ball. But he stayed on deck, holding together his cheeks with his hands and continuing to direct the fight, until a second shot struck him in the neck. He was taken below and Narbrough took over the command, but even then, the tough little man would not die. He lingered for days, and even seemed set fair for recovery, despite the gruesome wounds he had suffered. At last, though, he succumbed, and England lost one of its greatest heroes. I would have gone to his funeral, but by then I was already embarked upon a dark and desperate mission for my King. Mister Pepys of the Navy Board went, and later, he told me what transpired. He was about to get into the coach of Sir William Coventry, the Duke of York's secretary, when the two of them were approached by a tearful delegation from Myngs's crew, who spoke words to this effect:

'We are here a dozen of us that have long known, loved and served our dead commander, Sir Christopher Myngs, and have now done the last office of laying him in the ground. We would be glad if we had any service we could do for him, and in revenge of him. But all we have is our lives. If you will please to get His Royal Highness to give us a fireship among us all, here are a dozen of us willing to go in it. Choose any one to be her captain, and the rest of us will serve him, whoever he is. Then, if possible, we will honour the memory of our dead commander, and give him the revenge he deserves.'

Such is the true spirit of England.

But such, alas, is also the true nature of England's government: overwhelmed by the weight of business during wartime, Sir William Coventry simply forgot all about the offer.

* * *

With the fleet in desperate straits, I had only one thought, and only one duty: protect the flag. That meant defending the *Royal Charles*, and as the Dutch continued to breach the gaps in our line, I had Urquhart con the *Sceptre* into position off the flagship's starboard quarter, to protect her from any enemy ships which attempted a raking pass. Tromp himself approached in his mighty *Hollandia*, but both we and the *Royal Charles* gave him a hot reception with a shattering broadside.

'Flagship's hoisting the blue at the mizzen, Sir Matthew!'

'Very good, Mister Urquhart! Fall into her wake, as the instructions require!'

'She's wearing ship – coming round onto the other tack!'

'Then we shall do the same!'

My words might have sounded confident, but a dark fear gnawed at my heart. Francis Gale sensed it. As the ships around the *Royal Charles* wore around onto the other tack until we were bearing roughly south-east again, parallel to the rear of the Dutch, the *Sceptre*'s chaplain stepped over to me and spoke softly.

'You seem troubled, Matthew.'

'They tell us the days of miracles are passed, Francis, and that saints no longer walk the earth. But I think you need to pray for a miracle now, Reverend Gale. This manoeuvre is desperate. The duke clearly means us to sail to relieve the Blue Squadron, but what if Prince Rupert's ships don't follow suit, or go off to relieve Myngs and the *Victory*? I feared this, Francis – we all did. The consequence of having two commanders-in-chief in two separate ships. And what if the Dutch squadrons get to windward of us again and fall down upon us? Our fleet is divided and disorganised – but the Dutch are still in their line of battle. Once De Ruyter tacks back to the north, as he will surely do at any moment, we will be doomed.'

Francis said nothing. Instead he leaned against the starboard rail of the quarterdeck and closed his eyes.

Now, I am no believer in miracles. If they were disregarded then, in the simpler time that was the 1660s, they are ridiculed and reviled now, in these days when a German blockhead calls himself King George the Second and the only people who speak of miracles are the Jacobites, who need an almighty one to restore them to the throne. But whether it was a consequence of prayer, or, more likely, a glorious coincidence, that for the one and only time in their lives Rupert of the Rhine and George Monck had exactly the same thought at exactly the same moment – however it happened, we had our miracle.

'The Red's tacking!' I cried, once I was certain of what the Prince's ships were doing.

As soon as his ships fell in on their new tack, the tables were turned. Our ships were now sailing parallel to the Dutch – ourselves directly alongside them, firing broadside after broadside into Tromp's ships, while Rupert's stood further off to the west, to windward, thus preventing a counter-attack against us by any Dutch ships that tacked back to try to regain the weather gage. Meanwhile the Blue Squadron, which had seemed on the verge of destruction, trapped on the wrong side of the entire Dutch fleet, now lay directly ahead of Tromp, trapping him between them and us. Tromp had no alternative and fell away to leeward; in effect, his ships were dropping out of the battle.

Now our tails were up, by God! We Sceptres cheered ourselves hoarse at the sight of one of our fireships grappling on to a big Dutch frigate and igniting her. In what seemed like no time at all, she blew up, and we cheered even louder. I am ashamed to say that only Francis Gale was praying for the souls of all the brave Dutchmen who perished; for my part, I was cheering as loudly as the rest of them. Even Lord Rochester's monkey clapped and shrieked patriotically.

We joined with the Blue, and slowly reformed ourselves back into a full line of battle. The Dutch, by contrast, remained widely separated, their squadrons in disorder. Now we sailed between them, sometimes engaging a ship to windward of us, next one to leeward. Once again, it was a case of tack and tack again, pass and pass again, the firing at too much of a distance to make much impact. But in the middle of the afternoon, a decisive change occurred. Since being forced out of the battle by Rupert's and Albemarle's brilliant simultaneous manoeuvre, Tromp and the other detached Dutch ships to leeward of us had struggled to come back at us, break through, and rejoin De Ruyter. Now they made a concerted effort, but we were ready for them. We happened to be sailing parallel to the *Royal Charles*, only a cable's length or less off her starboard quarter, when I saw the unmistakeable stout figure of Albemarle, on the quarterdeck, pick up his voice trumpet and direct it toward me.

'Sir Matthew!' The loud Devonian voice carried easily across the water. 'We will close Admiral Tromp, there, and bring him to close action! Lead and second the *Charles*, if you please!'

I brought up my sword in salute. We put out studding sails, pulled ahead of the flagship and fell down on the wind toward the Dutch ships. Behind us came the best part of forty English men-of-war, Rupert keeping his ships to windward to deter a relieving attack by De Ruyter. There was no more speculative firing from a distance. We hammered into Tromp's ships, our heavier guns battering their weaker hulls. The *Royal Sceptre* came up against a smaller, but still substantial, Dutchman, and we unleashed two broadsides into her.

Richardson appeared before me. The carpenter was a rare sight on the quarterdeck, but he had been overseeing repairs to damaged planking on the forecastle.

'Begging pardon, Sir Matthew,' he said. Every word seemed to be a struggle for a man who much preferred silence. 'The Dutchman, yonder. The mainmast. Quivering and shaking, it is. I'll wager it's in a bad state. One good shot –'

'I take your point, Master Carpenter. Very well, then! Orders to Mister Burdett! Upper deck starboard battery to load with chain and bar, and to fire for the mainmast upon the uproll!'

We were approaching the Dutchman on the opposite tack, so there was precious little time. Boys ran up from below with the two different types of shot, and the gun crews on the starboard side loaded furiously. I went down into the ship's waist and stood next to Burdett. Wait – wait – judge the moment…

'Give fire!'

Our guns blazed and recoiled. Chain and bar shot whistled across the few dozen yards of water separating us from the Dutchman. Shrouds and sheets snapped and sprang away crazily in all directions. Several shot struck the trunk of the mast. I saw one unfortunate soul, in the wrong place at the wrong time, have his head taken clean away by a chain shot. The bleeding torso continued to stand for a moment, then fell down to the deck behind the ship's rail.

At first it seemed as though our shot had no effect. But as we sailed on past the Dutchman's stern, we heard a great crack like a peal of thunder.

'Well done, Mister Richardson, by God!' I cried. 'There she goes!'

Already weakened earlier in the battle, and now with most of the standing rigging that support it shredded by our broadside, the mainmast cracked a few yards up from the deck. It toppled slowly to larboard, pulling at the fore and mizzen masts. Yet more rigging snapped. The mainsail fell across the ship's waist, making it impossible to work the guns. The Dutch ship was easy prey for the ship following us – and that was the huge *Royal Charles*. Unable to fight or manoeuvre, and confronted with the titanic broadside of the flagship, the Dutch captain did the only sane thing he could do. His colours came down, and the *Dom van Utrecht*, as we later discovered her to be, surrendered.

All around us, the same story was being repeated. Our ships were wreaking havoc upon the enemy. Through my telescope I could see the *Hollandia*, Admiral Tromp's flagship, limping away to leeward, severely damaged. Other Dutch ships were scattering before one of our fireships, unwilling to meet the same fate as their compatriot earlier in the day. Others still were simply turning tail and running.

'Look there, Sir Matthew,' said Lord Rochester, beside Musk and I on the quarterdeck, 'De Ruyter comes!'

Contrary to appearances, the young man had sharp eyes and sharp wits. There, coming up from the south with all sail set, was the great admiral himself, the *Seven Provinces* leading the charge.

'So he does, My Lord. But he is surely too late – we have destroyed this half of his fleet. They are scattered and fleeing. And even if he does attempt to relieve them by attacking us, the Prince's ships are still over there to windward. They can fall down on him from the rear, trapping the Dutch between them and us.'

'Then have we won, Sir Matthew?'

'Funny kind of victory if it is one, My Lord,' said Musk. 'The *Prince* gone, and poor Admiral Berkeley, and all the other good men who've fallen. All the bodies we've slung over the side, or who jumped and drowned in the night battle. The maimed men down in the surgeon's cockpit, good for nothing now but hoping for charity from their parishes and begging on the streets when they don't get it. Aye, a funny kind of victory. As they all are.'

I said nothing, but continued to watch the unfolding scene. I had the leisure to do so: there was clear water around us, and no opponent within range. My men were lying down, resting and drinking beer.

If De Ruyter threatened to attack, of course, the warrant and petty officers would have them back at their quarters in an instant. But the Dutch ships were not coming at us. The great De Ruyter, the invincible De Ruyter, was passing our sterns. Our men, and those aboard the other ships near us, cheered feebly.

The Dutch were running for Holland.

I lowered my telescope and smiled at the Earl of Rochester.

'Yes, My Lord. Yes, we have won.'

Chapter Eight

THE FOURTH DAY, 4 JUNE 1666: 4 PM to 8 PM

Officers Slaine and Wounded:

Captains Whitty of the Vanguard, Wood of the Henrietta, Bacon of the Bristol, Mootham of the Princess, Terne of the Triumph, Reeves of the Essex, Chappell of the Clove Tree, Dare of the House of Sweeds, Coppin of the St George, all slaine.

Sir William Clarke, secretary to His Grace of Albemarle, slaine.

Sir Christopher Myngs, maimed, and since dead.

Captain Holles, his arm shot off.

Captain Miller, his leg shot off, since dead.

Captain Gethings, drowned.

Captains Jennens and Fortescue, maimed; Harman, hurt by the fall of a mast; Pearce, Earle, Silver and Holmes, all wounded

Sir George Ayscue, prisoner in Holland.

Sir William Berkeley of the Swiftsure, perhaps prisoner in Holland, perhaps slaine.

Lost on our side, 6,000 men.

Adapted from 'A Particular Account of the Last Engagement between the Dutch and English, June 1666': Bodleian Library, Oxford

Battle is a strange country, a nightmarish land full of unwanted surprises, unexpected vistas, foul smells and terrifying experiences. One can be talking to one's neighbour, and in the very next instant he is headless, his bleeding corpse slumping against you. The acrid, all-pervasive stench of gunfire is often complemented by the stink of men shitting themselves in fear. Men whom one thought stout and strong-hearted, like Lancelot Parks, are revealed by battle to be no more than gibbering half-men. Others whom one assumed to be weaklings and probable cowards, like Jack Rochester, prove to be veritable lions under fire. Above all, though, battle toys with the emotions. In one moment you can feel the greatest elation you have ever known: you are certain you have the victory, and there is no better, stronger feeling that any man can experience than the conviction that you have triumphed over your foes. That was how I felt when I saw De Ruyter's ships turning, apparently fleeing the battlefield, leaving the Navy Royal of England battered, bloodied, but victorious.

But no man can truly describe the feelings of a warrior who has the certainty of victory snatched away from him. In an instant, the weariness gnawing at the limbs after many hours of exhausting combat becomes unbearable. Wounds that have hardly been noticed are suddenly painful beyond measure. Above all, the heart seems to contract. It tightens, bringing on a kind of short-breathed blackness of the spirit. It is as if one has married the most beautiful woman in the world, only for her to turn to dust at the altar after the exchange of vows.

That is how it felt, that afternoon of the fourth day of the battle, when I realised with horror what I was witnessing. The Dutch ships that had sailed past us, the Dutch ships that had been fleeing away to leeward, the Dutch ships that had lost the battle – those same Dutch ships were now doing the inconceivable.

'De Ruyter is not fleeing,' I said to Musk, as I watched his ships put over their rudders, and saw their yards and sails swing round as they came back into the wind. Back toward us. 'He is regrouping. He is preparing to attack again.'

For once, the loquacious Phineas Musk had no words in response. Not even the world-weary, sarcastic Musk could comprehend what he was seeing. His shoulders slumped, and he looked like the old, recently wounded man that he was.

I heard groans from the gun crews in the waist and on the quarterdeck. These were men who had fought for four days, with precious little rest. They had given their all, and their exhausted bodies had nothing more to give. But somehow, they would have to rouse themselves one more time. Every man in the fleet would. For there, setting its course toward us on its new tack, was the *Seven Provinces*, the huge standard of Admiral De Ruyter streaming from the maintop.

My officers reported.

'Mizzen's shaky, Sir Matthew,' said Richardson, 'but God willing, I can fish her sufficiently so she'll hold.'

'Very good. Carry on then, Mister Richardson. How much shot left, Mister Burdett?'

The master gunner stood before me, looking sullen.

'No more than four or five balls for each gun, Sir Matthew. More of chain, bar and grape. Barely twenty barrels of powder.'

'Well,' said Musk, 'if we have a fifth day, perhaps we can lob mess-plates at each other.'

The Dutch came on. Now the *Defiance* swept past our larboard quarter, Sir Robert Holmes strutting the quarterdeck impatiently. He was close enough to shout out without needing a voice trumpet.

'With me, Matt Quinton! De Ruyter is making for the *Royal Charles*! I've got next to no powder or shot, but I'm damned if those butter-box cheese-fuckers are going to take our flag!'

'Directly in your wake, my admiral!'

We both laughed, though there was precious little humour in the situation. De Ruyter was no longer shunning close range duels lest our heavy cannon smash his ships to pieces. Now he was coming in close and hard, knowing it was his only hope of driving straight at the heart of our fleet. At the flagship.

The *Defiance* and *Royal Sceptre*, together with Will Jennens's *Ruby* and the valiant little *Sweepstakes*, formed a screen around the *Royal Charles* and waited for the Dutch to strike. A couple of Frisians came on first, but although the *Defiance* and *Sceptre* had little ammunition left, the *Ruby* had been with Rupert on his futile expedition westward, and thus had plenty of powder and shot to spare. She also had one of the maddest captains in the fleet: bragging, brawling, brave Will Jennens, whose wife (being even madder than he) had attempted to assassinate Oliver Cromwell, and whose niece became Duchess of Marlborough, effectively ruling the kingdom through bedding both its greatest soldier and its Queen, the late and unlamented Anna Regina. Will had managed to get his foremast repaired after our encounter with the Zeelanders earlier in the day. Now he placed the *Ruby* squarely in front of the Frisians and gave the first of them an almighty broadside, but the second veered away and raked him, smashing the fragile stern gallery and windows of the *Ruby* to pieces. Convinced he had defeated the *Ruby* and her captain, this fellow made directly for the *Royal Charles*, only to find the King's Prick in his way. Undaunted, he made to grapple and board us, steering directly for our beakhead.

'Sceptres, with me!' I cried, leaping into the ship's waist, sword in hand. 'Cutlasses, muskets and *grenados*, men! Let's give them a hot reception!'

Carvell, Macferran and three dozen or so other good men abandoned the upper deck guns and ran to the forecastle alongside me. But we were not the first there: not by any means.

'Brutus to him aloud thus spake.
What work (quoth he) mean you to make?'

Lord Rochester: who else? And who else in our fleet would have thought it appropriate to greet the Dutch, not with a volley of chain-shot and grape, but with his own translation of Lucan?

'Shall my fleet idle range the coast,
That you your marine art may boast?
We hither come prepared for fight,
Against our foes to show our might!
Come bring us therefore sword to sword,
Lay me the stoutest Greeks aboard.
These words of Brutus he obeys,
His broad side to the foe he lays!'

The libidinous Earl illustrated each couplet with a barrage of *grenados*. His aim had improved somewhat since the first day, but I noticed a number of our men still hanging back in case the noble young poet accidentally blew them to pieces. Strangely, though, the men immediately around him seemed to revel in the unconventional leadership of Lord Rochester and his monkey: our 'lieutenant' had even been dressed in a miniature baldric, hastily run up somewhere on the lower deck, and was throwing *grenados* with abandon. Across the water, the Frisians massed in their own forecastle clearly had not the faintest idea what to make of it all. Their warlike shouts and obscenities died away before the spectacle of a madman spouting Lucan and a monkey throwing bombs at them. The hesitation proved fatal, for on the other side of the Frisian ship, Will Jennens was bringing the *Ruby*'s bows back round into the wind.

I saw the glow of a linstock at one of the gun ports behind the *Ruby*'s beakhead, and knew what Will intended. His bow chasers, demi-culverins both, blazed and roared at once. He had charged them with grapeshot, the bags of musket balls, nails, and glass bursting as they struck the enemy. The men on the forecastle of the Frisian fell in their droves, some pieces of bloodied flesh even making it across the yards of water that separated us to fall on the deck of the *Royal Sceptre*. A small splash of Dutch gore struck my cheek. The Frisian fell away, and both the *Sceptre* and *Ruby* slowly edged our ways back toward the *Royal Charles*, now exchanging fire with a big North Quarter flagship. My quarterdeck came up level with the *Ruby*'s, and I could see that Jennens was bleeding profusely from a wound in the head which his surgeon was attempting to staunch.

'Fear not, Matt,' he cried, 'I'll live! Damned beef-witted hogen-mogens hit the least important part of me! And if Fresh Holles can live with his arm being taken off, I'm sure I can live even if this fly-bitten bum-bailey of a surgeon has to cut off my head!'

And with that, Will Jennens roared with pain as the surgeon drove a needle into his scalp.

* * *

Shocking as it was, I reassured myself that De Ruyter's unexpected charge was still suicidal. It could be nothing else. Prince Rupert and his ships were still to windward, most of them yet undamaged and with plenty of shot in reserve. They could come down on the wind, trapping the Dutch between us and them. The great Dutch admiral had surely made a terrible mistake. Just an hour earlier, he could have withdrawn to his own shore with honour, having fought us to a stand-still. Now, we would absorb his brief onslaught; then, once the Prince's ships engaged, we would annihilate him and his fleet.

But as the *Royal Sceptre* and *Ruby* resumed their positions protecting the *Royal Charles*, a gap opened up between the ships immediately to westward of us, giving me a view of Prince Rupert's ships sailing large toward us. Thus I happened to be looking directly at the *Royal James* when the disaster occurred. The Prince's flagship was a fine sight, bearing down with all sail set. She, and the rest of the windward ships, would fall down upon De Ruyter, trapping the Dutch once and for all between the two halves of our fleet. We would still win. We were…

The maintopmast went first, and that brought down the main yard and the great sail it bore. On its own, this double calamity would have been enough to disable the great ship for an hour or two. But her masts had taken an awful battering, and the effect of rigging being stretched and pulled apart by the collapse of the top half of the mainmast immediately pulled down the entire mizzen mast too. The *Royal James* stopped abruptly and wallowed, out of control, upon the main. The ships around her shortened sail; their captains were not prepared to attack without the talismanic Prince leading them.

'Switch your flag, Your Highness,' I screamed. 'In the name of God, move to another ship!'

But there was no sign of a boat leaving the *James* for one of the other ships. To this day, I do not know why Rupert, the bravest of the brave – aye, and often the foolhardiest of the foolhardy – did not shift his flag, resume command of his squadron, and bring it into action against De Ruyter. As it was, the Dutchman was emboldened by the sight of the catastrophe which befell the *Royal James*. A great red flag broke out at the foretop of the *Seven Provinces*. The bloody flag. De Ruyter was going for the kill.

The next hour was a kind of encapsulation of all the little hells of the entire four days of battle. The Dutch came again and again against the flagship and the tiny group of ships defending it. If they had been determined on the first three days, they were doubly ferocious now, the bloody flag and the sight of the crippled *Royal James* driving them forward like a host of avenging archangels. The sound of gunfire was all around, but most of it was coming from the Dutch; many of the English ships, our own included, were running out of ammunition, and were either attempting to conserve stocks for a final, desperate defence, or else had already run out. And now the *Royal Charles* was edging slowly north and west. At one point we were within voice trumpet range, and with one Dutch attack beaten off and the next one not yet launched, Albemarle was able to bellow across the waters.

'We're holed below the waterline, Quinton, and we're nearly out of powder. Keep on the larboard quarter – I've ordered Holmes to stay on the starboard. Cover our withdrawal.'

So there was to be no fresh tack, no attempt to counter-attack the Dutch. The battle, the great four-day battle that we had nearly won so many times, was lost, and this time there could be no retrieving it. I felt no despair, no shame; only relief that, God willing, it would soon be over, and no more would have to die.

I noticed that the fat old Duke was moving even more awkwardly than usual.

'You are hurt, Your Grace?'

'Grapeshot in the arse, Quinton. God knows what the court wits will make of that.'

Perhaps in the heat of battle, Albemarle had forgotten that perhaps the most vicious of the court wits was aboard my ship. Indeed, he was standing nearby, well within earshot. That same wit duly smirked.

'And lo,' said the Earl of Rochester as we pulled away from the flagship, 'in the midst of battle, a godsend to the poet. *Arse* will rhyme eminently well with either *Mars* or *farce*.'

But soon I had more serious matters to contemplate, for the withdrawal was a catastrophe. Our retreat on the previous day, before Rupert's ships rejoined, was an organised, almost impressive affair, with the fleet's strongest ships in the rear to ward off the Dutch attacks. Now, though, our dispositions during De Ruyter's last attack meant that the weakest ships were left at the rear of our retreat, and the Dutch fell upon them like furies. The *Black Bull* was taken, and the *Clove Tree*: Dutch prizes, these, so perhaps no great loss. But I saw the colours come down on the *Essex*, a stout man-of-war not much smaller than the *Sceptre*, and thus nearly as dreadful a loss as that of Will Berkeley's *Swiftsure* on the first day. We could do nothing but watch from a distance: our duty was to protect the flag, and that meant we were among the stronger ships in the van of the fleet, unable to respond to the carnage astern. God knows how much more havoc the Dutch might have wreaked under their bloody flag, had not England's unfailing guardian come to our aid: that is to say, the weather intervened. A little before seven in the evening, or two bells of the Last Dog, a thick fog came down. Under its cover, we ran for the King's Channel and safety. Some tried to dress it in fine words, but there is no doubting what it was: a chaotic, headlong retreat. The Dutch did not pursue us, but they did not need to. Their work was done. England's proud Navy Royal had been shattered and, worse, humiliated.

'And now the real battle starts,' said Musk, grey-faced and wheezing from his exertions during the great four-day fight.

'The real battle, Musk?' said Francis Gale, nursing a wound to his left hip that he had taken in our last fight with the Frisian.

'The battle to assign blame. The Prince will blame the Duke. The Duke will blame the Prince. Parliament will blame the King. The King will blame Parliament. Minister will blame minister – Clarendon will say it was all Arlington's fault, Arlington that it was all Clarendon's doing. There'll be riots in the streets as the mob blames whoever they can think of. Who ordered the fleet divided? On what intelligence? The country won't be happy until someone swings for this.'

It was a gloomy assessment, but I knew enough of our court, and the mind of the Englishman, to know that Musk spoke nothing but the truth. And in an England where the crown had been restored barely six years before, where many still looked back nostalgically to what they called the triumphant days of Cromwell, who could say what the effects of such a catastrophe might be?

For the moment, though, I had rather more immediate concerns. We still had to get into the river, but my ship's master, a fellow of Trinity House who knew these waters as well as any man, was dead. Although Urquhart, the erstwhile boatswain, seemed confident in his command of the charts, he was a Scotsman, familiar with Forth and Tay but rather less so with the Thames. I had visions of us surviving the great Four Days' Fight, only to perish as the *Sceptre* broke her back, ploughing onto an unseen sandbank. So although we had nearly all sail set and wetted, we sounded every fifteen minutes, and kept a careful watch on the ships ahead of us. Slowly, though, the fog thinned a little, until at last it was possible to make out a shore, a few miles to starboard.

'The Naze seamark bears west by north, five miles, Sir Matthew!' cried Urquhart, in his thick Scots accent.

There it was, by God! England's dear, blessed shore. It was some moments before I realised that the sight had brought me to tears of joy and relief.

Truly, never was any Englishman happier to see Essex.

Part Two

THE NORE, LONDON, AND PLYMOUTH

5 JUNE - 21 JULY 1666

Chapter Nine

Now joyful fires and the exalted bell
And court gazettes our empty triumph tell.
Alas, the time draws near when overturn'd
The lying bells shall through the tongue be burn'd;
Paper shall want to print that lie of state,
And our false fires true fires shall expiate.

Marvell, *Third Advice to a Painter*

The shattered fleet lay at the Buoy of the Nore. The *Royal Sceptre* was quite close to Sheppey's shore, the squat tower of Minster Abbey clearly visible almost due south of where we swung at single anchor. The carpenter's crew swarmed over the forecastle, removing the remnants of shattered timbers and hammering their replacements into position. Other men were in the waist, sewing up shot-holes in the sails or fixing patches where the holes were too large to be sewn. On every tide, barges were bringing down shipwrights and planking from the dockyard at Chatham, or barrels of powder from the ordnance store at Upnor Castle. Only the ships with the very worst damage were going up to the dockyard itself. Depending on wind and tide, it could sometimes take days to negotiate the tortuous channel of the Medway in each direction; besides, Chatham could only have four ships in its dry docks at any one time. Better by far to bring the dockyard to the fleet, especially as time was at a premium. We had to repair the ships and put to sea once again before the Dutch could follow up the advantage they had gained in the Four Days' Fight. Thus there was no shore leave, an edict that caused not a few murmurings on the lower deck. Every hand was needed for the businesses of repairing, revictualling and rearming.

I paced the deck impatiently, giving words of encouragement here and admonishing men to work faster there. I was hardly recognisable as a captain and a knight of the realm: with most of my wardrobe having been sacrificed to douse the flames during the fireship attack, I was clad in a slop shirt and breeches. Somehow, though, it seemed more appropriate gear for the urgency of our work, and it was that, rather than the inadequacy of my wardrobe, which made me turn down Captain Kit Farrell's invitation to dine with him aboard the *Black Prince*, moored off Queenborough. I was determined that the *Sceptre* would be ready to sail with the fleet, but I also had a more personal reason to be at the Dutch again as quickly as possible. Put simply, I was determined to avenge Will Berkeley. My friend had died to redeem his honour; instead, the latest intelligence out of Holland stated that his decomposing corpse was on display in a sugar-chest in the Hague, no doubt being mocked by every mean Dutch moneylender and fishwife. Almost as bad, it was said that the captured Sir George Ayscue had been painted, had a tail stuck on him, and been paraded through the streets to suffer the derision of the rude Dutch. It was too much for any Englishman of honour to bear. Admiral Michiel De Ruyter and their High Mightinesses of the States-General would pay for their disrespect. On that, I was determined.

(As is the way with such 'intelligence', which is swiftly embellished by every idle rogue who frequents inns, coffee houses, brothels, and Parliament, it all proved to be so much cant, as we later learned: in truth, Ayscue was treated with respect, while Will's body was embalmed and laid to rest reverentially in the Great Church of the Hague before being returned later in the year for burial at Westminster Abbey. But I find that the truth accords only rarely with the mood of those intemperate, irrational beasts, the English. Even so, the same truth would not have mattered much to me back then, in the middle days of June, 1666. The Dutch could have canonised Will Berkeley and built a vast shrine to him, but I would still have been set on avenging my dear friend's pointless death. I could not wreak vengeance on the man I really held responsible for his slaughter, namely George Monck, Duke of Albemarle, so the Dutch would have to do.)

A small squadron of victualling hoys was in sight, coming out of the river from London. Urquhart stood at the starboard rail of the quarterdeck, watching them intently through his telescope; a new lieutenant was to be commissioned to the *Royal Sceptre*, or so Prince Rupert had told me, but he was still to join the ship.

'Let us pray that one of them is bringing our beef and beer, Mister Urquhart' I said. 'Another day of old biscuit and mouldy cheese, and I fear we shall have mutiny on our hands.'

Urquhart seemed not to hear me. 'Strange, Sir Matthew – one of the royal yachts sails in their wake.'

'Flying a standard?'

'No, sir. Neither that of the King nor the Lord Admiral.'

'Then I expect she bears despatches from Whitehall for the generals.'

'Her course isn't set for the *Royal Charles*, Sir Matthew. It's set for us.'

He handed me his telescope, and I focused on the distant fleet of hoys. There, indeed, was the yacht. Her men were sheeting home her sails as she moved out from behind the victuallers, bearing down on her new course. A course that was plainly set directly for the *Royal Sceptre*.

I kept the telescope fixed on the yacht. She was a trim little craft, one of the newer ones that the King had had built for his amusement.

Her captain brought her smartly under our lee and handed what appeared to be a letter to the Marine on duty at the port. The missive was brought to me on the quarterdeck. I recognised the seal well enough; the familiar coat of arms should have been reassuring, but in the circumstances, it was anything but. I broke the seal, unfolded the letter, and read the contents.

I was aware of Urquhart's eyes upon me. I looked up and essayed a smile, although I suspect it might have been an unconvincing attempt.

'I am to go to London. Immediately. In the yacht, yonder. My belongings to be sent up to town after me. Until the new lieutenant embarks, you have the ship, Mister Urquhart.'

* * *

Ravensden House, the London seat of the Quinton Earls, was a decrepit, rambling establishment. It consisted principally of a middling Tudor merchant's house, backing on to older, ramshackle outbuildings and a gimcrack new wing thrown up some seventy years earlier by a villainous, incompetent builder who fleeced my grandfather mercilessly. Much of the house had been closed up since old Earl Matthew's death in 1645; my brother, whose tastes were spartan, maintained only a few rooms for himself. But during the winter, the Jacobean wing had been opened up, cleaned, and transformed into the new quarters for Sir Matthew Quinton and his Dutch wife. There were several reasons for this. Firstly, the landlord of our previous rooms near the Tower had increased the rent dramatically, reckoning that now Sir Matthew was a knight of the realm, he could afford to pay whatever ludicrous price the rogue demanded. Secondly, brother Charles, too, had meditated upon the implications of my elevation, and decided that Ravensden House was a more fitting residence for the newly-knighted heir to the earldom. Thirdly, and most importantly, my wife Cornelia was never content in one place for very long, and decided that her new status demanded a home rather closer to the court at Whitehall. Thus I had returned from my previous command of the *Cressy* to find that which the French term a *fait accompli*. Cornelia was resident at Ravensden House, and therefore so was I.

The yacht had landed me at Tower Wharf, whence a waterman rowed me up to Queenhithe, a relatively short walk from our new home. I found my wife in the parlour, vomiting into a bucket.

'Cornelia, my love!' I cried, rushing to her side and holding her gently. 'What ails you?'

It was less than a year since the plague had swept through London like a malevolent tide of death, carrying away thousands before it. Deep down, every Londoner watched every cough, every sweat, every stool, every vomit, for signs of its return. That was my first thought; I discounted the possibility that she might be with child, for after eight barren years of marriage, even the optimistic Cornelia seemed to have accepted our fate. She had even found a kindred spirit in her new friend Elizabeth, the French wife of Mister Samuel Pepys, Clerk of the Acts to the Navy Board, to whom all of the navy's sea-captains reported; similarly childless after an even longer marriage, the worryingly outspoken Elizabeth Pepys had become a great solace to my wife.

'Matthew!' she cried in surprise, looking up from the bucket and wiping her mouth on her sleeve. 'An undercooked chicken, nothing more. But how can you be here, husband? Why have you come away from the fleet?'

'A summons from Charles, to meet him here. He said nothing of it to you?'

'I have not seen him for three days. Besides, husband, your brother shares his business with no man, let alone with any woman.'

She stood up, looked me up and down, prodded me about the ribs, then clasped me tightly and kissed me vigorously (on the cheeks; even the enthusiastic Cornelia realised that my mouth needed to be out of bounds after her so-recent evacuation).

'You were truly not wounded, then?'

Inevitably, that was the moment she chose to fling her arms over my shoulders. I nearly cried out in agony.

'Bruising,' I said, gasping for breath. 'A fall. Nothing worse, thanks be to God.'

'Amen, husband!' She lowered her arms, holding me tightly around the waist instead. 'But it must have been horrible – four days of it, Matthew? And all those good souls dead, on both sides... Poor Will Berkeley, above all! *God in hemel*, I pray that the reports from Amsterdam about the treatment of his body are not true.'

Cornelia and I held each other for some little time, during which her new lady's maid, a simpering girl named Lettice, entered, blushed, curtsied, and then discreetly removed the sick-bucket.

'You are sure you are well?' I asked.

'I have told you so,' said Cornelia with a flash of indignation. 'Chicken. No more.'

But she did not meet my eyes, and I wondered if she was keeping something from me. Any thought I might have had of pressing her on the matter was extinguished by the arrival of my brother. As was Charles's way, there was no ceremony or noise about his entry; one moment he was not there, the next he was, his slight, stooped figure standing silently by my side.

'You have been an unconscionable time getting here, brother,' he said in his familiar, quiet and slightly breathless way.

'My apologies, My Lord. The yacht came upstream as quickly as it could, given the state of wind and tide.'

Charles Quinton, tenth Earl of Ravensden, shook his head. He was an exceptionally intelligent man, but he had some kind of void in his mind when it came to anything relating to the sea. The fact that a ship simply could not move when or where it willed, after the fashion of a man upon a horse, was to him at best a damnable inconvenience, at worst a significant flaw in God's creation.

'We must ride to the King,' Charles said. 'At once. My apologies, Cornelia.'

My brother took his good-sister's hand and kissed it. In such niceties, at least, he was always the perfect gentleman.

The stable-boy of Ravensden House had already saddled two horses, mine being a lively grey that I had ridden twice or thrice before. We made our way out onto the Strand, negotiating a path through the endless stream of carts and coaches, riding west toward the Charing Cross.

All the way, Charles said not a word; no hint at all of why the King required our presence. I knew better than to raise the subject. My brother was a quiet soul, guarded in his words and actions: a man who lived with the bodily pain of the musket-balls that had smashed into him at the Worcester fight, and the mental pain of knowing that he was, perhaps, not the rightful Earl of Ravensden at all, but rather the bastard son of Charles the First, King and Martyr. Yet there was another side to him, too, one known only to very few. Using the alias of Lord Percival, Charles had been one of the most feared and successful Royalist agents during the usurpations of Cromwell and the Rump Parliament. The war against the Dutch, along with the myriad plots of disaffected men and betrayal by the woman he had been persuaded to marry by his friend and putative brother, the King, brought Charles's mysterious other self back to life. Thus I wondered who it was who rode beside me as we made our way down through the Holbein Gate of Whitehall Palace: the elusive sibling twelve years my senior, or the ruthless and secretive Lord Percival?

We rode down the length of White Hall, the public thoroughfare that bisected the sprawling, irregular palace of the same name. It was soon apparent that we were not going to turn off into one of the yards of the palace, to make for any of the rooms where the King was invariably to be found. Curiosity got the better of me, and I asked my brother where we were bound.

'The Abbey,' he said, nodding toward the great shape that loomed above the south-west corner of the palace, the stonework of its multitude of buttresses lit brilliantly by the setting sun. 'His Majesty is at prayer.'

We rode on, out through the gate and into King Street, but I could not prevent one persistent and disloyal thought from lodging in my mind.

If King Charles the Second, England's crowned libertine, felt the need to be at prayer in Westminster Abbey, then things were desperate indeed.

* * *

We entered the great Abbey church by the north door. This was guarded by two pikemen, who stood to attention as we approached. Within, one man stood in the transept: a red-cheeked old man with large, penetrating eyes, wearing an expensive brown periwig designed for a man thirty years younger. Will Chiffinch, keeper of His Majesty's private closet and page of the backstairs, had only recently succeeded his dead elder brother in the role, but it was as though there had been no change at all. Both brothers were utterly discreet and devoted to their master. This was just as well. The Chiffinches shepherded new royal mistresses to the King's bed, carefully ushering out the old in due time by another stair. The Chiffinches controlled the King's most secret incomes and expenditures. The Chiffinches literally held the keys to the kingdom's best kept secrets.

As if to prove the point, the new Chiffinch bowed to my brother rather more deeply than was necessary to an Earl, thus proving that he was entirely aware of the strong possibility that Charles Quinton was actually a son of King Charles the Martyr. Then he bowed to me rather more deeply than was necessary to a knight, thus proving that if the first possibility was true, I was the rightful Earl of Ravensden, and worthy of such deference. Without a word, he turned and escorted us into the main body of the Abbey, where the flickering candlelight cast strange shadows upon the pillars and monuments. We walked up into the Choir, past the High Altar, and Chiffinch indicated a tall man standing in the darkness beyond the side-chapel of Saint Paul. We approached, and bowed.

Charles Stuart, second of that name, King of England, seemed at first to ignore us. He was a very tall man – as tall as myself – and truly ugly, a vast nose set within a face so dark that the king had been nicknamed 'the black boy' since childhood. His attention seemed to be fixed entirely on the huge table tomb before which he stood. Although the light was very dim, I knew full well whose tomb it was: I had been here many times before. I could just make out the stern features carved in the white marble, the vast ruff about the neck and chest, the sceptre in the right hand and the orb in the left, the crown of state upon the head.

'What would she have made of it, I wonder?' said the king, still not turning to face us. 'A defeat on such a scale. A calamitous judgement upon the land. What would she say to me, if she could?' The king looked long and hard at the features of his predecessor, and shook his head. 'Methinks it would have more of vitriol about it than even the sharpest of My Lady Castlemaine's reproofs.' Finally, Charles Stuart turned toward us, away from the effigy of Elizabeth the Great, Gloriana, the Virgin Queen: the monarch in whose name my grandfather had sailed out against the Spanish Armada. 'Charlie, Matt, I tell you this,' said King Charles the Second. 'I will not be a new Harold, a king who loses his kingdom. I will not be a new Henry the Sixth, a weakling who allows his realm to descend into chaos.' He nodded toward the tomb. 'And above all, I will not be the king who fucks up her legacy.'

For a man who enjoyed the act so much, Charles Stuart rarely uttered the word; it was one of the strange paradoxes of this most enigmatic of monarchs that he favoured refinement of speech even when some of his other faculties were guilty of the worst excesses.

'Tell me, Sir Matthew,' said the King, turning fully toward me at last, 'what do the men of the fleet say about how it came to be divided?'

Careful, Matt…

'Very much what men always say when there is some great calamity, Your Majesty. There are those who think it mere misfortune – simple error or chance. Others… others see darker causes.'

'And they would be?'

Even more careful, Matt.

'Many believe there must have been some great conspiracy – that treason was committed by those who wish ill to Your Majesty's affairs. Others still see it as God's – that is, as divine judgement –'

'Oh, spit it out, Matt Quinton! Men see it as divine judgement upon me, for my weaknesses as a man. For what they would call my indiscriminate whoring. For the so-called degeneracy of my royal court. Is that not so?'

Being invited by Divine Majesty to call him a whoremaster to his face places a man in a somewhat delicate and unenviable position. I swallowed hard, and said nothing.

'Your brother is a discreet man,' said the King to Earl Charles. 'But his recent shipmate Jack Rochester is anything but discreet, and that noble lord has delighted in telling me exactly what the men on the lower deck of your ship have been saying.'

I could imagine it all too easily: the Sceptres were not a reticent crew, least of all some of my long-serving Cornish followers, and even Rochester would have had no need to embellish their words.

The King looked down once again on the marble features of Queen Elizabeth the Great. For a moment he seemed to be lost in thought; perhaps it was a trick of the light, but I thought I saw a whispered apology upon his lips. Then he turned to us once more.

'Two mysteries, then,' he said. 'Firstly, how did the fleet come to be divided? The French fleet was approaching, we were told. A French army was poised to invade Ireland, we were told. But in truth, the fleet was no nearer than Toulon, and there is no army. We have been deceived, but was that deceit witting or unwitting? Secondly, how did we come to have no intelligence of the Dutch being at sea? Those are the questions. It is for you, the brothers Quinton, to answer them for your king. To answer them for England.'

In those times, a royal command was still akin to the word of God being inscribed in flaming letters fifty feet high. My brother and I could make only one response. We both bowed our heads before Sacred Majesty.

'If there has been treason, then there must be a traitor,' continued the King. 'My Lord Ravensden, you will remain in London. I wish you to investigate the failure of intelligence from Holland, and the decisions taken by my ministers that brought about the division of the fleet. You will act in my name, and with my authority. All papers will be open to you, and all men – from the highest to the lowest – will be under orders to speak to you.'

My brother nodded, his face a mask. But I knew that this unlooked-for responsibility would sit heavily upon his shoulders: to investigate the king's ministers for possibly treasonable failure was a sure way to make a host of new and powerful enemies.

'And you, Sir Matthew,' said Charles Stuart, preferring formality to 'Matt', which was what he had called me ever since my first audience with him, aged fifteen: 'you will interrogate the two men who are our most likely traitors – the men who either provided the false intelligence that divided the fleet, or else betrayed the fact of the division to the enemy.'

It is not fitting to quibble with a royal command, but I could sense that my expression was quibbling to the point of outright rebellion. I was no inquisitor, I was a sea captain. Interrogation of potential traitors was my brother's world, not mine. But perhaps there was a consolation in the king's words. Only two men? Surely that would take no time at all, and in the meantime I could live at Ravensden House with Cornelia, regaining my strength after the rigours and horrors of the four-day fight, reassuring myself that her mysterious sickness truly was nothing serious…

'By chance, the men in question are far from London,' said my brother, dashing my hopes before they were even properly raised, 'but by an even greater chance, they are all within a few miles of each other.'

'Chance,' said the king, 'or proof of a deep-rooted plot, hatched in a remote land notorious for its rebelliousness and disloyalty during the late civil war? That will be for you to discover, Matt.'

Far from London. A remote land. An appalling thought occurred to me. 'Sire, I am the captain of the *Royal Sceptre* –'

'And, God willing, you will be captain of her when she next ventures out against the Dutch. It will take several weeks to repair the fleet, Matt. Ample time for you to go where you have to go, and do what you have to do.' Charles Stuart raised his arm and snapped his fingers. Chiffinch appeared, as if from nowhere, carrying two small bundles of papers in his hands. He handed one to my brother, one to myself. 'Your instructions and authorities,' said the King. He bowed the royal forehead towards us, a sure sign that Majesty was about to depart. 'Find me a traitor. Find me someone I can hang, draw and quarter, to placate the mob. Find me someone whom England can blame for this disaster.'

* * *

Charles and I watched the King and Chiffinch depart. A distant door closed. Nothing stirred in the great church. In the dim candlelight, surrounded by all the royal tombs, there was an eerie sense of the entire weight of English history pressing down upon we two, the Quinton brothers.

'Yes,' said the Earl of Ravensden at last, 'His Majesty wants someone who England can blame – someone, anyone, other than himself.

After all, it is not meet for governors to appear fallible in the eyes of the governed. Especially not as fallible as this, in such a time as this.'

'But what if there proves to be no guilty man? No traitor for the king to scapegoat?'

'Oh, the world is full of traitors and guilty men, Matt. The law is simply the means by which crimes are fastened upon them, like the planks of your ship to its ribs. The King commands us to find such men, and in my experience they are two a penny – the ones who are neither innocent enough nor clever enough to avoid the hangman's rope.'

With that, Charles went over to the nearby tomb of Mary, Queen of Scots, and placed the papers that Chiffinch had handed him on top of the monarch's effigy, so much simpler than that of the cousin who had ordered her execution. My brother opened the first of them, leaned against the tomb, and began to read. I was shocked by my brother's apparent disrespect toward the remains of a divinely ordained monarch, even one as foolish, headless and Scottish as Mary Stuart; but then I realised to my astonishment that if the dark legend of his royal paternity was true, my brother was merely resting upon the grave of his own great-grandmother, whose ghost would probably indulge one of her own flesh and blood.

I moved into the light of a small group of votive candles, and opened the papers addressed to me.

My heart grew heavier, almost at the sight of each new word. I was to be transformed into a creature I despised: a soldier. I was to venture into perhaps the only part of the known world where my good standing in Cornwall would be positively dangerous to me: that is to say, Devon. Worst of all, one of those who I was to interrogate happened to be a good friend. If the evidence against him proved sufficiently damning, I was to be the instrument of his destruction. If I made him a scapegoat for the division of the fleet, which was clearly what the king wished, then I would be condemning him to a traitor's fate. In darker moments, I still blamed myself for the death of Will Berkeley. Was I now to be the instrument of another friend's death? If so, then it seemed there was a high price to pay for friendship with Matt Quinton.

Chapter Ten

When civil dudgeon first grew high,
And men fell out, they knew not why…
When gospel-trumpeter, surrounded
With long-eared rout, to battle sounded;
And pulpit, drum ecclesiastic,
Was beat with fist instead of a stick;
Then did Sir Knight abandon dwelling,
And out he rode a-colonelling.

Samuel Butler, *Hudibras* (1662)

The government of England is like a very old dog: lazy, forgetful, incontinent, and beset by vermin. But when it rouses itself, the ancient hound can yet outrun the impertinent young pups, its bark can terrify all and sundry, and its bite can still tear apart beasts or men. Thus was the government of England in that summer of 1666. Shaken by the calamity of the Four Days' Battle, the old dog suddenly stirred and looked about it. It remembered what it was, and what it could do. It stretched its limbs, shook off the fleas, and set to with a will. All was activity, all was purpose. The most indolent clerks of the Navy Office, rarely seen at their desks for more than an hour a day, were now scribbling before dawn and still hunched over their quills after midnight. Foppish courtiers strode the corridors of Whitehall with grim-faced martial determination, hands resolutely clasping the hilts of newly-bought swords, and volunteered for the fleet in their droves. Kit Farrell's letters from the *Black Prince* recorded how Chatham dockyard, that veritable temple to idleness, was transformed into a hellish cacophony of sawing and hammering. Every hour of every day and every night, men who would down tools in a trice if their breakfast-time was curtailed by so much as a minute worked with Herculean resolve to repair the shattered ships, the *Royal Sceptre* among them.

So it was on my journey to the west. I was accompanied only by the smallest of retinues – four men, Francis Gale, Macferran, Carvell and Ali Reis, competent horsemen all, and two additional horses laden with our effects – so we travelled light and very fast. But at every stage, our change of horses awaited us, already paid for: prime racing stallions, not the arthritic carthorses passed off by so many ostlers. We needed two overnight stops, and the inns that awaited us were the finest that Andover and Chard had to offer. The best rooms had been reserved for us (which, at Chard, involved ejecting a disgruntled baronet), and paid for in advance at substantially above the asking price. Innkeepers, justices of the peace and parish constables fell over themselves to present their compliments to the Most Honourable Sir Matthew, to establish whether the Most Honourable Sir Matthew had any requirements, to enquire whether the Most Honourable Sir Matthew might be interested in bedding their daughters, sisters, wives or mothers.

The small size of my party, and the need for it to move as swiftly as possible, meant that I was forced to leave Musk behind. In truth, though, this suited both of us. He was uncharacteristically quiet after the Four Days' Battle. I had known Musk since I was five years old, and he had always seemed to be ageless and indestructible. Suddenly, however, he seemed much older, and it was clear that his exertions in the battle, allied to the wound he received earlier in the year, had taken their toll on the old rogue. But if truth be told, both of us had other motives. I remained concerned about Cornelia's health, and allowing Musk to return to his nominal duties as steward of Ravensden House would allow him both to watch over her and to send me word by express if her condition worsened. In any case, Musk had a proprietorial attitude to my wife – as he did, indeed, to all the Quintons – and accepted my instructions with enthusiasm. But we both knew he had yet another reason to remain in London. If my brother was to unravel the secret machinations that brought about the division of the fleet, he would undoubtedly resume the persona of Lord Percival: the secret identity that he had used in Cromwell's time, when he was one of the most successful and feared Royalist agents, and which he had taken up again during the previous plague-summer to thwart a most heinous plot against the kingdom and our own family. And Lord Percival's faithful, if somewhat obstreperous, assistant, was the same Phineas Musk whom I left behind in our London house.

It was the Earl of Ravensden, too, who insisted that Francis Gale should accompany me to the west.

'You will need a man of letters who can take oaths,' Charles had said, 'and I am sure you would rather depend upon Francis than some erstwhile rebel of a Plymouth lawyer.'

'Of any lawyer,' I replied indignantly. 'Nothing did more to bring about the civil wars in this realm than the plotting of that avaricious profession. And as the King said, Devon was notorious for its malignancy – a veritable nest of serpents.'

'Indeed. And you should not assume that all the serpents were extirpated at the Restoration, Matt. Remember who rules in Devon nowadays, who serves as its Lord Lieutenant, who has his men in every nook and cranny of the government of the county.'

Realisation came as a shock from the blue.

'Albemarle,' I said.

'Our illustrious kingmaker. Quite. And as you have told me enough times, Matt, he is no friend to you. So be careful, brother. God be with you.'

'And with you, My Lord.' I smiled. 'May I ask, though – is it to be My Lord Ravensden or My Lord Percival in this affair?'

Charles pursed his lips. 'Ah, Matt. Do you know, I find it ever harder to tell those two apart?'

* * *

The town of Plymouth sat upon a hill to the north and west of a broad harbour thronged with shipping. The gate-tower through which we rode, and the walls on either side of it, still bore the unmistakeable signs of shot-marks and other damage inflicted by the siege artillery that, twenty years before, had attempted to batter Plymouth into submission to its lawful king. Upon seeing my approach, the guard at the gate, a lazy red-coated brute, sprang up from the stool on which he was lounging and doing nothing more than shouting ribald insults at passing wenches and goodwives. For, uncomfortable though I was in my new finery, I must have been an awesome sight indeed. Mounted upon a large grey stallion, I wore a broad-brimmed, befeathered black hat, knee-high cavalry boots, a yellow tunic and a wide black baldric. Behind me came my little troop, as diverse a soldiery as that of the largest army: the black-skinned Carvell, brown-skinned Ali Reis and red-haired Macferran, all clad uniformly in yellow tunics and lobster-pot helmets, with muskets slung over their shoulders. And as if to emphasise the fact that no ordinary entourage was approaching the gates of Plymouth, our fifth horseman was a black-cassocked clergyman, who nonetheless looked just as much a soldier as the rest of us.

The guard tentatively levelled his musket and shouted a challenge. 'Who goes there?'

'Sir Matthew Quinton, Major of the Lord Admiral's Marine Regiment!'

We did not slow the pace of our horses. If the fellow had done his duty, he would have shot me dead there and then; but as he knew full well, the men at my back would have cut him to pieces long before he could reload. Instead, he came awkwardly to attention and shouted 'Pass, Sir Matthew Quinton!'

We rode on, into the heart of the town.

It being a Sunday, there was little doubt where most of those whom I needed to inform of my arrival would be found. A large church stood high upon the slope overlooking the inner harbour, the bells were ringing, and the crowds flocking toward it suggested that a service was imminent. I was in no mood for delay, or for reticence in announcing my arrival: I wished to complete the unpleasant business as swiftly as possible, then to return to my wife and my ship.

I left Carvell to arrange accommodation for the men. As one of the most cosmopolitan seaports in the land, Plymouth was one of the few places where such exotic creatures as an erstwhile Virginian slave, a Moor and a red-headed Scotsman would attract little comment or attention. Meanwhile, Francis Gale and I made our way up toward the church, receiving some curious stares as we did so. More than curious, too, in not a few cases: I could see hatred in some eyes, especially in those of the old, those who remembered the late times. I had been prepared for such a reception, although it still came as a shock to be regarded as an enemy in one's own land. But Plymouth had been one of the staunchest strongholds of the rebellious Parliament during the civil wars. Some of the widows who now gave me the evil eye would undoubtedly have lost their husbands in battle. To them, the young officer standing proud in a yellow uniform-coat and black baldric would have seemed the epitome of the Cavaliers against whom the men of Plymouth fought.

We came to the Church of Saint Andrew, a vast structure which dwarfed Ravensden's cramped parish church, where Francis ministered. My friend looked up appreciatively at the large tower.

'Recent,' he said. 'No more than two-hundred years old. Proof of the wealth of the town. The incumbent will be a fortunate fellow – the tithes here must make him nearly as rich as Croesus.'

I nodded. Further proof of Plymouth's prosperity could be seen all around us, in the grand merchants' houses that lined the streets, in the cut of the clothing of the townsfolk making their way through the north door, in the confident air given off by men and women alike.

We made our way through the porch, into the main body of the nave.

I have fought in countless battles. I have encountered deadly foes at swordpoint. I have known fear. I have been under the surgeon's knife more often than I can remember. Truly, though, few experiences are more unsettling than walking into a strange church for the first time. I never felt that peculiar sense of isolation and terror more keenly than in Saint Andrew's church of Plymouth. The hubbub of conversation ceased at once. All eyes turned towards the door, towards Francis and me. We were appraised, frankly and critically. I felt uncomfortably akin to a prize stallion being assessed at a horse fair, but Francis was in his element. Indeed, even as my eyes scanned the crowded nave for a pew with even a modicum of space, the Reverend Gale was looking around keenly.

'Puritanical,' he stated, loudly enough for at least half the congregation to hear. 'To be expected in this den of rebels, of course. No altar rails, candles or genuflection, the curate not even in a chasuble. Low Church, Sir Matthew. So damnably low, its arse scrapes the floor.'

With that, he began to stride boldly down the aisle, toward the very front of the congregation. I followed, rather less certainly, but deciding that there was nothing to be gained by modesty; indeed, the grandeur of my uniform precluded it. There were some gasps and growls as we made our way past the serried ranks. Those in the very front pews, the great men of Plymouth (and their even greater women, at least in girth), turned their heads toward us and glowered. One of them, a gross and self-satisfied creature, wore a chain of office around his neck: the mayor, no doubt. Next to him sat a strongly built, square-faced fellow, dressed simply in the black garb favoured by the so-called godly in the days of the Commonwealth. He sat by what could only be his wife, a great, fat creature similarly clothed in black, a white bonnet crowning her vast head and ugly, scarred face. The mayor's expression was furious, but that of the man with the titanic wife was cold and calculating.

Now, though, I could see that we had at least one ally in this place. Across the aisle from the mayor sat a stout man of middle years, bewigged and sporting a great nose not unlike that which adorned the ugly face of the king. His wide eyes met mine. We exchanged a nod of recognition, although for the moment I could not quite place where or when I had met him. But his red uniform coat and sash identified him as an army officer, and the fact that he was alone in his pew suggested that he was very nearly as out of place amid this hostile congregation as I was. I began to make for the vacant space beside him.

Francis Gale could never be out of place in any church, though. From the lowest chapel to the greatest cathedral, each and every church was Francis's stage. He marched boldly into the choir, brushing past the bemused curate, and genuflected in front of the altar, making the sign of the cross as vigorously and publicly as he possibly could: actions calculated to cause the utmost offence to the Puritanical hordes among the congregation behind him.

While Francis remained kneeling before the altar, seemingly deep in private prayer and oblivious to the hostile hubbub behind him, I came up beside the army officer.

'Sir Matthew,' my ally said, bowing his head.

'Begging your pardon, sir, you have me at a disadvantage –'

'De Gomme,' he said, and now I could identify his strong Flemish accent, so similar to that of my Zeelander wife Cornelia. 'We met at the Tower last year, when you were arming the *Merhonour*.'

'Sir Bernard,' I replied, reciprocating the bow. No mere officer, then: the King's Engineer, no less. And I knew full well the nature of the 'engine' he was now building here in Plymouth. So did every man, woman and child in the congregation of Saint Andrew's church; and that was precisely why Sir Bernard De Gomme sat alone and friendless in the front pew.

At the east end of the church, Francis's words were suddenly interrupted by the arrival of the incumbent Vicar of Saint Andrew's, a stooped, elderly man who must have experienced, and been shaped by, the bitter religious schisms of thirty and forty years before. His simple cassock and stole revealed his taste in religion as surely as if he had written a five-hundred page book setting out his theology. He whispered angrily at Francis, who merely smiled beatifically at him before genuflecting to the altar once more, turning, and taking his place beside me.

'Latitudinarian,' said Francis loudly, thus deploying one of the vilest insults in his vocabulary. 'But one step away from atheism. Remind me to mention it to my friend Billy Sancroft, on our return to London. He will be only too pleased to take it up with the Archbishop.'

* * *

The service went on; and when it seemed it could go on no more, it went on longer still, grinding into dust the patience of the less Puritanical members of the congregation (namely, ourselves). The incumbent of Saint Andrew's evidently had a liking for the lengthier psalms and for more collects than a moderate man might consider reasonable. His sermon, upon an obscure passage in the Book of Nehemiah, was interminable. Sir Bernard whispered to me from time to time, naming some of the leading personages of Plymouth. The mayor, it seemed, was a nonentity, entirely in thrall to the black-garbed man sitting to his left: Ludovic Conibear, the navy agent in the town during Cromwell's day, who had enriched himself mightily by serving the usurping republic and who was casting frequent, suspicious glances in my direction. But although he lost his great landed estate up-river when the king returned, Conibear had somehow managed to retain both his position in the navy and much of his ill-gotten wealth. According to De Gomme, the 'somehow' was not unconnected to the fact that the navy agent was a creature of George Monck, Duke of Albemarle. Thus Ludovic Conibear was still a power in Plymouth, and a markedly dangerous man.

At length, Bernard De Gomme exhausted his catalogue of dignitaries whose names he felt I needed to know. Yet still the sermon continued. I assumed that Francis's eyes were closed to enable him to concentrate on following the impenetrable drift of the vicar's argument; but then he gave out a great snore, and I, along with the rest of the congregation, realised that he was fast asleep. In time my mind, too, drifted away from the vicar's dreary words. Indeed, it drifted away from the church, and even from Plymouth, seeking solace in a vision of Cornelia unclothed and lying, provocatively spread-eagled, upon our marital bed. If God can truly read our innermost thoughts, and takes account of the time and the place in which we think them, then he must have been especially outraged by my contemplation of such undeniable impurity in his own house, as his own Word was expounded by one of his own ordained priests…

'The hell-hound!'

The shout came from the south porch, and at once every head turned in that direction. The minister of Saint Andrew's stopped in mid-sentence. Francis woke with a start. I looked around. A youth of perhaps twelve or thirteen stood in the doorway, a tall, gangling lad, evidently out of breath from hard running. He pointed behind him, toward the south: toward the sea.

'The hell-hound has returned! He has come into the very Sound itself!'

The first to stand was the strong, calm man alongside the mayor. Sir Bernard De Gomme followed suit, then Francis and myself. As the youth turned and ran out of the porch, back in the direction from which he had come, we began to run after him. Running towards the hell-hound.

Chapter Eleven

Thou nere wilt riddle neighbour John
Where ich of late have been a;
Why ich have been at Plimouth, mon,
The like hath never been a,
Zich streets, zich men, zich huge zea,
Zich things, zich guns, there rumbling,
Thy zelf like me would bless to zee,
Zich bomination jumbling.

Anon., *A Devonshire Song* (published 1665)

With much of the congregation hot on our heels, Francis, De Gomme and I followed the running youth through the streets of Plymouth. It was only a matter of yards downhill to the town wall, a pitiful old rampart that displayed tell-tale signs of having been battered by cannon-fire during the civil war, and rebuilt with cheap materials and shoddy workmanship. We ran through the gate tower, then uphill again onto the large area of high, open ground known as the Hoe.

As I reached the crest, I saw an astonishing vista open up before me. Ships of mine had anchored in Plymouth Sound before, but strangely, I had never been up to the famous headland. Thus I had never before looked in this direction, nor seen this particular view. The Sound was a great, broad bay, with the high coast of Devon stretching away to the east and that of Cornwall to the west, toward Rame Head. The Hoe itself was the promontory of a peninsula jutting out into that bay, flanked by the rivers Plym to the east and Tamar to the west. Fairly close to the shore, towards the mouth of the Tamar, was a prominent island, upon which stood a small fortress. As I drew breath, I saw fire and smoke belch from one of the cannon on its ramparts, and a moment or two later I heard the sound of its firing. The shot was only a gesture, and the gunner on the island would have known it; his target was simply too far out into the bay. And his target, I could now see, was the proverbial hell-hound.

There in the Sound was a man-of-war, cut at a quick estimate for twenty-eight guns. She had all sail set and was steering north-east, very nearly beam on to the stiff breeze from the south-east. She was a sleek, slim craft with no forecastle, but even so, it was easy to recognise her for what she was. Her unmistakeable lines, the familiar colours at the stern, and the large numbers of men lining her rails and in her rigging, gave her away. She was a Dunkirk-built Dutch privateer – a caper, as they called such craft – and she was about to run down two fishing boats that were attempting to flee from her by getting into the mouth of the Plym.

'Captain Jacob Kranz,' said De Gomme, 'and his *Duivel*. They have been plaguing this coast for months, taking prize after prize in sight of land, even raiding ashore. The man's impudence knows no bounds, and he seems to have an uncanny knowledge of where the King's forces await him. When ships sail to intercept him in Lyme Bay, going on certain intelligence that he is there, he appears off Fowey instead. When the militia marches to Salcombe, believing him to have landed there, he attacks Bridport. Credulous folk and men in their cups in the taverns say he is in league with the devil. For certain, he has a huge black dog with him aboard the ship, and its howling can be heard off the coast at night – some even say Kranz and the dog are one and the same creature, witchcraft enabling the one to turn into the other at will.'

Francis rolled his eyes. 'Dogs that turn into men. Do the folk of Plymouth also still believe that one can create mice by sealing grains of wheat and a dirty shirt in a jar?'

But I was intent only on examining the hell-hound's ship. The Dunkirk privateers had been famous – or rather, infamous – for a century. Swift, well built and heavily armed, they served whichever nation was prepared to grant them letters of marque to attack its enemies. If no such patron came forward, the Dunkirkers served themselves. They fell on the ships of all nations as they made their way through the English Channel, and often roamed further afield. Dunkirk captains were renowned as some of the boldest and best seamen to sail the seas. But Dunkirk was now tamed, having come under the unbending control of France a few years earlier. The port's fast, sleek ships were either sold on to new owners, or else the crews and captains had gone over en masse to whichever foreign state would employ them. Such, it seemed, was the case with the *Duirel*.

As we watched impotently from the Hoe, the caper, as was inevitable, rapidly overhauled the fishing boats, which were forced to heave to. Boarding parties left the *Duirel* to take charge of her new prizes. And on the Hoe, women sobbed and men raged bitterly at this injustice, this heinous disgrace, committed in England's own waters, very nearly under the walls of an English town.

Ludovic Conibear approached us.

'Well, Sir Bernard,' he said in a loud, strongly accented Devon voice, 'where is the king's power now? What use are your new ramparts against that?' He pointed out to sea, towards the triumphant *Duirel*. An angry crowd gathered behind him. I heard words spoken against the king, and in praise of Oliver Cromwell. A truly ancient man, bent almost in two, shuffled to the front of the crowd and stared at me intently. 'And the king's ship in the harbour?' Conibear demanded. 'Tell me, Sir Bernard, why does she not sail to give battle to the Dunkirker? A nor'easterly, yet her cowardly captain stirs not! Just as he has not all these last weeks!'

This was not my business. The hell-hound was of no concern to me; I was in Plymouth upon a very different affair. A much greater affair, at that, namely discovering the cause of the division of the fleet. Yet I could just see the topmasts of the king's ship in question away to the east, beyond the shallow ditches, low earthern banks and scaffolding that would one day dominate Plymouth Hoe and its Sound: the vast new royal citadel that Sir Bernard De Gomme was building, ostensibly to protect Plymouth from the likes of Kranz, but in truth to overawe the obstreperous town and ensure that never again could it rebel against its rightful king. That distant ship, and the so-called coward who commanded her, was very much a part of my business.

'Perchance, Mister Conibear,' I said, 'the captain is even now making his ship ready for sea. Or if he is not, there might be a hundred reasons to detain a royal man-of-war in harbour. If I were you, sir, I would not be so swift in coming to judgement.'

Conibear stepped forward brazenly, until he was barely inches from my face. Behind him, the mob advanced. We were three men, three Cavaliers, against three score.

'If I were you, swordsman,' growled Conibear, 'I would not be so swift in defending a craven and a popinjay. Do not lecture me on what might or might not detain ships in this harbour, for I have known it since before I could walk, long before you were born.' The mob behind him murmured their approval of his words. 'And in the year fifty-six, I was aboard the *Marston Moor* down there in the Cattewater when she put to sea in half an hour to despatch a Dunkirker seen off the Rame.' Louder murmurs, and the pointing of fingers at the *Duirel* and the topmasts of the warship in the harbour. Conibear turned to them, nodded, and then turned to face me once again. 'But your name, swordsman, if you please? And the yellow uniform that you wear – what strange new confection is that, pray?'

I would have damned the man's impudence, if not run him through, although that might have led in short order to my being torn apart by the angry mob at his back. But before I could speak, a strange thing happened. The old, bent man, who had been staring at me from the front of the crowd, stepped forward and pointed a gnarled finger at me.

'Quinton,' he said in a broken voice. 'Quinton of Ravensden. Thanks be to God for bringing back my old captain, England's last true hero.' He stumbled forward, and I saw that his cheeks were moist with tears. He took my hand and said, 'Heale, My Lord. Do you not remember? I served with you in the *Constant Esperance* in the year eighty-eight, when I was but a child, a cabin boy. Joined the ship with you at Deptford, and sailed her here with you. I was near this very spot when you and the mighty Drake stood yonder. When you looked out toward the dread Armada's forest of sails. When the two of you resolved that you had time to finish your game of bowls and beat the Don still. And so you did, My Lord. So you did.'

As he ran his hands over mine, and the mob – aye, even Conibear – looked on in stunned astonishment, the old man's words suddenly took on meaning.

I took hold of the ancient's chin, and lifted it gently until we were looking into each other's eyes. 'Mister Heale,' I said, 'you pay me a great compliment, but I fear you have confused me for my grandfather. Although I, too, am named Matthew Quinton.' I looked toward Conibear, and on that plot of ground, of all the sods of earth in England, I knew I could only speak as my grandfather would have done. 'My uniform is that of a Major of the Lord Admiral's Regiment, Mister Conibear. I was recently captain of His Majesty's Ship the *Royal Sceptre* in the great four-day fight with the Dutch. I am grandson to the Earl of Ravensden who sailed from this very harbour to defend

England against the Invincible Armada, and brother to the present Earl. Aye, by God, my name is indeed Quinton, Mister Conibear. Sir Matthew Quinton. Mark it well.'

The crowd behind Conibear was startled and confused by these revelations. They might still have no love for me, or for the king I served, but my rank, title, and the abiding legend of my grandfather, were sufficient to awe them, if only for the time being. What was more, at least some of them evidently did have a deep well of love for old Heale, who was still looking up at me in wonderment. If he truly had sailed with my grandfather against the Armada, he had to be ninety years old or more. Over the years, I had encountered several who claimed to have been with old Earl Matthew on the *Constant Esperance* in 1588, but they were all swiftly exposed as rogues seeking to wring some coin from my brother or myself. But Heale was different. For one thing, he had knowledge that none of the pretending vagabonds possessed: namely, the strange similarity between my own appearance and that of the only portrait of my grandfather as a young man. Painted shortly after he became Earl, when he was a year or so older than I was then, this adorned the wall of the library at Ravensden Abbey; a room that my mother never entered, for she made every effort to avoid looking upon the image of the father-in-law she detested. Heale could never, ever have seen that portrait, which meant there was only one possible explanation for his mistaking my identity.

Conibear had plainly wrestled with similar thoughts, and had come to a conclusion. He looked at me anew, smiled, and bowed his head. 'Sir Matthew,' he said obsequiously, 'I beg your forgiveness for my most intemperate words. I was distressed by the Dunkirker's attack – we all were. Plymouth is honoured by your presence, just as it still honours the name of your illustrious grandfather.'

I doubted the truth of every single one of his words, but it was a moment to be gracious. 'I thank you, Mister Conibear. I trust there shall be no further, ah, misunderstandings between us.'

But as we exchanged further empty pleasantries, I could see the hell-hound sailing away to the south-east, her two prizes following in her wake. Not my business, I reminded myself. Not my business at all.

* * *

Francis and I found my three men down on the quayside known as the Barbican. The stallholders, fishermen and whores who thronged the narrow streets were evidently giving my miniature army a wide berth. As had been the case with Conibear, this would have been their first sight of our unfamiliar yellow uniforms, and there was suspicion and downright fear in nearly every pair of eyes. No doubt some feared that we were really a pressing party, come to make up the numbers that the fleet had lost during the four-day fight.

'Requisitioned rooms at the Turk's Head, Sir Matthew,' said Carvell. 'Took a little persuading, the landlord did. Mighty reluctant to take the King's gold, and mighty afraid of the King's uniform. Like everyone else in this town, it seems. And as you requested, I've hired a boat. That took some finding, too.'

I nodded, and could well imagine the measures that Carvell and the others had resorted to in order to overcome the reluctance of the good townsfolk of Plymouth.

With a long June evening stretching ahead, I saw no reason to delay the unpleasantness that I had been dreading throughout the journey from London; dreading, indeed, since the moment when the King had given me his written instructions in Westminster Abbey, and I read the name inscribed upon them. I recalled my brother's words to me later that same night, when he explained the reason for the uncomfortably hot uniform I was now wearing.

'As you know better than I, Matt, your commission as a King's captain only has force while you actually have that command. So if you go down to Plymouth as you are, you are but a private individual. Yes, you are a knight and my brother, but neither of those distinctions will be of much use to you in your dealings with the sort of men you are likely to encounter there – mayors, aldermen, magistrates, army officers, all the puffed-up office holders one finds in any county. In Devon above all, where many of them owe allegiance to the Duke of Albemarle. So you will need a high military rank, both to give you status in the eyes of the good people of Devon, and to make you clearly the superior officer of the man you need to investigate. The man we suspect of having brought about the division of the fleet. Your erstwhile friend, brother.'

'He will not dispute my authority –'

'Matt, if you seek to arrest him on a charge of high treason, who knows what he might dispute? Your friendship will count for nought then, I suspect.'

My heart sank at the very thought: *a charge of high treason*. A charge that I would bring against one of my dearest friends, and arrest him for it. An arrest that would inevitably lead to trial, conviction, and if the King was merciful, a swift beheading. And if the King's mercy was exhausted? The terrible spectacle of hanging, drawing and quartering. I had witnessed the regicide Harrison's execution not long after the Restoration, when that exact sentence was carried out. I saw him hanged, then cut down alive, his guts sliced open, the entrails torn out and flung into the fire, the body decapitated. The memory was hellish; the prospect of the same fate awaiting a good friend, and at my own instigation, was beyond any hell.

The boat taking me across the harbour was a long rowing skiff manned by large, silent identical twin brothers. They looked on me warily throughout the short voyage. Perhaps they could divine my thoughts, which speculated on why such fine specimens were not in the king's service, either voluntarily or by pressing.

The brothers rowed me across the Barbican harbour, a busy waterway thronged with coastal shipping, a few foreign-going vessels and entire fleets of fishing craft, similar to those that the *Duirel* had seized within sight of the shore. Carvell, Ali Reis and Macferran briefly watched the boat's passage from the quayside, then turned and marched purposefully through the door of the nearest inn. I had no doubt that by the end of the night, they would be roaring drunk; all except Ali Reis, who remained true to his Mahometan faith in that regard if not in others, although strangely, he always seemed to be at the centre of any fight and the instigator of many a debauch. Meanwhile, Francis Gale was already bound for the Turk's Head and his bed. He was no longer a young man, as he often said, and preferred a good sleep to a good bottle.

Once past the breakwater, the boat was out into the broad, open reach known as the Cattewater, where I looked upon a familiar sight. Ahead, over toward the shore of Mount Batten, lay the hulk, an old Spanish prize from Cromwell's war that served as the navy's jetty here in Plymouth; several times, I had been on ships that moored to her. Alongside her was a Fifth Rate frigate, secured fore and aft, her sails furled and her cannon hidden behind closed gunports. A very familiar frigate.

I had never thought to set foot on her deck again. For in that hull, I first met Francis Gale. In that little wooden world, I commanded the likes of Carvell and Macferran for the first time. She was the ship that I had commanded in my first battle. The ship whose deck had been stained with my blood.

The *Jupiter*.

But it was not just the ship that was familiar. Several men were upon deck, watching our approach with some curiosity, but only one of them stood on the quarterdeck. Only one of them was attired in a silk dressing gown and a large white periwig, holding a delicate glass of red wine in his hand. He was a bluff fellow, a year or two older than me but already starting to run to fat. Suddenly, recognition dawned upon his face. He disappeared below, shouting as he did so at several of the men in the *Jupiter*'s waist.

By the time my boat came alongside and secured, a side party awaited me. The boatswain's whistle piped me aboard, and as I hauled myself up onto that so-familiar deck, my successor as the *Jupiter*'s captain doffed his hat in salute. He had discarded the dressing gown for a breastplate and baldric, but even so, he possessed about as much military bearing as a pheasant. He smiled broadly, and I could not help but grin in return. Despite what I was about to do, it was good to see him, for I had thought him dead. The whole English navy had thought him dead. My last sight of his ship had been of it being engulfed by the entire Dutch fleet during the early part of the Battle of Lowestoft, the summer before.

'*Sir* Matthew,' he said with emphasis, 'I give you joy of your knighthood. Belatedly, but my joy is not diminished by time.'

'And I give you joy of your freedom, Captain Harris. Nor is mine diminished by time.'

With that, we embraced, and the *Jupiter*'s side party cheered. Beaudesert Harris, my very good friend, whom I had thought to be sailing the lake below. But even as we clung to each other, I thought upon the irony of it. I had given Beau joy of his liberty, yet perhaps I was about to snatch it away from him once again. Indeed, perhaps I was the angel of death who would consign poor Beau Harris to a traitor's fate.

Chapter Twelve

New captains are made that never did fight,
But with pots in the day and punks in the night,
And all their chief care is to keep their swords bright,
And is not old England grown new?
Where are your old swords, your bills and your bows?
Your bucklers and targets that never feared blows?
They are turn'd to stillettos and other fair shows.
And is not old England grown new?

Anon., *Old England Grown New* (1660s song)

The captain of the *Jupiter* raised the glass that he had been drinking from on the quarterdeck, and which had already been refilled several times since my arrival in the ship's great cabin.

'To Will,' he said simply.

'To Will.'

'And may God give us the ships, the guns and the men to avenge him!' Beau virtually threw the contents of the glass down his throat.

'Amen,' I said, and took a rather more measured sip from my own glass.

I had not seen Beau since before the Battle of Lowestoft, just over a year earlier. It took some weeks for the intelligence to reach England that, finding himself surrounded by the enemy fleet, Captain Beaudesert Harris had prudently surrendered his command, the *House of Nassau* – a ship that had been mine earlier in the year. Taken prisoner, he was housed in reasonably tolerable conditions in a Dutch castle until early in the new year, 1666, when the intermediaries of the two governments agreed to an exchange. In one of those peculiar ironies that God sometimes devises, the man for whom he was exchanged was my brother-in-law, Cornelis van der Eide, a bold and skilful captain of the Zeeland Admiralty, who had surrendered to me during the Battle of Lowestoft; and much as I loved Beau, I could not help but feel that it was anything but an equal exchange. Nevertheless, Beau Harris was duly released. But by the time he returned to England, I was at sea in command of the *Cressy*, tasked with bringing home the mast fleet from Gothenburg. And when I came home in my turn, Beau already had the command of the *Jupiter* and was at sea, cruising the Soundings from his base here in the Cattewater. As I say, I loved Beau as a true and amiable friend; even so, I thought it perverse that a man who lost his ship due to a catastrophic error of judgement on his part, which he then compounded by surrendering to the enemy, should be granted another command immediately. But during one of our last conversations before he lost his life making an even more fatal charge into the middle of an enemy fleet, Will Berkeley explained the matter succinctly.

'One, Beau may not know one end of a ship from the other, but he has the heart of a lion and the blood of a true Cavalier, traits valued highly by the King. Two, he makes Lady Castlemaine laugh, which endears him even more to our sovereign lord. Three, his father controls two parliamentary boroughs, which endears him to both our sovereign lord and Lord Chancellor Clarendon. Thus Beau's continuation in the service is assured, and I'll wager you a guinea to a groat that he'll outrank us both one day soon. Besides, Matt, it is not as though he is being given a ship in the fleet itself, to repeat his blunder of last summer. Your old *Jupiter*, cruising in the mouth of the Channel, far from the real action of the war – not even Beau can make a pig's ear of that command.'

Poor Will: if the charges laid at Beau's door in the papers given to me by the King were proven, the pig's ear was grown so large that it had very nearly crushed the navy of England beneath its monstrous porcine weight. It was certainly more than sufficient to put paid to the life of Vice-Admiral Sir William Berkeley. Moreover, it now seemed to be intent on giving Captain Jacob Kranz, the hell-hound, free rein in the waters of south-west England.

Beau was holding forth on the iniquities of his Dutch captors during his imprisonment, although as far as I could tell, this was principally annoyance at their refusal to supply him with a whore or two whenever he demanded. Finally, I could hear no more and interrupted him.

'Beau, why did you not even attempt to sail when the caper came into the Sound this afternoon? Is your ship damaged, or undermanned? The wind was favourable –'

He tapped the side of his nose. 'All part of my plan, Matt.'

'Your plan?'

Beau looked mightily pleased with himself. 'I am lulling him, Sir Matthew. Making him think that the *Jupiter* will not put to sea to oppose him. Encouraging him in the belief that her captain is a craven and a fop, who prefers to stroll the deck in his dressing gown. Tempting him to grow bolder, and bolder still. One day soon, he will become too bold, and he will make a mistake. Then I shall have him, Matt.'

Beau was no seaman, but then, he was no fool, either, and he was certainly no coward. There was a logic to his design, although I wondered whether he had the skill to execute it.

'And how many honest traders and fishermen have to suffer before you consider him sufficiently lulled?'

Beau bridled at that.

'I command the *Jupiter* now, Sir Matthew,' he said, stiffly. But Beau Harris could not be querulous for very long. He poured more wine into my glass and smiled. 'You seem in ill temper, Matt. That never suits you. Come, let us celebrate the reunion of two old friends, and raise toasts to absent ones.'

Beau was evidently intent on getting fuddled as rapidly and comprehensively as he could. The temptation to join him in a wake to honour Will's memory was powerful, but I resisted. If I followed him into his cups, it would only make worse what had to happen before the night was out. Best, then, to grasp the nettle as quickly as possible.

'Beau, there is something I have to ask you. Something that I am commanded by the King to ask you.'

His face fell.

'Commanded *by the King?* Then is this why you have come, Matt?' I said nothing; what could I say? And, as I have just observed, Beaudesert Harris was no fool. 'Of course. The hero Sir Matthew Quinton taken away from his great ship, to suddenly appear in distant Plymouth dressed as a soldier. I should have known you had not come here in that garb for the air or the society. Out with it, then, Matt. What has Beaudesert Harris done to offend the King's Majesty?'

How to word it? But at bottom, there was no easy way. Best to open the mouth and pray that the correct words spilled out.

'When you were cruising to southward, at the start of May, you spied a fleet off Lisbon, did you not? A great fleet?'

Beau was clearly confused by this. 'Of course I did. Every man knows that! I saw the French fleet, plain as day. The Duke of Beaufort's fleet, come out of the Mediterranean.'

'You are sure it was the French fleet?'

'God's wig, Matt Quinton, I may know less of the obscurities of sea-business than you, who have made such efforts to turn yourself into something akin to the roughest Rotherhithe tar, but even I can tell a French fleet when I see it! I saw the white Bourbon colours, plain as day.'

'And you reported that – when?'

Beau brightened. 'Ah, now that I can tell you. I may have many faults, but stinting on my correspondence is not one of them – unlike my idle oaf of a purser, who was put in solely because he's some sort of relation to the nursemaid of Lady Castlemaine's bastard by the King. Yes, truly.' He went to his sea-chest, and began to rummage through it. 'The idiot can't tell one end of a quill from the other. So I don't entrust any of my papers to him, Matt, nor to any of my servants. Here we are. Copies in my own hand of my out-letters from the *Jupiter*. This is the one you want –' He handed me a sheet written out in his familiar, nearly illegible scrawl – 'my letter to Sir William Coventry, the Lord Admiral's secretary, dated from this very cabin on the twenty-second day of May, as soon as we came into Plymouth Sound. It was even printed in the *Gazette*! I have the copy here.'

He produced the familiar paper and waved it at me, but I ignored it; although the *London Gazette* was still a new innovation, having appeared for the first time barely a year before, it already seemed to have existed for an eternity. Then, of course, the *Gazette* stood alone. Nowadays the streets are full of these so-called 'news-papers', though God knows why, for they barely deserve the name; every week seems to vomit forth a new title into the world, full of the same scurrilous untruths as all the others, penned by low-life incapable of following a more respectable trade, the columns crowded out with rewards offered for lost dogs or advertisements for coffee houses that no honest man would dare frequent. Yet the gullible amongst our nation – that is, very nearly every man of it – devours them all, thus feeding the demand for more. But some of them have their uses; I find the paper the printers use for that rancid mountebank Dick Steele's *Spectator* has a texture particularly pleasing to my ancient arse.

My younger self, though, had little time or use for the *Gazette*, which reported in detail the doings of the Pope, or the Margrave of Brandenburg, or the Khan of Samarkand, but said nothing whatsoever about what every man and woman in England really wanted to know: namely, precise details of the fornications of the King and the great lords and ladies of the land. Besides, I was intent on reading Beau's letter to Coventry. It was unequivocal, and tallied with the evidence of the summary of official correspondence that had been among the papers handed me by Chiffinch in Westminster Abbey. Beaudesert Harris, captain of His Majesty's Ship the *Jupiter*, had seen the French fleet off Lisbon, and duly reported that fact to Whitehall. There was only one difficulty: the French fleet could not possibly have been off Lisbon. The papers I had seen contained categorical proof that when Beau wrote his letter, the French fleet was no nearer England than Toulon. That meant Beau could be one of only three things: a blockhead, a liar or a traitor. And as my brother had said, if one cannot find a genuine traitor to hang, draw and quarter, there are plenty of blockheads and liars on whom the charge can be pinned instead.

Beau could see me reading and re-reading his letter, and my expression must have hinted at my thoughts.

'They think it was me, don't they? The great men in Whitehall. They think it was my intelligence of the French fleet that brought about the division of our own. But there's proof, Matt! The man who reported the French army at La Rochelle, ready to invade Ireland! His story corroborates mine, and he's here, in Plymouth –'

'Nathaniel Garrett. Yes, Beau. My men have put out word around the town requiring him to attend me. When we find him, Francis Gale will take his deposition.' I hesitated, but there was no way of concealing or dissembling. 'And in due course, he will also take yours.'

I saw the realisation dawn on Beau Harris's face.

'Depositions? Are you turned lawyer, then, Matt Quinton? No, I see it now. Not a lawyer, indeed. You are turned a hanging judge.'

'It will not come to that, Beau –'

'Really, Matt? How many Englishmen were lost in your four-day fight? Five thousand? Six thousand? Even here in Plymouth, scores of widows and orphans weep for loved ones who are either at the bottom of the ocean or rotting in Dutch gaols. The people cry out for revenge, both upon the Dutch and upon those responsible for the division of the fleet. And in this town, they also blame me for not sallying forth and destroying the hell-hound. I hardly dare set foot ashore as it is. Besides, if I did, and laid accusations against those – ah, what does that matter? For if they come to believe that I caused our defeat in battle too… they'll hang me from a gibbet on the Hoe, Matt, and won't bother with the niceties of courts and juries.' He essayed a smile, but it was grim and forced. 'So come, Sir Matthew Quinton. Let's drink while we can – you, who is set for glory and an earldom, and me, who is set for the gallows.'

Chapter Thirteen

Beaufort is there, and to their dazzling eyes,
The distance more the object magnifies…
Beaufort is in the Channel! Hixy, here!
Doxy, Toulon! Beaufort is ev'rywhere!

Marvell, *Third Advice to a Painter*

'And here, Sir Matthew, will be a demi-bastion, modelled upon the very latest French practice!'

De Gomme was unconscionably proud of his creation. We had already spent most of the morning, the third after my arrival in Plymouth, touring the foundations and earthworks, and there was as yet no trace of his enthusiasm waning. With no sign of Nathaniel Garrett coming forward, despite placards having been placed around the entire town and my men asking after him from inn to inn, I could not in conscience avoid the engineer's invitation to come up to the Hoe to view the vast building site. Hundreds of stonemasons, carpenters and labourers were hard at work. Great ditches were being dug, strong ramparts erected. The Citadel would be a formidable fortress: that much was clear.

'And this will be the Katherine Bastion, named for Her Majesty, of course –'

De Gomme enthused on, but my mind was far away. It was with the men of my ship, racing against time to get her repaired and fit for sea once again. It was out at sea, imagining De Ruyter's mighty fleet probing our defences, seeking a way to come up the Thames and wreak havoc, perhaps even to invade – for this was what all the newsletters from London, eagerly opened and read aloud in Plymouth's inns, spoke of. It was with my brother and Musk, burrowing into the rotten heart of government to see what dark secrets lay there. And above all, it was with Cornelia, hoping and praying that she was well. It was…

'Sir Bernard!'

The shout came from the side of the new Citadel nearest to the Barbican. There appeared to be a commotion under one of the new ramparts, with several men standing around, pointing excitedly into the ditch.

De Gomme and I strode across the future parade ground as rapidly as dignity permitted. We clambered up onto the new rampart and looked down. Two men were down in the bottom of the ditch, turning over what appeared at first to be a sack of some sort. Then I saw an arm, and a bloodied hand.

'It's a body, Sir Bernard!' cried one of the men in the ditch. 'Stabbed many times. Near hacked to death, God help us!'

'A woman's body, or a man's?'

'Man's, Sir Bernard! Seaman, by his garb!'

'I will make a wager with you, Sir Bernard,' I said, although the thrill of gaming was the last thing in my mind. 'I'll wager that we have just found the missing Nathaniel Garrett.'

* * *

I sent word to the *Jupiter*, plainly visible across the Cattewater, and to Francis Gale, who came up from the Turk's Head with the rest of the men. Francis said prayers over the body before permitting Carvell, Ali

Reis and Macferran to carry it down into Plymouth Castle, the crumbling old keep on the harbour side of the Citadel which was destined to be demolished once the new fortress was complete.

'We should inform the Mayor,' said De Gomme. 'There will need to be a coroner's court, and a hue and cry for the murderer.'

'As you say, Sir Bernard. But before we do that, I think we need to prevent a riot.'

The *Jupiter*'s longboat was coming across the harbour, steering for the quay at the foot of the Lambhay Hill, on which stood both the old castle and the warehouses which Conibear used for naval stores. A crowd was already gathering at the quayside, and the shouts of both women and men carried clearly to the ramparts of the citadel.

'Coward, for not sailing against the hell-hound!'

'Ignorant gentleman captains, all of your kind!'

'I could command yonder *Jupiter* better than you!'

'Coward, that struck to the Dutch in the Lowestoft fight!'

'Coward! Coward!'

The taunts angered me. As the longboat approached the quay, they grew louder and louder.

'Fuck the *Jupiter* – a runt of a ship and a cunt of a captain!'

'Damn the whoremaster King! Here's to the Commonwealth's halcyon days!'

My eyes seemed to turn red. They could insult my kind. They could even call Beau Harris a coward: that was the last thing he was, and he was strong enough to rise above that demeaning word. But they would not insult the ship that had made me what I was, nor all the gallant men who had died in her. Above all, they would not insult and demean my King, even if the charge of whoring was wholly true. I drew my sword and began to run down the slope toward the quay.

I heard De Gomme behind me, calling to me to stop, to wait for him to assemble a file of infantrymen. I was vaguely aware of Francis behind me, but I knew he was unarmed, and I doubted whether the ugly Puritanical mob ahead of us would pay heed to an Anglican Churchman. I simply charged down the hill, heedless of all dignity, making directly for the mob.

The bawlers, denigrators and fishwives were all looking the other way, toward the *Jupiter*'s boat. Only at the very last moment did those at the very back of the mob, and at the side, turn and see what must have been the extraordinary spectacle of a single yellow-uniformed, red-faced senior officer charging at them. I struck out with my fists and the flat of my blade. The sheer force of my charge carried me clean through the mob, down to the edge of the quay, where I turned and held up my sword.

'The next man or woman who calls out learns the taste of steel!' I bellowed.

Nowadays, of course, I could simply call for a reading of the Riot Act, that monstrosity of a law passed when German George came in – a vile travesty that seeks to prevent Englishmen from gathering to insult their fat Teutonic masters and the timeserving lickspittle ministers who serve them. Then, though, the sight of a single sword was sufficient to disperse the mob, whose members moved away slowly, scowling and murmuring. Those who might have been inclined to argue the case were swiftly disabused by the arrival of Ali Reis, Carvell and Macferran, running down from the castle: a little army at once so unsettlingly exotic and so determinedly ferocious of countenance (not to mention armament) that even those who fancied themselves the hard men of Plymouth slunk away shamefacedly.

I turned in time to see Beau disembark from his longboat. For once, he was not overdressed, wearing merely a simple buff jacket over his shirt, and no wig.

'I did not think you could run so fast, Sir Matthew.'

'It is an honour to exhaust myself for your safety, Captain Harris.'

Beau laughed. 'Come, then, Matt – come, Francis. Show me our corpse. I need to study the condition, for if my corroborating witness is truly dead, then I think I will be in the same state soon enough.'

* * *

Beau, Francis and I stood in what had once been the lord's chapel of Plymouth Castle, looking down on the remains of the man who had once been Nathaniel Garrett.

'It's him,' said Beau.

'You met him?'

'Only the once, just after we came into harbour after the cruise to Lisbon. Sir Bernard brought him to me, saying Garrett had important information about the French which had been sent up to London.' Beau grimaced at the memory, and at the sight of the bloodied face before us. 'He was one of the crew on a Plymouth ship, taken by a Frenchman last winter when she was on passage home from Alicante. His ship was taken into La Rochelle, and the crew were held prisoner there until an exchange was arranged and they were sent home. But as they were being paraded down to the dock, he said he saw a great army drawn up, all around the town. He asked why they were there, and was told the army was going to invade Ireland.'

'One man's word?' said Francis, clearly incredulous.

'He saw the army with his own eyes,' said Beau. 'He swore it upon oath.'

But that was not what Francis had meant. He and I exchanged glances, but held our peace.

'And this intelligence had already been sent up to London when you returned from Lisbon?'

'At least two weeks earlier,' said Beau, 'while I was still escorting the convoy. But it made sense, when I came to send my own letters to Sir William Coventry and My Lord Arlington later that same day.'

'Sense, Beau? How did it make sense?'

He smiled in the way that benevolent schoolmasters do when patronising a backward pupil.

'Why, Matt, it made sense of my fleet at Lisbon. It had to be the Duke of Beaufort, heading for La Rochelle to embark the invasion army.'

Francis closed his eyes: whether in prayer or in anguish, I could not tell.

'Yes, it makes perfect sense, Beau. Apart from one thing. It was not Beaufort's fleet. The noble Duke had not even left Toulon when you saw what you saw off Lisbon. So we have a phantom fleet, a phantom army, and a phantom invasion. And because of all those phantoms, Rupert was sent west with some of the best ships in our fleet, leaving the rest of us at the mercy of De Ruyter.'

Beau was strangely unapologetic.

'A mystery indeed, Matt. But surely, the King and our great ministers – Clarendon, Arlington, all the rest of them – would not have divided the fleet on my word alone, or that of poor Garrett here?'

I said nothing. I stood there, looking down at the increasingly pungent corpse of Nathaniel Garrett, and tried to stifle my growing suspicion that this was exactly what England's rulers had done.

Chapter Fourteen

The Town is pitcht with shingle stone,
Do glisten like the ze-a,
The zhops stand ope, and all year long
A Vair I think there be a;
The King zome zwear himself was there,
A man or some such thing a.

From *A Devonshire Song*

I sat on a markedly uncomfortable oak chair in my room at the Turk's Head. It was very late and very dark, but three candles still gave me enough light to pen a report to my brother. I did not write down my suspicions about the intelligence provided by Beau Harris and Nathaniel Garrett: even if the ascetic Charles Quinton, Earl of Ravensden, did not read between the lines of my letter, the calculating and ruthless Lord Percival most certainly would.

There was a gentle knock on the door, so indistinct that I barely heard it.

Following the morning's events at the quay, it was entirely possible that some young hothead or old rebel meant to stick a blade into my guts. Thus I took up my dagger, took my bearings on the room where my men were quartered in case I needed to call out, then walked across the room and lifted the latch.

A very thin and very young girl stood there. She was poorly clothed in an ill-fitting smock that must once have belonged to an older woman – a dead mother or sister, perhaps? – but her face and hands were clean, which seemed to be a rarity in Plymouth. She could not have been more than fourteen, and at that time of night, I assumed there was only one thing she could be.

'I have no need of you,' I said.

She cocked her head to one side and looked up at me strangely.

'I have no need of you either,' she said, with unbridled impudence for one so young. Her accent was broadest Devon. 'You're Quinton?'

'I am Sir Matthew Quinton, child. Address your betters properly.'

'*Sir* Matthew Quinton. My apologies, *Sir* Matthew Quinton.' But her expression was not in the least apologetic, and she seemed to take a particular pleasure in pronouncing 'Sir' in the West Country manner, very nearly as 'Zir'. 'You're to come with me.'

It should have screamed of a trap, but there was something disarming about this strange, brazen child. If I was being led into a trap, surely my intended assailants would have sent a rather different kind of messenger?

'Come with you? And why would I do that, child?'

'If you want me to address you as Sir Matthew, you'll stop addressing me as child, this very instant, that you will. My name's Isabella Mendez. Father was Spanish, but he's dead. Mother was from Stonehouse, but she's dead too. So are you coming or not? He wants to meet you.'

'And who is he?'

She crossed her arms impatiently. 'He who wants to meet you, of course! Are all knights of the realm so stupid? Well, are you coming or not? I don't have all night.'

I thought of donning my uniform; I thought of summoning my men. But for some reason, I did neither. I paused only to buckle on my sword, then followed the mysterious Isabella out into the night air.

She led me down toward the harbour, ever deeper into a warren of narrow lanes running between tall houses with overhanging upper floors, after the old fashion. Despite the hour, the Barbican was still very much alive. Shouts and songs came from the inns, the screams of children and angry wives from some of the houses. Two or three beggars, crippled in the previous year's fighting at sea or perhaps in even earlier wars, still shambled along the streets, asking hopefully for alms. If there was a night watch in this part of Plymouth, it was a markedly ineffectual one.

At last, we came before a house which seemed to be entirely dark. The child Isabella looked around several times, as though she was checking to see that the alleyway behind us was empty, then knocked on the door: a rhythmic, patterned knocking, presumably some kind of a signal to whoever was inside.

The door opened to reveal a very round, squat woman, as unlike the girl as two creatures of the same gender could be.

'This is him, Aunt,' said Isabella. 'This is *Sir* Matthew Quinton. Too tall and not enough hair for my liking, even if he is a knight.'

'Be off with you, Bella!' The broad woman's voice was gruff, almost manly, and I had difficulty following her strong Devon accent. 'Sir Matthew,' she said, with markedly more deference than her niece had managed. 'You are welcome. He is just through here, Sir Matthew.'

She led me through the entirely dark front room, then down a narrow passageway and into a small, low room at the back of the house. This was better lit in the sense that it had both a solitary candle and a blazing fire, the latter despite it being the second half of a markedly warm June. In front of the fire, sitting on a large settle, was Heale, the ancient who had sailed with my grandfather.

He stood, albeit slowly and with obvious discomfort. 'Sir Matthew. God be with you, and also with the soul of your noble ancestor, the late Earl. I trust Bella did not lead you astray?'

I thought, *in what sense?*, but dared not utter the words.

'She was an excellent guide, Mister Heale. Your granddaughter?'

'Great-granddaughter. A blessing that she still lives, Sir Matthew. There is no greater trial to a man than to have to bury not only most of his children, but many of his grandchildren too.'

He gestured for me to sit on a rickety old stool opposite the settle, very nearly next to the fire. I felt myself back in the heat of battle on the deck of the *Royal Sceptre,* and could feel the rivulets of sweat running down my back.

'Well, Mister Heale? What business is worth bringing me here, at such an hour as this?'

'I was told that Garrett was dead. Killed, and dumped in the Citadel moat.'

'You knew Garrett?'

'He was a good man. A steady man. So few in this town are. But that was why Conibear had him killed, of course.'

'Conibear?'

'There is much you do not know about our so-called Navy Agent, Sir Matthew. The corruptions in which the man is involved are legion. He has half the town in his pocket, and fleeces the navy itself mercilessly.'

'I have yet to meet a naval supplier who does not, Mister Heale. But why would that make Conibear kill Garrett?'

The old man coughed violently.

'Garrett had been at La Rochelle. He knew of Conibear's dealings there.'

'*Conibear* has dealings at La Rochelle? Mister Heale, this is a matter of importance to the kingdom!'

'Sir Matthew, I swear to you upon the honour of my family and your noble grandfather, Conibear's duplicity is boundless. Inspect the warehouses – the navy warehouses, on the Lambhay. Let me tell you –'

Whatever he intended to tell me was swallowed by another racking cough. Bella Mendez appeared, and gently stroked her great-grandfather's bent back.

'You've overtaxed him,' she said. 'If you live to be his age, Sir Matthew Quinton, you'll know how easily that happens.'

I have; and I do.

But Heale was clearly impatient to tell me more, and I was eager for him to do so. It made no sense. If Conibear was somehow involved with the French army at La Rochelle, why was the old man insisting that I inspect the Lambhay storehouses? Through the coughs, Heale continued to gesticulate with his hands. But it was to no avail. I waited…

Waited until the loud hammering on the front door began. Bella's aunt appeared in the doorway of the room.

'Conibear's men! Quick, Bella! Get him out the back!'

I drew my sword and followed Bella Mendez out into the tiny yard at the back of the house. A shape moved ahead of us – I saw the glint of a blade – I lunged with my sword, heard a gasp and the gurgling of blood in a throat, then ran on.

Back out into the maze of narrow lanes. Which way? The Citadel was nearest, but the town wall lay in the way, and the gates would be locked…

'Too far to the Turk's Head!' Bella shouted. 'They'll know to cover that way too, although if she can, Aunt Joan will send word to rouse your men.'

I now knew enough of Plymouth's geography to realise that we were running down toward the harbour-side. But surely that gave no way of escape…

Out onto the wharf, a few score yards inland of where I had berated the mob. Without hesitation, Bella ran up the gangplank of the vessel alongside the wharf, a wide-hulled and grimy Welsh collier by the looks of her. She took hold of the shrouds and began to pull herself upward.

'Come on then, Sir Matthew! If you're a King's captain, you'll have been aloft!'

'The commission does not require it,' I said, but followed her example nonetheless.

In truth, I had been aloft no more than half-a-dozen times since I first went to sea. Not only was it beneath the dignity of a captain: I also had a markedly weak head for heights.

I followed Kit Farrell's advice and kept my eyes upward, never daring to look down. I could hear the shouts of men on the quay, could hear them running hither and thither, but whether they were pursuing us or their own private quarrels, it was impossible to tell.

Bella reached the yardarm of the collier and embraced it as confidently as any topman in the Navy Royal, pulling herself along the spar. I followed suit, although I wondered what in the name of God she had in mind. My chest, stomach and groin pressed against the yardarm as I pushed with my arms and legs.

'That's it, Sir Matthew!' she cried. 'Just like swimming!'

She was at the end of the yardarm already, and now I saw her intent. The ships on that side of the harbour were moored three deep, their yardarms almost touching. Almost, but not quite. The ship outboard of the collier was smaller, her yardarm perhaps five or six feet below that to which we clung. The motion of the ebbing tide and the fair breeze made the spar sway away from us, then back again.

'Come on, Sir Matthew! Fortune favours the bold!'

With that, Bella let herself drop over the end of the yardarm, clinging to it with her outstretched arms. She dangled there for what seemed an eternity, but could only have been a few seconds as she judged the motion of the outboard ship. Then she planted her feet on the other spar, let go, and fell, all in one motion, wrapping herself around the smaller ship's yardarm as though embracing a lover.

I edged along to the end, then repeated her actions. I let myself fall away from the yardarm, keeping a tight grip of it…

And pain seared through my entire frame. My shoulder, bruised when the *Royal Sceptre* struck the Galloper during the third day of the battle, erupted in agony. Nearly every instinct in my body screamed at me to let go.

Thankfully, though, not quite every instinct. I held on, and being taller than Bella, my feet found the lower yardarm without my needing to jump. I fell, gripped the spar for dear life, and rested the aching shoulder.

'Easy, isn't it?' said Bella, up ahead of me, standing upright against the mainmast of the smaller ship. 'Played this game since I could walk. Come on, Sir Matthew.'

With that, she scuttled off across the yardarm toward the outermost of the three ships. By the time I caught up with her, she was staring upwards.

'Too high, even for me.'

The third ship was higher out of the water, and the yardarm must have been some eight feet above the one to which we were clinging. Unlike the two we had already negotiated, this one had a footrope; but it also had a cursedly tidy crew, who had wrapped that rope tightly around the spar while the ship was in port.

I edged my way along to where Bella was.

Do not look down, Matt Quinton.

But I did. In the darkness of the night, the deck far below looked like an inviting black carpet, tempting one to move one's head just a little to lay down on it.

Do not look down.

There was but one way for us to get onto the yardarm of the next ship.

'Get behind me,' I said.

Nimbly, Bella crawled across my back. I had a sudden, vivid memory of my long-dead twin Henrietta and I playing upside-down pick-a-back in the gardens of Ravensden Abbey when we were children.

I pushed myself up until I was perched on the spar like a monkey, gripping it tightly with my hands and feet. I judged the movement of the outboard ship, took a deep breath, stood, and at once jumped for the third mainyard. My scabbard slapped against my thigh as my hands gripped the spar. My shoulder protested again, and for a moment I dangled there, like a prisoner of the Inquisition strung up on a dungeon wall. Then I pulled myself up and clung for dear life to the higher yardarm.

'Wish I was that tall,' said Bella, clambering back to the end of the yard below and stretching out her hand.

I reached down and pulled her up, then turned, drew my sword, and slashed at the lashings of the footrope. It duly fell into position.

'An easier passage, Mistress Mendez.'

'Easier indeed, Sir Matthew.'

We hauled ourselves across, around the mainmast, and onto the larboard half of the spar. From this new vantage point, we could see our next objective: the two ships that lay against the wharf on the opposite side of the harbour. Get across them in the same elevated fashion, then we could get back down to the ground, with only a short distance to go to the Turk's Head and Conibear's men still looking for us back on the other side. But there was a problem.

'Bigger gap than I thought,' said Bella. 'They must have moved the Topsham lugger to a new berth on the last tide.'

A good twenty feet separated us from the outboard vessel on the other side.

'Perhaps we should have swum for it,' I said.

'And now he chooses to tell me he can swim,' she said. 'Never met a man of breeding who could swim before. But it wouldn't have done us any good – nowhere back there to get into the water without diving, and the splash would bring them after us in an instant. So what do we do, then, Sir Matthew?'

I looked around. There was nothing – no way at all of moving forward. All we had was the spar, the rigging, the footrope…

I smiled.

'Did your great-grandfather tell you anything about what my grandfather was like, Mistress Bella?'

'A great captain, he said, and brave, but the maddest man on earth.'

'Oh, madder than that, if even half the stories are true. Like the story of how he took the *Virgen de Guadalupe*, a great galleon twice the height of his own ship. There was no way of boarding her, his officers told him. Until my grandfather did this. Off the footrope, Bella, and grip the mainmast.'

With that, I pulled myself onto the spar alone, drew my sword, reached down, and severed the footrope from its fastening by the mainmast. Then I gripped the loose end, checked I was clear of all standing rigging, and launched myself into space.

The standing rigging of the vessel dead ahead seemed to fly toward me. I reached out with my right arm, grabbed for the shrouds, and missed. I swung back toward the ship where Bella was.

A child swinging from a rope tied to an oak-tree branch.

I felt the old familiar thrill. I braced my knees, struck the oak-trunk – rather, the mainmast – with my feet, and pushed hard. Again I soared above the black waters of the Barbican harbour, reached out for the rigging, and this time caught hold of it.

I could just make out the slight form of Bella, still standing at the junction of mainmast and yardarm. She had no need to follow me now; she was unlikely to be of concern to Conibear's men, even if they were still searching the wharves and lanes on the far side of the harbour. But she was beckoning for the rope, and I knew nothing would stop her seeing her self-appointed mission to its end. So I took aim and hurled the erstwhile footrope back toward her. It took three failed attempts, but on the fourth, she caught hold. Bella leaped from the yardarm, swung across the water, and reached out. I caught her and pulled her in.

'Why, Sir Matthew!' she squealed. 'And I thought all you men of rank were good-for-nothing sluggards.'

'I am glad to disabuse you, Mistress Mendez! But come, we still have two yardarms to cross –'

But she climbed down instead, stepped onto the deck of the outboard ship, looked around, then beckoned me to follow her.

'Would it not have been easier just to go across the decks of those on the other side of the harbour, too?' I said, as I stepped onto the deck.

'Easier for Conibear's gang, too. And we might have encountered a watch-on-deck who took exception to us and raised the alarm. Besides, Sir Matthew, men usually keep their eyes to the earth, and hardly ever think to look upward. Was that not what saved the King himself, when he hid in the Royal Oak?'

She was a strange girl, this one, but astute.

'So it did, Bella Mendez. So it did.'

We went ashore, walked down the side of a warehouse, turned a corner, and there found Francis Gale, Julian Carvell, Ali Reis and Macferran emerging from the Turk's Head.

'Sir Matthew!' cried Francis. 'Praise God, you are alive!'

'That I am, Reverend. All thanks to this gallant girl –'

I turned, but Bella Mendez was already running off, back into the dark streets of Plymouth.

Chapter Fifteen

Should thou that had no water past,
But thick same in the meer a;
Didst zee the Zea would be agast,
Vort did zo ztream and rore:
Zo zalt did taste, thy tongue would think,
The vire were in the water:
And 'tus so wide, no land's espy'd,
Look nere so long thereafter.

From *A Devonshire Song*

The next morning, Plymouth was in turmoil once again. I had been there only a very short time, but this was sufficient to establish that turmoil seemed to be the town's usual condition. The people were excitable and peevish: they made the citizens of London seem like masters of serenity and self-control, which was a mightily difficult thing to do. On this particular morning, they were greatly exercised by intelligence coming into the town from west and east at once.

From the west came news that the hell-hound had been flaunting himself off Looe only the evening before. He had even dared to run in close and loose off a few balls at the town. Then he steered away toward the Rame, the great headland that lay between Looe and Plymouth Sound.

'Aye, and the vast black hound was howling from the quarterdeck before it turned back into Captain Kranz!' cried a fishwife, authoritatively.

'The shame of it!' bawled another. 'The *Jupiter* lies idle in harbour while this cursed Dutchman parades up and down the Channel, without a care in the world!'

'Damn this Captain Harris, who cares only for his wine and the whore he keeps aboard!'

This took me aback at first; I had seen no evidence of a whore during my time on the *Jupiter*. But knowing Beau, and upon reflection, it did not surprise me in the slightest.

From the east came the London postboy, whose arrival at the Guildhall I witnessed: I was up early to meet with De Gomme at the Citadel, and was passing by on my way to the vast building site. One particularly forward creature – a dissenting preacher, by his look and garb – grabbed eagerly at the letter proferred to him, tore it open, and began to read aloud to the fast-growing audience around him.

'The Dutch fleet rides unchallenged in the mouth of the Thames! They have embarked an army, and look to invade England's fair shore! At Amsterdam and all through Holland, they light bonfires and beacons to celebrate their great victory over us! They have burned an effigy of the king in the shape of a dog, with the crown upon his head! Aye, and so should we – only why should we be content with an effigy, good people of Plymouth?'

The mob around him growled in approbation. Several scowled at me, for both in rank and in proximity, I was the nearest thing they had to the king at that moment. Until only a very few years before, I would have berated the idle preaching rogue, or even drawn my sword on him; but the mob around him was large, I was alone, and even for Sir Matthew Quinton, honour no longer always won out over discretion. I took the two letters addressed to me from the postboy and made my way up to the Citadel, where De Gomme and his men were already hard at work.

'Well, Sir Matthew,' said the royal engineer, 'shall we resume our tour, and pray that this time it is not interrupted by any more corpses?'

'Gladly, Sir Bernard. But I would crave your indulgence for a few minutes, while I digest my letters from London.'

De Gomme was obliging, and put at my disposal the hut that served as his temporary headquarters while the garrison commander's house was being erected.

I opened Cornelia's letter first. Her English was as unique as ever, and her garrulousness on some matters was rivalled only by her silence on others. Upon the matter that concerned me most of all, there were but four words: '*Husbant, I am wel.*' She was more forthcoming about the letters she had received from her father, in the town of Veere in Zeeland, regaling her with news of her twin, who had apparently distinguished himself during the four-day fight. But Cornelia ended ominously:

'My father says all the talk in Veere is of the humbling of the proud English. Admiraal De Ruyter looks to com into the Tames itself and to burn London. I wd rather welkom you home than entertyn him, husbant, so speed you bak to yr Cornelia.'

This troubled me. In all our years together, and however distant I was from her, Cornelia had never before ended a letter to me with a request to hasten back to her as swiftly as possible. It was unlikely that she seriously believed Michiel De Ruyter and the Dutch Marines would come marching up the Strand; and even if she did, Cornelia was both intrepid and sensible, and would hardly have anything to fear from her own countrymen. So her ostensible reason for seeking my return could only be a pretence. In which case, why was my wife so eager for me to come home?

Troubled in mind, I turned to the letter from my brother, which was in cipher. I took out our secret code-book, *The Legend of Captain Jones* (a fantastical tale, albeit one founded upon the no less fantastical life of my grandfather), and slowly translated the words. As ever, the letter from the tenth Earl of Ravensden was a masterpiece of brevity, marked more by what Charles did not say than by what he deigned to report.

'Brother. The King's ministers deny any wrongdoing, as was to be expected, and despite the most rigorous enquiries by myself and by Musk (you may imagine the nature of his particular rigour, Matt), as yet we have discovered no proof of any. It appears that the said ministers met on the thirteenth day of May to discuss the news of Beaufort's fleet being at sea, and on its way to England, as was generally believed; but My Lords of Clarendon and Arlington do dispute what was said. '

No surprise, this: Lord Chancellor Clarendon and secretary of state Arlington heartily detested each other, principally because the latter sought to bring down and supplant the former, and the former knew it. As Musk had presciently foreseen at the end of the battle, each would undoubtedly be seeking a way to blame the other for the calamity that had occurred.

'Some time thereafter, it seems, word was received from your friend Harris that he had seen the French fleet off Lisbon. Arlington also had firm intelligence from Holland that the Dutch fleet was not at sea. So His Grace of Albemarle was strongly in favour of sending His Highness the Prince away to look for Beaufort before he could join with De Ruyter, and the Prince, for his part, was equally keen to go.' Of course he would be, as I – *'Then word also came from your man Garrett at Plymouth that he had seen a French army massing at La Rochelle, and that this was intended to invade Ireland. This seems to have convinced the doubters: how could so much intelligence, from different and disinterested quarters, possibly be wrong? Thus it stood, brother, when order was given to divide the*

fleet, that being upon the twenty-second day of the month. It seems, though, that from that day onward for a week, no intelligence at all was received from Holland, the west wind preventing the sailing of the packet boats. Thus the fact that your fleet got no word of De Ruyter being out was no dark conspiracy of evil men, and no failure by our spies in Holland either; it was simply a consequence of the weather, Matt, and God knows how often that has played a part in the history of our kingdom. When word finally came on the thirtieth that the Dutch had sailed, orders were sent at once to recall Rupert. So in short, brother, I cannot yet see anything that smacks of treason here in London. If there was such, it must lie where you are, with Garrett or with Harris. God be with you, Sir Matthew.'

I put down my brother's letter with a heavy heart. If there was no likely scapegoat in London, it could only mean, as Charles had said, that he had to be found here, in Plymouth. So as I toured the Citadel with De Gomme, my mind was very far from the ravelins, demi-bastions and salients over which the engineer enthused.

* * *

I returned to the Turk's Head just before noon. Going in through the door and entering its principal room brought on the strangest feeling: it was as though I was transported four years back in time. Julian Carvell, Macferran and Francis Gale, all veterans of my own time in command of the *Jupiter*, were carousing with another very familiar face from those memorable days: Thomas Penbaron, the tiny but redoubtable ship's carpenter, who still held the same position under Beau Harris.

'Mister Penbaron!' I said.

'Sir Matthew,' he said in his Cornish brogue; he was a man of Mevagissey, I recalled. 'I give you belated joy of your knighthood, and of all the honour that has come to you since we served in the *Jupiter*.'

'I did not know you were still in her, Mister Penbaron. I thought you would have had a bigger ship by this time.'

Penbaron was the only one of the ship's warrant officers to survive the bloody battle that the *Jupiter* fought in the waters off the west of Scotland. As a standing officer who stayed in post whether the ship was in commission or not, he had gone with her into the Ordinary at Portsmouth, spending a couple of years in the relative idleness of shipkeeping.

'Solicited for many a post when the war began, Sir Matthew, but there were few vacancies in the bigger ships. Expect there'll be plenty more now, though, after the four-day fight.'

'You can rely on my recommendation. And it is good to see you, man –'

But the urgency in Penbaron's eyes told me that this was not a social call to catch up with old shipmates.

'A word with you in private, Sir Matthew, if you will permit it?'

'Of course.'

I raised an eyebrow at Francis Gale, but he shook his head. Whatever the carpenter's business was, he had not confided in any of the others. I took him aside, to one of the small private rooms at the back of the inn.

'Speak, then, Mister Penbaron.'

'It is a matter most delicate, sir. It concerns –' The little carpenter averted his eyes, as though he were having second thoughts about the words he had meant to utter.

'Out with it, man!'

He looked up and fixed me with his rheumy eye.

'Very well, Sir Matthew. Your talk with Captain Harris aboard the *Jupiter* – well, sir, you remember what the old ship's like. Any conversation below decks can be overheard easily enough.'

'Especially if men are listening out for it?'

'That's as maybe, Sir Matthew. But the truth is, what you said to

Captain Harris is common knowledge aboard the *Jupiter*, as is what he said to you. And that is the devil of it, you see.'

'The devil, Penbaron? How so?'

The carpenter shuffled his feet, and looked away.

'It is a terrible thing to have to do this, Sir Matthew. I like Captain Harris. He's no seaman, it's true, but he's kind to the men, and a fair man, not like –'

'Not like most of our fellow gentleman captains, you mean? Come, Penbaron. We fought and bled together, remember? You can say anything to me in confidence, and it will go no further.'

'But that's the very devil of it, Sir Matthew, as I said. It has to go further, you see. It can't do otherwise. I thought long and hard on whether I should tell you, but I knew that if I did not, one of the other officers or men would tell someone less honourable than yourself. And it's my duty to tell you. My duty to Cornwall, to England, to the King, to all the poor souls who perished in the four-day fight.'

I said nothing. The man was plainly in agonies of conscience, wrestling with his very being.

'It was the fleet, you see, Sir Matthew. The fleet that we sighted off Lisbon. I've sailed the Iberian and Mediterranean seas for most of my lifetime, sir, as you well know. So I know the difference between a French man-of-war and one of the Don's.' Penbaron shook his head. 'I tried to tell Captain Harris, but he would not listen to me, a mere ship's carpenter – a dull and lumpen shipwright, as he often says when he thinks I am not within hearing. He could see the French colours, you see. I tried to tell him it was the Spanish, and that they were flying false flags to confuse us. I reckoned it was because they knew us to be allied to the Portuguese, so didn't want us to betray their position to them. I tried to tell him all of that, but he wouldn't listen. Why, Sir Matthew, he even said something about a talk you and he once had, where you told him some story of your grandfather.'

'My *grandfather* –'

And then I remembered. A drunken night of quaffing Madeira aboard Beau's command, the *Falcon*, in Bantry Bay, when I had the *Happy Restoration*: a few weeks before that unfortunately misnamed ship was wrecked through my error on the rocks in the entrance to Kinsale Harbour, killing nearly all of her crew. I was regaling Beau with one of the many colourful tales of my grandfather, the eighth Earl of Ravensden, the piratical old sea-captain in the late Queen Elizabeth's time. Apparently he and Drake had been arguing, as they did about nearly everything. In this case, my grandfather was of the opinion that the men-of-war he had sighted in some harbour of the Caribbee were really Spaniards, flying false French colours, and thus prime targets for plundering by that notoriously rapacious old war-horse, the eighth Earl of Ravensden.

'Don't be a fucking fool, Quinton,' Drake is meant to have said to him, 'the English and French fly false colours upon a whim, but the Don thinks it beneath his honour to be so underhand. A Spaniard will only fly his own ensign, no other.'

My grandfather being the man he was, he ignored Drake's advice, attacked the ships at anchor, and thus very nearly brought about a war with France. I recalled Beau being greatly amused by the story, and saying he would remember it.

'Captain Harris was so certain in his judgement,' Penbaron continued, 'and so excited by what he thought he had seen. And the other officers would not contradict him, for fear that he might refuse to recommend them for promotion, even though they knew as well as I did that all of the ships we could see were Spaniards –'

The old man's voice trailed away, as though he was overwhelmed once again by the enormity of the charge he was bringing against his captain. But he had no need to complete his statement. I had heard more than enough.

Oh, Beau: poor, dear Beau, was as unlikely to be able to distinguish a Spanish ship from a French one as between two peas in a pod. He had convinced himself that the fleet he saw off Lisbon was that of King Louis, and that the news of it which he bore to England was thus of the utmost importance to our kingdom's wellbeing. To its very survival, indeed. Relying on my secondhand retelling of my grandfather's anecdote from eighty years before, he had also convinced himself that no Spanish man-of-war would ever be so underhand as to fly French colours. Thus to his mind, the great fleet that he saw off Lisbon, flying the white fleur-de-lis banners of the Bourbons, had to be the French fleet.

But it was not the French fleet at all.

It was the Spanish.

Chapter Sixteen

The Gods then let us imitate,
Secure from carping Care and Fate;
Wine, wit and courage both create:
In Wine Apollo always chose
His darkest Oracles to disclose;
'Twas wine gave him his ruby nose.

Anon., *A Song of Sack* (published 1687)

'The Spanish? Sweet Jesu, Matt, I will dangle for this.'

Beau and I stood upon the crumbling parapet of Plymouth Castle. Neither the captain's cabin of the *Jupiter* nor even the busy Turk's Head offered the privacy that this conversation demanded, while the Citadel was all noise and bustle. But with a strong westerly blowing and whipping up the waters of the Cattewater, our words were carried offshore at once, with no chance of being overheard.

'It need not come to that, Beau.'

'Of course it will come to it. You know that full well, Sir Matthew. The King is changeable, and will readily sacrifice anything or anybody so that he may sit securely upon his throne. And the Duke of York has never liked me much. With so much at stake, and with so many having died, do you really think that either of them will lift a finger to save me?'

There was nothing I could say to reassure him.

'I will have to take you to London, Beau. Those were my orders from the King. If there seemed to be a case against you, then I was to take you before him for you to answer to His Majesty in person.'

'Before I am taken to the Tower in chains, and thence to the scaffold. Yes, Matt. That is what you must do, and I do not blame you. But I would ask just one thing.'

'If it is in my power, Beau.'

'My plan against Kranz, the hell-hound, is very nearly ready to come to fruition. Give me time, Matt, and give me your sword. The time is very nearly right to carry out my scheme, and your presence here gives me the means to do it. I'd have needed to approach De Gomme, otherwise, and although he may be a fine engineer, he's not a man for hand to hand fighting -'

A slight movement seen out of the corner of my eye – a brief flurry of movement – I drew my sword – the blur of a small figure, running past me…

Bella Mendez flung herself into Beau's arms. She was weeping profusely.

'No!' she cried. 'No, they will not hang you!'

Behind her, at the head of the spiral stair up to the wall walk, stood Ali Reis, out of breath, and waving his hands in what I took to be a Moorish gesture of apology.

'Sir Matthew,' he gasped, 'a thousand pardons, she was past us in the blink of an eye –'

I sheathed my sword.

'No matter, Ali Reis. I myself have witnessed the resourcefulness of Mistress Mendez, here. Go below, man, drink some water and recover your breath.'

The loyal Moor saluted and went back into the castle. I turned to face my friend and his distraught young lover.

'In God's name, Beau,' I demanded, 'how could you take one so young?'

'It was more a case of her taking me,' said Beau, somewhat abashed. 'There seems little that Plymouth maidens of any age do not know, or dare not venture.'

'You cannot take him away, Sir Matthew! You cannot let the King kill him!'

I had no answer for her. Beau stroked her hair tenderly, and kissed her forehead.

'Now, Bella,' he said, 'you must not fear for me. And I have done a mighty wrong, there can be no doubt of that. All those thousands of deaths rest upon me.'

She continued to sob plentifully. The scene touched me beyond measure, but there was nothing I could do. By his own admission, Beau was guilty at best of serious negligence and incompetence; and I had no doubt that some devious prosecuting counsel could easily twist any words of Beau's in his own defence into proof of high treason.

Yet even in such a desperate strait, Beau remained steadfast.

'Just a day or two, Matt. That's all I need to fight this one last battle against Kranz and his allies.'

'You envisage such a fight?'

'I do. So are you with me, Matt Quinton?'

I thought hard upon it. My duty as a loyal subject was to return to London at once, taking Beau with me for his interrogation by the King, and perhaps ultimately for trial and execution. My duty as a sea-captain was to return to my ship as swiftly as I could. My duty as a husband was to establish the condition of my wife.

But there was my duty as a friend, too.

'If the plan seems sound, and does not delay us for very long, then yes, Beau, I am with you.'

'Good. Then there are things you need to know about the hell-hound, but above all about our friend, Conibear. Isn't that so, Bella?'

The girl looked up with damp, loving eyes. 'That's so, my captain,' she said.

'She told me of it, you see,' said Beau. 'She and her great-grandfather pieced the story together over these last few months. And it's quite a story, Matt. Above all, the legend of the hell-hound is not what it seems to be.'

* * *

The next morning, I marched confidently up the Lambhay hill, Carvell, Macferran and Ali Reis at my back, Francis Gale at my side. The navy storehouses nestled under the cliff upon which stood Plymouth Castle; they looked out toward the east, where the *Jupiter* still lay alongside the hulk.

Conibear stood on the slope in front of the storehouses, arms folded. Behind him stood a dozen of his men, all carrying cudgels or knives. Quite a crowd was already gathered round about: the good people of Plymouth had a taste of violence. I spied Bella Mendez, who grinned at me. It took a considerable effort of will on my part not to respond in kind.

'Mister Conibear,' I said, 'I would be grateful for an opportunity to inspect the storehouses, yonder.'

'Can't have that, Sir Matthew. I'm Navy Agent here at Plymouth, appointed by the Lord High Admiral through the recommendation of the Duke of Albemarle himself. My responsibility, and mine alone.'

'Well, Mister Conibear, that may be so. But I think when it comes to a charge of treason, His Grace of Albemarle would be the first to insist on a full and proper enquiry.'

'*Treason*, Sir Matthew? There is no treason here!'

'That is what you say, Mister Conibear. But others say differently.'

'Who, then? Heale, that old fool? He's so ancient, even the grave has given up on him! You'll believe his senile rambling over my word? Besides, a charge of treason requires two witnesses for proof, and you'll never find a second man to testify against me! Not here – not in Plymouth! And if you want a traitor, look across the water, to that preening, periwigged coxcomb of a captain on the *Jupiter* – he who brought about the division of the fleet, and the slaughter of so many proud English lads!'

The mob behind Conibear, and not a few of the onlookers, growled in approbation. Carvell casually unshouldered his musket, followed with equal insouciance by Ali Reis and Macferran, and the crowd fell silent.

'If there is no treason, as you say,' said Francis, 'then surely you can have no objection to Sir Matthew inspecting the storehouses.'

'You can choose to do so now,' I added, 'or you can choose to do so in an hour's time, when I have all of Sir Bernard's garrison from the Citadel at my back. Or you can do so in a day's time, when I have a warrant from Sir Jonathan Skelton, the Lieutenant-Governor of Plymouth. Or you can do so in a week's time, when a warrant for your arrest on the charge of high treason has come down from London, and you are conveyed there in chains. But your co-operation now, Mister Conibear, would count strongly in your favour.'

I could see Conibear struggling with his thoughts. He was a man unaccustomed to being crossed; a man who had lorded it over this, his little private fiefdom, for long years on end. If he had managed to survive the restoration of a monarchy that he hated, he must have reckoned that he could survive anything.

Finally, he looked me directly in the eyes.

'My pleasure, Sir Matthew,' without displaying any hint of that emotion. 'I have nothing to hide.'

My men shouldered their muskets again, and we went inside.

* * *

I had already been inside many naval storehouses, and would go into very many more, but few were as orderly as those of Plymouth. Whatever else Ludovic Conibear might have been, he was clearly a man of method. The spare yards, cables and ropes on which the

King's ships in the west depended were stacked neatly against the walls. Barrels of tar and pitch were kept well apart from those of flour, beer and cheese. Unlike in the great dockyards, though – in, say, the great storehouse in Deptford – where all of these commodities would have been kept in their own rooms, here they were crammed together in a range of low, nondescript buildings. The resulting smell was truly unique. The very remembrance seems to bring it into my nostrils once again, to bring me very nearly to the point of retching as it did all those years ago, in the hot summer of 1666.

There was one very strange thing about the Lambhay storehouses, though: very strange indeed.

It was Julian Carvell who articulated the thought.

'Never seen so much wine in one place,' he said. 'Not in the warehouses in Jamestown back in old Virginia, not even in London. Every man jack on the King's Prick could have his fill ten times over.'

'Not just on the Prick, neither – begging pardon, Sir Matthew,' said Macferran. 'There's enough here for an entire squadron, for an entire campaign.'

'Naturally, Sir Matthew,' said Conibear, a few paces behind us. 'Remember, Plymouth is almost always the final port of call for the King's ship heading to the southward, for the Mediterranean or other distant seas.'

'I know that amply well, Mister Conibear,' I said. 'My own ships have called here in the past. You would have dealt with my pursers aboard the *Wessex* and the *Seraph*.'

'Well, then, Sir Matthew, you'll know that the victualling allowance prescribes that below the latitude of thirty-nine degrees north, the King's ships should give men an allocation of a quart of wine instead of their daily eight pints of beer. Thus we have to keep a large store of wine here at Plymouth, to satisfy that demand.'

'Aye,' growled Carvell, 'but the victuallers' wine's always piss – begging pardon, Sir Matthew.'

I had seen the English seaman shot at. I had seen him go unpaid for years on end. I had seen him flogged mercilessly by brutish officers. But the single thing most certain to move him to mutiny was bad drink.

I looked around the storehouses once again. Nothing was out of place; everything that should be there, was there. No doubt Conibear and his men embezzled on an undetectable scale, selling naval stores to merchant ships or local merchants; but that was the hallmark of every man involved in the administration of the navy, and I had even heard the King declare it a just perquisite to compensate for the inadequate wages he was able to pay them. But there was rather more to Conibear's corruption, and thanks to Beau Harris and Bella Mendez, I knew exactly what form it took.

'Sceptres,' I said to Carvell, Macferran and Ali Reis, 'you've all served enough time in the King's Navy, and drunk enough of his wine – excepting yourself, Ali Reis.' The Mahometan inclined his head in thanks. 'Look around you. Compare these barrels, here at the front, with all of the others stacked behind them.'

My men stepped forward and studied the evidence before them with the gravitas of eminent physicians inspecting a particularly interesting corpse. Even Ali Reis, who had never sampled the contents, had helped haul enough barrels of wine over the side of a ship and down into the hold to be something of an authority upon them.

'These here, Sir Matthew,' said Carvell, 'these are the victualler's, all right.' He scraped his finger along the seepage from one of the barrels, then licked it. He grimaced. 'And this is the victualler's wine. No mistaking it.'

Macferran was in among the barrels further back toward the wall. He, too, had spotted a barrel with a slight leak, and was dipping his finger into the wine seeping from it.

'But this isn't,' he said, in his rough Highland brogue – *this isnae*. 'Try it for yourself, Sir Matthew.'

I went over to the barrel and tasted the wine.

'This is very good,' I said. 'Very good indeed, albeit new, not vintage. Gascon, without doubt.'

I turned to look at Conibear. He was staring at me, but the confidence had drained from his expression.

'New Gascon wine?' said Francis Gale. 'How might that be, Sir Matthew, when we have been at war with France these six months? When not a drop of French wine has come into England – not legally, at any rate?'

'A good question, Reverend Gale. A very good question indeed. Perhaps it's a question that Mister Conibear would care to answer?'

My men unshouldered their muskets. I drew my sword. Conibear still had the numbers, but his men knew full well that if they charged us, up to half of them would be dead before the next five minutes were up. And even if the other half reached us, a large number of townspeople were crowded around the outer doors of the storehouses, able to see and hear everything. To witness everything. Bella Mendez stood in the very front of the crowd, and she knew, just as Conibear's men did, that if they rushed us, that crowd contained more than enough enemies of Ludovic Conibear to ensure that every one of his men would hang.

First one, then two, then all of Conibear's men dropped their weapons.

'Now, Mister Conibear,' I said, 'we are going to talk, you and I. You are going to tell me about this most excellent wine, and how quite so much of it comes to be in the navy's storehouse. Is that not so, Mister Conibear?'

The navy agent of Plymouth stared at the floor, no doubt hoping some magical passageway would open beneath his feet and allow him to escape. But none did.

* * *

I stood upon the Hoe, watching the *Jupiter* put to sea. A captain always feels a special bond to his old ships, and I felt a particularly strong one to the Fifth Rate edging out of the Cattewater under courses alone. The *Jupiter* was a fine, trim ship, and as she moved into the Sound, I reflected on how little I had known when I first set foot aboard her, and on how much I had learned during my command. Learned at the cost of spilling some of my own blood, it was true; but I had learned that for a sea-officer of the King, those were the best lessons of all.

The *Jupiter* moved out into the Sound. Her topsails fell, and were made fast. She steered a southerly course, skirting the Devon shore toward Bovisand. Word was out in Plymouth that Beau Harris intended to cruise as far as Guernsey in search of the hell-hound, then back toward Portland. The old seamen in the taverns mocked him, saying he had a better chance of finding El Dorado then the *Duirel.* But then, they did not know what Ludovic Conibear had said in an attempt to save his miserable skin. They did not know the contents of the urgent message that I had despatched to an ale-house in Bodmin. And above all, they did not know the true reason why I left the Hoe and made my way west by the coast road, as casually as though I were out for a ride in the country. I had given out that I wished to inspect some land over by the river of Hamoaze as a possible site for a new royal dockyard; a prescient lie, as it happened, for that was very nearly the exact place where the present Plymouth yard was established, many years later. Thus I duly rode down to the water's edge in the lee of a small, rocky peninsula. Close by a ruined fort, a familiar brown-skinned figure emerged from the trees.

'*Salaam alaikum*, Sir Matthew,' said Ali Reis.

'*Salaam alaikum*, Ali Reis. Everything is in hand?'

'Three boats, as you ordered.'

'There looks to be a hellish tide-race in that channel.'

'Hellish enough for the people here abouts to call this place Devil's Point, Sir Matthew. But on the ebb after dusk, we should launch with no difficulty.'

I nodded. God willing, the night would herald death and victory.

Chapter Seventeen

Britons, strike home!
Revenge, revenge your Country's wrong.
Fight! Fight and record. Fight!
Fight and record yourselves in Druid's Song.
Fight! Fight and record. Fight!
Fight and record yourselves in Druid's Song.

John Fletcher, arr. Henry Purcell,
from *Bonduca, or The British Heroine* (1695)

Muffled oars cut through the dark waters of Cawsand Bay. The night was black and moonless, ideal both for smugglers and those who sought to intercept them. I could just make out the dark shape of the *Duirel*, at anchor close in, under the cliffs of Rame. And there, just visible on the pale strand of Cawsand's beach, was Kranz's longboat.

I gesticulated with my hands. The two boats behind us carried straight on, making for the beach, while Julian Carvell steered my own directly for the darkened cottages of Cawsand village. The silence was eerie: it was as if the entire population had fled, or been carried off at once by a sudden plague. But I knew they would be there, cowering in the darkness, fearful of the vengeance of the hell-hound.

A few feet from the shore, I stepped up onto the wale and jumped into the shallow water, then waded onto the beach. The two dozen men with me followed, keeping total silence. Four or five carried muskets, the rest of us blades alone. This was not a night for my father's sword, a fine old cavalry rapier. Instead, I gripped a cutlass in my right hand and a long dagger in my left. Francis Gale, alongside me, held a distinctly un-clerical back-sword.

We crept through the narrow lanes of Cawsand, over the hillock, then down toward the beach. I could just make out our two other boats, stealthily approaching the shore. It was a miracle that Kranz's men had not spotted them – the Dutch had to be asleep…

There was a shout, a pistol fired in warning, and all was pandemonium. From all along the beach came the flashes and dull blasts of matchlocks being fired. The men on our incoming boats replied.

I turned and shouted at my men.

'Jupiters, with me!'

We charged downhill, out onto the beach, hitting the Dutch from the flank just as our other men were starting to come ashore from the boats. I slashed right and left with my cutlass, trading metal with a half-dozen or so. I wounded at least one, caught at the shoulder by the downward slash of my blade. I felt my metal slice into flesh and strike bone, heard the man's scream as he fell away in agony. I did not tarry over him, or any of my opponents: I was running for the head of the beach. I wanted Kranz.

I saw him at last, coming down toward the shore, a cutlass in his hand. A score of men massed behind him…

And then another score. And another.

'He's landed most of his crew!' I cried. 'Conibear must have got word to him!'

Quite how Conibear had done so from his confines in Plymouth Castle would require investigation, if we won the day; but given how much of the town he had in his pocket, it was perhaps hardly surprising.

'That will make Captain Harris's task easier, even if ours is harder,' Francis replied.

I saw him nod toward the open sea, and glanced across in the same direction. A ship was coming round the headland, her hull just visible in the darkness, her white sails filling with the breeze as she came round. The first of the *Jupiter*'s bow chasers fired, sending an almighty echo around the bay. The cruise toward Guernsey, word of which had been deliberately disseminated throughout Plymouth, was but a ruse. Beau Harris was bearing down on the *Duirel*.

The beach was a battlefield. We were all at close quarters now, fighting hand to hand. Two men came at me, both stabbing with half-pikes. I parried the one with my cutlass, then shifted my weight, rushed in under the guard of the other and stabbed him in the throat with my dagger. Blood spouted over my hand and blade. The Dutchman fell away, clutching his neck.

But the Dutch had the advantage of numbers. We were tightly packed now, being pressed steadily backwards towards the water's edge. If the enemy overwhelmed us, Kranz might still have time to get back to the *Duirel*, which was raising her anchor and starting to unfurl her sails. She was a smaller, nimbler ship than the *Jupiter*, so it would still be possible for the hell-hound to outrun her inshore and get back out into the Sound, thence to the open sea.

I could see Kranz, a few feet away, further up the beach. He was directing more of his men into the fight, but there were no others behind them. He had committed his entire shore party to the fight, confident that victory was his.

'Now!' I cried.

Ali Reis raised his cornet to his lips and blew two shrill notes.

Nothing.

My plan had miscarried. Kranz's men would cut us all down…

Then, from just inland, came an answering trumpet note, the same two notes, sounded from a deeper and larger instrument. Some of the men surrounding us turned, looking uncertainly over their shoulders.

There was a great shout from behind the nearest cottages of Cawsand, and a tide of men erupted onto the beach. Red-coated soldiers and rough-shirted sailors together raced across the sand, swords waving in their hands. Leading them were two unmistakeable figures: Sir Bernard De Gomme, the engineer turned warrior for one night, and the crop-headed Martin Lanherne, unofficial leader of my Cornish following, sometime coxswain of the *Jupiter*. My letter to the inn at Bodmin had borne fruit in ample measure. Lanherne brought with him not only his own reassuring presence, but some three-dozen sturdy and heavily armed Cornishmen.

'For England and King Charles!' I shouted, and hacked my way forward. The Dutchmen surrounding us fell away, some of them trying to run for their boats, others throwing down their arms and surrendering.

But not Kranz. He and some half-dozen of his men were trying to launch a small skiff, perhaps still believing they could reach the *Duirel* and make their escape. Their ship was getting under way, but there could only have been a skeleton crew aboard, and whoever was in acting command now made a fatal error. He tried to run in closer to the beach, perhaps to cut the distance for boats trying to flee, perhaps trying to turn the tide of the battle by firing a broadside into our ranks. But the *Duirel*'s bow suddenly rose up out of the water, and a great tearing roar came from her hull.

'He's struck a rock!' Carvell bellowed.

'Now, Beau,' I murmured, 'prove what my dear ship can do.'

As the *Duirel* lay helpless, the *Jupiter* came up astern of her. It was strangely silent on the beach now, the sounds of battle dying away as more and more of the Dutch lay down their arms. So we could clearly hear the sound of the gun-carriage wheels on the deck of the *Jupiter* as the demi-culverins were run out. A pause – the momentary flash of linstocks – the tongues of flame spewing from fifteen cannon of the *Jupiter*'s larboard battery – the noise and feel of the blast – the great cloud of smoke, momentarily obscuring the entire bay…

And when it rolled away, it was obvious that the *Duirel* was shattered and ablaze. Her mainmast, already weakened by the collision with the rock, toppled into the sea. Flames broke out from stem and stern, illuminating the men jumping into the sea. There was one last, unearthly sound: the howling of a great dog, Kranz's hell-hound itself, the beast which he had used to sustain his legend. It wailed its lament for one last time. Then the magazine exploded, and the ship was ripped apart. The flames illuminated great timbers, tossed into the air like paper in a breeze, and the remains of men riding the flames that carried them to hell.

A few yards away, De Gomme, Lanherne and their men were surrounding the last Dutchmen in arms. Both parties were still prodding swords toward each other, but the Dutch were outnumbered ten to one.

I stepped forward.

'Surrender, Kranz,' I said in Dutch. 'The days of the hell-hound are done.'

'Perhaps, Sir Matthew,' he replied in English. He was a stocky man with a great black beard, after the fashion of half a century before. 'But perhaps not. Even now, De Ruyter lies in the mouth of the Thames. God willing, we Dutch will conquer England before the summer ends, and I will be a free man again.'

'Then we shall have to hang you quickly,' said De Gomme. 'And summer hangings always bring out bigger crowds. The entire town of Plymouth will turn out to see you swing from a noose.'

Kranz continued to hold his sword in front of him, like a gladiator about to face the final onslaught.

'Do not be so certain, Sir Bernard,' he said, laughing. 'Half of Plymouth is in my pocket. Besides, not even England would hang a legitimate privateer, carrying official letters of marque and reprisal from the Admiralty of the North Quarter.'

'Do not be so sure of half of Plymouth,' I said. 'Your ally Conibear languishes in prison. It was his false information that brought you here, into our ambush. A trap that he was very willing to collude in, once it was suggested to him that it might be the only way to save his miserable neck from the noose.'

Kranz shrugged.

'Conibear is weak, and an avaricious fool. You English will call him a traitor, naturally. He served his purpose, but I will be glad to be shot of smuggling, despite all the gold it brought me.'

'So you will testify against him?'

Kranz laughed.

'And why would I do that, Sir Matthew Quinton? As I say, I am a properly accredited captain of a private man-of-war.'

'Ah,' said Francis Gale, 'your precious letters of marque and reprisal from the Admiralty of the North Quarter. And where might those letters be, Captain Kranz? I see no pockets in your shirt or breeches. You have no coat. So might they, perhaps, have been in your cabin aboard your ship?' Francis nodded toward the blazing remains of the *Duirel*. 'Without papers, of course, you are no better than a pirate. True, confirmation of your story might be sent for from the North Quarter Admiralty, but in war, such communications take an eternity. Or it might not be sent for at all. In either case, Captain Kranz, the chance of your being hanged for piracy are high, I would imagine.'

The confident Kranz was evidently stunned by this revelation. He turned to look at the flames that marked where the *Duirel* had been, and must have known in that moment that Francis spoke nothing but the perfect truth.

'One thing more,' I said. 'Perhaps one last chance for you to save your neck, Captain Kranz. You took on your wine at La Rochelle? And that would be – when?'

'The last cargo?' The Dutchman was still reluctant, but every second must have served to make his predicament more obvious. He breathed hard, then looked up. 'About the fifteenth of May – the fifth, by the calendar you English use.'

'And there was a French army at La Rochelle at that time? An army designed to invade Ireland? You will not serve your country or yourself by lying about it, Kranz. But the truth may yet save you.'

Kranz frowned in puzzlement.

'To invade Ireland? Why –' He fell silent, and was clearly thinking hard. But Jacob Kranz was a highly intelligent man; the creator of the dark legend of the hell-hound would be no fool. At last, he understood the true significance of the questions posed to him. '*God in Hemel*, is that what you believed? Is *that* why you English divided your fleet?' He began to laugh, but the laughter was bitter, and it was directed at me. 'Yes, Matthew Quinton, there is a French army at La Rochelle. Yes, there is indeed. Oh, you English!' Tears of mirth were now flowing down Kranz's cheeks. 'You think the world revolves around you. King Louis is deploying regiments at Rochelle, so they can only be aimed against your vain, preening apology for a country! But the truth, Sir Matthew? Shall I tell you what the truth is? The men at Rochelle were the honour guard for a wedding, nothing more – the proxy wedding of the Duke of Nemours' daughter to the King of Portugal. Much good it will do either of them, because he's impotent and a lunatic. Ask your Queen if you seek confirmation, as she's his sister!' For a prisoner with a possible death sentence hanging over his head, Kranz was still extraordinarily merry. 'The wedding is public knowledge, but the English choose to ignore all of that. Oh, no. The English choose instead to believe that the troops being lined up for nothing more than a ceremonial wedding parade are preparing to set sail to invade and conquer them. Oh, Sir Matthew Quinton – what gullible fools you English are!'

I raised my hand to strike the impudent Kranz, but stayed it at once; for even in that moment of blind anger, I could see that he was right. Truly, one of the greatest flaws in our English national character is our willingness to believe only that which we wish to believe. One lone sailor – great God, *one sailor and one alone* – informs the king's ministers that the army at La Rochelle is intended to invade Ireland, and behold, within the blinking of an eye it becomes a tablet of stone, the foundation for all policy, and for the division of the fleet! Poor Will Berkeley and all the other fallen heroes of the Four Days' Fight, that they should have died in such a cause.

'And yet, you had Nathaniel Garrett killed for spreading a falsehood that could only benefit your country's cause!'

Kranz looked genuinely puzzled.

'Garrett, Sir Matthew? Who is Garrett?'

The truth came to me then, and I cursed myself at once for my blindness and stupidity. This was what old Heale had wanted me to know; this was what Bella Mendez had hinted at.

'Garrett was not killed for his false intelligence of the French army,' I said. 'Conibear had him killed for stumbling across your arrangement with him, while Garrett was at La Rochelle. Your very lucrative arrangement to smuggle French wines into Devon under cover of the legend of the hell-hound, the devil who terrorises the coast. The arrangement that he explained to us in some detail, after we raided his storehouse – he hoped to save his neck by confessing all, but he did not quite confess all, did he, Captain Kranz? For it is no wonder that you could operate when and where you pleased and avoid the king's ships, when you had the Navy Agent at Plymouth himself supplying you with intelligence of their movements!'

'It is one of the many reasons why you will lose this war, Quinton. No Dutchman would ever betray his country in that way, simply to supply the sots of his province with embargoed wine. You believe in phantom armies, invisible fleets and hell-hounds, and you have a whoremaster for a king. Thank God I am Dutch.'

I gestured to two of the men to tie Kranz's hands and take him away. I looked about: after the discomfiting discourse with the hell-hound,

I had need of good company. Francis Gale was properly engaged in saying prayers over the dead, but Martin Lanherne was close at hand.

'My thanks, Mister Lanherne,' I said. 'Your arrival was timely, and your men did well.'

'Volunteers to a man, Sir Matthew. Couldn't press a good man for love nor money from Saint Just to Saint Germans, but once word went out that there was a chance to do for the hell-hound once and for all, men flocked in. That Kranz had wreaked such havoc all along the coast, there probably weren't a family in the county that hadn't lost money on his account. So the men were mad for revenge, sir. Reckon a few of them had been hiding out on Bodmin Moor to escape the press, but if there's one thing a Cornishman hates more than the King's Shilling, it's some dirty foreigner invading Cornwall's fair shore.'

'And you are excepting the English from that, Mister Lanherne?'

He smiled.

'Now that's a question, Sir Matthew. But seems this war's made some unlikely alliances – the Dutch and the French, the hell-hound and friend Conibear, and the Cornish and the English.'

'I won't dispute that. But tell me, Lanherne – have you had your fill of pressing? Are you ready to come to sea once again?'

'If you have a vacancy, Sir Matthew. I'd be honoured to serve with you again, and I reckon at least a few of the brave Cornish lads yonder would say the same.'

'The *Royal Sceptre* will need a boatswain, and I think the capture of the hell-hound should give me enough credit with the Lord Admiral to have my candidate put into the place.'

'Very well, Sir Matthew. The *Royal Sceptre* it shall be. Reckon the men call her the King's Prick, though?'

'Not in my hearing, Mister Lanherne. Rarely in my hearing, at any rate.'

At last, I walked to the water's edge, and looked out to sea. The *Jupiter* had dropped anchor, and by the light of the flames from the

Duirel, I could see Beau's longboat approaching.

My old friend waded ashore, and we exchanged formal salutes.

'Deaths?' he asked.

'Two of ours. Perhaps ten of theirs. And I think Kranz will testify to all of it – the smuggling, the collusion with Conibear. Indeed, I think the Reverend Gale will be kept busy for a day or two, taking the sworn depositions of all concerned in this business.'

'Then it's done. The coast is safe from the hell-hound at last, and my reputation is redeemed. A part of my reputation, at any rate.'

We were silent; we both knew what had to happen. At length, it was Beau who spoke the words that had to be said.

'I shall need to make ready to ride to London, I take it? To appear before – who?'

'Yes, Beau. Take the *Jupiter* back into harbour, say your farewells to Bella Mendez, and then we ride. And you will appear before the King, in person.'

I did not tell him of the truth about the army at La Rochelle. Beau would realise at once what it meant: Nathaniel Garrett would have been the other obvious scapegoat for the division of the fleet, but he was dead. So if one man alone was going to be offered up as a sacrifice to the mob, as the King wanted, then that man could only be Beau Harris.

It would be a bitter journey to London.

Part Three

THE ST JAMES'S DAY FIGHT

21-25 JULY 1666

Chapter Eighteen

By this means, when a battle's won,
The war's as far from being done;
For those that save themselves, and fly,
Go halves, at least, i' th' victory;
And sometimes, when the loss is small,
And danger great, they challenge all;
Print new additions to their feats,
And emendations in Gazettes…
To set the rabble on a flame,
And keep their governors from blame,
Disperse the news the pulpit tells,
Confirm'd with fire-works and with bells…

Butler, *Hudibras*

We stood before the King of England in a room on the landward side of the palace of Whitehall, in the block between the tennis court and the tilt yard. The small window gave a view over Saint James's Park, but none of us – Beau, my brother, and I – had any leisure to admire it. We were all in awe of a King whose demeanour was akin to that of a lion moving indolently toward a kill.

Charles the Second stood behind a small table. On it were two ship models.

'Behold, Captain Harris. This ship, to my right, has a large gallery at the stern, to enable her captain or admiral to take the air.' The King pointed toward the feature in question. 'Such galleries are characteristic of Spanish men-of-war, and Spanish men-of-war alone. Now, this ship, to my left, has no gallery. You will perceive that she has finer lines, more sheer aft – you do know what sheer is, Captain Harris? – and sits higher out of the water than either the Spaniard or any of our English ships. Are you content with that, Captain Harris? Do you *now* see the difference between a Spanish fleet and a French one?' Beau bowed his head miserably. Since we entered the King's presence, he had been the very image of dejection. 'Very well. Let us now consider what you reported –'

All through the King's tirade (which was already approaching perhaps ten minutes' duration), a thought nagged away at the very edge of my mind. Slowly, this tiny thought chipped away at the other, more prominent ones: notably my near-treasonable rumination that it was surely hypocrisy for this King, who had enthusiastically granted commissions to gentleman captains like Beau and myself, now to denounce one of his own creations for an ignorance of the ways of the sea that His Majesty had done nothing whatsoever to remedy. Even that thought was progressively driven out of my mind by the other, more urgent, more elusive, one. It was something important, something I had missed, something I should have seen. But however hard I tried to concentrate, I could not quite grasp it.

'You saw the Spanish fleet off Lisbon on the fourteenth of May,' the King was saying, 'and on your return to Plymouth you immediately sent an express to London –'

There. There it was, emerging into the light. You fool, Matthew Quinton: you poor, stupid fool, for not seeing it until now.

'Wait, Your Majesty,' I said.

The King peered down his remarkably long and ugly nose, fixing me with one of his coldest and most imperious stares.

'It does not do to interrupt Majesty, Sir Matthew Quinton.'

'I crave Your Majesty's pardon. But is there a copy of the *Gazette* to hand? The copy that contains Captain Harris's letter?'

'The *Gazette*?' said the King. 'What light can that tedious rag possibly shed upon this business?'

'Trust me, Sire.'

The King gave me what seemed remarkably like a royal evil eye. I was taking an almighty risk; all Charles Stuart had to do was to stand upon his royal authority, to reject my imprecations, and to damn me for an impudent scoundrel who dared to contradict the will of God's anointed upon Earth. But I had the credit of having undertaken this distasteful mission for him, and my brother had the credit of being, perhaps, the king's own sibling. If Charles the Second could not trust the Quintons, then his throne rested upon feeble foundations indeed, and at last, that simple truth seemed to win out. The king beckoned one of his pageboys to him, and sent him scuttling away.

The minutes passed. Beau, Charles and I stood there, unable to move without the King's express command. And the King sat, stock still and impassive, almost as though he had been turned to stone by an invisible Medusa.

At length the lad returned, and handed me the copy of the *Gazette*. I opened it, read, and handed it directly to the King.

'Behold, Your Majesty. Proof that Captain Harris is entirely innocent of any wrongdoing.'

Both Beau and my brother looked at me in utter astonishment. But the King simply read, then re-read, the page in front of him.

'I do not see it,' he said. 'It is his own letter to Coventry, reporting his sighting of the French fleet. The fleet that proved to be the Spanish. The letter that I fully intend to upbraid him about.'

'Quite, Your Majesty. Captain Harris's letter of the twenty-second of May, from onboard the *Jupiter* in the harbour of Plymouth. My Lord?'

I turned to my brother. The Earl of Ravensden seemed nonplussed, but then he blinked. He had caught my meaning.

'The twenty-second of May was the very day that Your Majesty and your councillors took the decision to divide the fleet,' he said.

'But a letter could never get from Plymouth to London on the same day!' cried Beau. 'It must have been two days, perhaps three, before my letter reached Whitehall!'

'That can only be so, Your Majesty,' said my brother.

There was a long silence. Although it was a warm day in July, the room suddenly seemed chill beyond measure.

'Yes. It can only be so.'

There was a curious note in the King's voice, and an equally curious aspect to my brother's expression.

'And the publication in the *Gazette* proves it,' said Charles Quinton. 'The mob may blame Captain Harris now, because the only evidence they have of how the fleet came to be divided is this published copy of his letter. But if they were aware of all the facts, they would see that this evidence also exonerates him. And, of course, those facts could be brought to light in any trial of Captain Harris for treason. Would that not be so, Your Majesty?'

'It would be so,' said the King, with evident bad grace.

From being like a statue upon his chair, Charles the Second was now shifting uncomfortably and fidgeting.

At last, I realised what I was witnessing. The King would have known full well that he and his ministers made the decision to divide the fleet long before Beau's letter arrived in London. At first it must have seemed like a godsend: proof that the French fleet was sailing for the Channel, and that a decision taken with considerable reluctance had turned out to be correct after all. But there was an unintended consequence of the letter's arrival, and the decision to publish it in the *Gazette*. The intelligence of the fleet off Lisbon was the single piece of information that the government made public. The people of England duly assumed that the division of the fleet was founded upon Beau's letter. So when the King learned, through me, that Beau had mistaken the Spanish fleet for the French, he must have thought that he had the perfect scapegoat, the ideal sacrifice to offer up to the baying mob. And that is how it might have been, but for the inconvenient fact that publishing the letter in the *Gazette* also set the date of its despatch in stone, and proved beyond doubt that Beau Harris could not possibly have caused the division of the fleet.

Of course, I could say none of this in that room, at that moment. Openly to accuse the King of England of being prepared to have an innocent man executed to serve his own dubious ends would undoubtedly have seen me changing places with Beau. But I did not need to say it. I could see in my brother's expression that he thought it, and I could see in the king's face that he knew full well what my brother – *who was, perhaps, also his own brother* – was thinking. That was sufficient.

'Very well, then,' said King Charles the Second, as though he had tired of the entire matter in the blink of an eye. 'Captain Harris, you may return to your ship at Plymouth. We are well pleased with your actions against the privateer Kranz, and are glad that our coasts have been rid of such a pest. We are also certain of your future discretion in this matter of our, uh, slight misconception of your actions.' Beau bowed. He was a staunch Cavalier, and no man would ever hear of the king's duplicity from his lips; every one in the room knew that. 'But take heed of this lesson. Learn seamanship, as your friend here has done. Above all, Captain Harris, learn how to distinguish the ships of one nation from another.' The King turned his gaze toward me. 'Sir Matthew, you may return to the fleet. If the reports coming to me are accurate – if they have been dated correctly, and so forth

– then it should be weighing from the Buoy of the Nore upon the next tide.'

I bowed. Beau and I left the room, leaving my brother to embark upon what must have been a particularly strained conversation with the King.

'Well, Matt!' Beau was not one to dwell on things: he was already in remarkably good spirits, for a man who had been staring at the gallows barely five minutes before. 'By God, Sir Matthew Quinton, I owe you my life! You are a new Nostradamus, or a Merlin – a veritable seer! How could you know that the dates did not match?'

'I should have realised long before, when I received intelligence from my brother giving the date of the decision to divide the fleet. But it is an odd thing, is it not? One can stare things in the face, yet not see they are there.'

Quite suddenly, the colour seemed to drain from Beau's face, and he swayed upon his feet. He reached out and steadied himself upon the oak panelling that covered the wall of the corridor. In that moment, Captain Beaudesert Harris must have realised what had very nearly happened, and how lucky he had been. But as a loyal Cavalier, he voiced no criticism of his King. None whatsoever.

'I am eternally in your debt, Matt – and that of the *Gazette*, by Heaven!' he said instead. 'Think upon it, my friend. Just a year ago, before the *Gazette* existed, I would surely have hanged, for my letter would have been lost somewhere here in the palace, never to be seen again. Thank God for the news-papers, then, Sir Matthew!' His colour returned, and with it his usual, unabashed good humour. 'And I'll not take the Plymouth road before buying you a fine dinner, Matt Quinton, and pouring enough ale and wine down you to float a fireship!'

'Another time, Beau. I must go to Cornelia before I leave for the fleet. But when you return to Plymouth, my friend, be certain to pass my compliments to Mistress Mendez!'

Beau grinned.

'The fair Bella. Yes, I will. A bewitching little creature, is she not?'

'Be careful that you are not bewitched too far, Beau. She is much too young and much too clever for you, Captain Harris!'

* * *

Phineas Musk's familiar form lurked in the entrance hall of Ravensden House.

'Sir Matthew.'

'Musk. You are ready to return with me to the King's – to the *Royal Sceptre*?'

'Sea chest packed and already on its way to Tower Wharf, Sir Matthew. Looking forward to sea air and killing a few Dutchmen after this last business with your brother. Too much politics, and you know my feelings about that sorry world of scabrous blaggards and whoremongers. Too much of trying to wring the truth out of shifty clerks in the secretary of state's office, too. Took a lot of wringing, some of 'em.'

'As you say, Musk. A bad business altogether. It very nearly went badly for Captain Harris.'

'But it wouldn't have been him, would it, even if they'd chopped him into pieces on Tower Hill. Way I see it, the Duke and the Prince were each determined to be on their own. If it hadn't been the tales of the French fleet and army, it would have been something else. Especially for Prince Rupert. Never could stomach anyone else's authority, that one. Everyone said as much, back in the wars, your uncle Tristram at the head of them. Rupert would have found a way to have his own fleet, mark my words.'

A dark thought struck me, but I suppressed it. I was in a desperate hurry to see Cornelia and to return to sea, so I pressed on, through the warren of corridors and low, narrow doorways that characterised Ravensden House, up to the room that Cornelia had appropriated for her own.

'Matthew!'

She flung herself into my arms and kissed me profusely. She had a better pallor than when I saw her last; indeed, she seemed radiant. She had also put on weight.

'Thank God you are well, husband! Your business in Plymouth was not dangerous?'

I thought of swinging from yardarm to yardarm with Bella Mendez, and fighting desperately against Kranz's men on Cawsand beach.

'No, my love. Not dangerous at all. And you are well? Truly well?'

She pushed herself away from me.

'Do I not look well, Matthew?' She grinned. 'Do I not look as well as you have ever seen me?'

'That you do.'

'It has a cause, husband. The miracle we prayed for has finally happened. I am with child, Matthew.'

I stood there, stock still, as the room vanished all around me. I felt myself begin to sway, but somehow I remained upright capable of speech.

'With child? Great God in Heaven – Cornelia, a *child*? How long…?'

'Three months, perhaps.'

I thought back to my brief time at home after returning from Sweden with the Gothenburg convoy and before taking command of the *Royal Sceptre*. It had been a loving and vigorous time, but no more so than many of our other times together, when we had hoped in vain for success in conceiving our long-desired child.

I gathered her in my arms, and suddenly realised I was weeping profusely. I could find no words; none at all. It was as well that she could.

'He will be Earl of Ravensden one day.'

'It might be a girl.'

'Or twins. Remember you and I are both twins, Matthew.' She never usually spoke of this; my own twin, Henrietta, had died when we were thirteen, and she knew I still grieved for her loss. 'But I am certain it will be a boy, and he will be an Earl one day.'

Neither of us thought to suggest that Charles might marry again, and father a son. After all, his experience of marriage, in a perverse alliance engineered by the King for his own ends, had been calamitous. It had also run contrary to his own instincts in every conceivable way.

'If it is a girl, I will be well content as long as she is like her mother.'

She looked up at me with an uncommon seriousness in her damp eyes.

'Boy or girl, husband, the child will need a father. Do not get yourself killed in the next battle, Matthew. Do not let my countrymen deprive our child of you.'

'Fear not, love. Remember I am the only captain in the fleet that sails with three indestructible talismans – Phineas Musk, the King's Prick, and Lord Rochester's monkey.'

Chapter Nineteen

What's that I see? Ah, 'tis my George agen!
It seems they in sev'n weeks have rigg'd him then
The curious heav'ns with lightning him surrounds,
To view him and his name in thunder sounds…
Stay heaven a while, and thou shalt see him sail,
And George too, he can thunder, lightning, hail.

Marvell, *Third Advice to a Painter*

'Did you ever see the like, Musk?'

'Course I did, Sir Matthew. Saw old General Blake's fleet put out against the Dutch in the year Fifty-Three. A grander sight still, that was.'

The old curmudgeon and I were on the deck of the *Bezan Yacht*, sailing north-east towards the King's Channel. There, dead ahead, was a remarkable sight; and despite Musk's attempt to belittle it, I could see that even he was awestruck by the spectacle that lay ahead of us. The Navy Royal of England, beaten and shattered less than seven weeks before, was in magnificent order, a vast line of ships perhaps ten miles long, the White Squadron leading the Red and then the Blue to sea. Ensigns and pennants streamed proudly in the south-westerly breeze. The dockyards had done an astonishing job. Not only were all the damaged ships from the four-day fight repaired: new ones had joined the ranks, and only a few of them were feeble hired merchantmen brought in to make up the numbers. As we passed through the fleet, the sense of determination was palpable. The navy was sailing to avenge its humiliation and its fallen heroes, to pay back the Dutch for all the death and suffering they had inflicted. There was the *Royal Charles*, the great Union Flag streaming out from her main top, but I had little regard for her; my heart was leaping at the sight of the ship directly behind the flagship. There was the *Royal Sceptre*, immaculate and with no sign of the damage she had sustained, keeping station a few hundred yards ahead of the *Black Prince*, Kit Farrell's command. My old friend doffed his hat and grinned as we sailed past, and while I replied in kind, Musk waved boyishly to his old shipmate. But I requested the *Bezan*'s captain to put some searoom between ourselves and the *Sceptre*. I did not think I could bear the sights and sounds of my crew's greetings before doing what had to be done.

The yacht came alongside the *Royal Charles* and secured to her larboard side, allowing me to board her by way of the entry port.

The flagship's great cabin was very much like a court room. The portly Duke of Albemarle sat behind a table, his back to the stern windows; beyond them, the bow wave of the *Royal Sceptre* surged at the cutwater as she kept her station astern of the flagship. Albemarle seemed entirely intent upon the papers in front of him. Prince Rupert was at the stern, at the larboard side, looking out at the fleet, apparently oblivious to everything that was happening in the cabin. I took a deep breath. I had new responsibilities now, or soon would have: the responsibilities of a father. And yet I was about to do the most irresponsible thing I had ever done in my life. Somehow, though, it was if I could hear my grandfather whispering in my ear.

'Courage, boy. Remember, above all, that you are a Quinton.'

And fortunately, I was not the last and only Quinton. Tucked into my sleeve was the note that my brother had sent to me from Whitehall, just before I set off for the fleet.

Finally, Albemarle looked up and acknowledged my presence.

'Sir Matthew,' he said, politely enough. 'Your appearance is somewhat... shall one say, unanticipated? You were expected back long before the fleet sailed from the Buoy of the Nore. Your absence forced us to appoint a new captain for the *Royal Sceptre* - Captain Marks, a good man. I do not intend to put him out to accommodate you. You are welcome here aboard the *Charles* as a supernumerary or volunteer, but you cannot expect special privileges, and certainly not a cabin –'

'No, Your Grace.'

To my surprise, I found contradicting a Duke, the Captain-General of England no less, an easy thing to do; very much akin to reprimanding a naughty child, in truth. And I would need practice at that.

'No? *No?* You dare 'no' me, Quinton?' Incredulity at my interruption gave way to rage. 'I am Albemarle, by God! How dare you, a jumped-up, insolent gentleman captain, say nay to me! I will –'

'No, Your Grace. I will have back the command of the *Royal Sceptre*. As I recall, Captain Marks is a Devon man, is he not? A client of yours, Your Grace, who fought under you during the wars in Cromwell's time? Another member of your Devon coterie?'

Albemarle's fat face was a vivid red.

'God's blood, Quinton, I will have you court-martialled for this – you and that gross incompetent Harris, who couldn't tell the French fleet from the Spanish and deserted his command to go up to London with you –'

'No you will not, Your Grace. You see, any action you take against us will force my brother, the Earl of Ravensden, to bring certain papers to the attention of His Majesty and the Lord Chancellor, as head of the judiciary. The papers consist principally of affidavits, taken and sworn by the Reverend Francis Gale, while we were in your native Devon.' It was easy now: out poured all my hatred of this man who hated me, and whom I held responsible for the death of my friend Will Berkeley. 'Papers relating to the collusion of Ludovic Conibear, the navy agent at Plymouth and another client of Your Grace's, with the notorious Dutch privateer, Captain Kranz, the so-called hell-hound. Papers which connect Conibear directly to the murder of Nathaniel Garrett, whose unwitting testimony was one of the principal causes of the division of the fleet. Testimony which you chose to accept, Your Grace, despite it being the unsupported, second-hand account of just one man. Papers which prove that many of the gentry of Devon, including some of your own family, knowingly bought wine smuggled from France by Kranz and Conibear, in contravention of the embargo imposed by the Privy Council. And papers which implicate Your Grace in an attempt deliberately and unjustly to smear Captain Harris as another principal mover in that unfortunate calamity –'

Albemarle slammed his hands on the table, pulled himself to his feet and leaned forward menacingly, his vast bulk shaking with rage.

'You damnable, impudent, arrogant pup – I have had men shot for much less –'

'Sit down, George, and be silent.'

Prince Rupert's strong German accent made the reproof seem even more abrupt and brutal than it was. The Prince turned away from the stern windows, and stepped toward Albemarle.

'*What?*'

'Sit. Be silent, you great blockhead.'

'But I am Albemarle –'

'Indeed you are, Your Grace. But I am Rupert. *Prince* Rupert. I was born in the palace of Prague Castle, to the King and Queen of Bohemia. My brother is the Elector Palatine of the Rhine, one of the select eight who choose the Holy Roman Emperors. I am cousin to Charles, King of England, whom you restored and who made you Duke of Albemarle, as you might recall. Who are *your* brothers and cousins, George? And where were you born, pray? Great Potheridge, was it not?

Why, in lowly Prague they speak of nothing but Great Potheridge, of what a mighty and noble city it is.'

Albemarle's mouth opened and closed, but no words emerged. The Duke swayed on his feet, staring impotently at Prince Rupert. Rage battled against deference. But the sometime George Monck, younger son of an obscure Devon knight, had no refuge. Albemarle had brought royalty back to the British kingdoms, and that very fact ensured he could make not even the slightest protest against a scion of the blood royal he had elected to restore.

'Your Highness,' he said, and bowed his head slightly. Thus did the proud and powerful Duke of Albemarle acknowledge defeat.

'I propose that we adopt a different view of the present situation,' said Prince Rupert. 'I suggest that while Captain Marks has many excellent qualities, they surely do not exceed those of the heir to Ravensden, a man knighted for his astonishing valour in the Lowestoft fight. And as the *Royal Sceptre* seconds our flagship, it is surely only right that a man of honour, from one of the finest families in the kingdom, should command her. I suggest that Captain Marks should be compensated with the command of the next frigate sent to cruise off Heligoland, where he will stand a better chance of taking wealthy prizes – perhaps even a fat Dutch Indiaman or two. You concur, Your Grace?' Albemarle waved a flabby hand, but said nothing. 'Very well. Sir Matthew, return to your command. God willing, very soon we will be avenged on De Ruyter and the Hollanders.'

* * *

Back aboard the *Royal Sceptre,* I was huzzah'd to the heavens. Men waved their Monmouth caps and dangled from the shrouds, shouting themselves hoarse. Even a number of the toughest old veterans in the crew were in tears. However, Francis Gale, who had returned to the ship before it sailed from the Buoy of the Nore, quickly disabused me of the notion that their enthusiasm might have been born entirely of love for me.

'A sign of His Grace of Albemarle's entire lack of grace,' he said. 'Who but he would have thought it suitable to appoint a Devon man, and a former rebel at that, to command a crew made up chiefly of Cornishmen, the stoutest Cavaliers in the kingdom? And even if they were not, they would hate a Devon captain on principle. I suspect that Captain Marks found his chaplain a trial, too. He seemed to me to have anabaptistical tendencies, which is probably why he appeared not to find my sermon upon our God-given duty to baptise infants entirely to his liking. Upon which subject, Sir Matthew, I give you and Lady Quinton joy of your news.'

The stolid Captain Marks had disembarked into the *Bezan* only a few minutes before. He did not seem sad to be going, although whether that was because of the antipathy of the chaplain and crew or because of the presence of the wholly amoral Lord Rochester and his accursed monkey remained to be seen. The beast in question, still attired in its miniature lieutenant's baldric, glowered at me from the top of a quarterdeck demi-culverin, seemingly the one living creature aboard the ship that was not delighted by my return.

I looked about me. It was good to feel the gentle rise and fall of a deck beneath my feet, good to see and hear the wind in the sails, good to smell the tar and the timber. It was good to have abandoned the yellow uniform. In short, it was good to be a king's captain again, to be sailing into battle against the enemy, and to contemplate fatherhood. I even felt benevolent toward Lord Rochester's monkey, and patted the creature on its head.

The ungrateful beast bit me.

Chapter Twenty

25 JULY 1666

There happened of late a terrible fray,
Begun upon our St James's Day,
With a thump, thump, thump, thump, thump
Thump, thump, a thump, thump
Where Rupert and George for Charlemaign
Swing'd the Dutch again and again
(As if they had been the French or the Dane),
With a thump, thump, thump, thump, thump
Thump, thump, a thump, thump

Sir John Birkenhead, *A New Ballad of a Famous German Prince and a Renowned English Duke, Who on St James's Day One Thousand 666 fought with a Beast with Seven Heads, call'd Provinces…* (1666)

'The Dutch are a shambles,' said Lord Rochester. 'Even I can see that, by God.'

'We should not underestimate them, My Lord,' I said. 'They will still fight like tigers.'

'Too many bloody Dutchmen in the world,' said Musk. 'That's what I say, at any rate. Like that beast in legend, whatever its name was. Keep cutting off its heads, and still it grows new ones and comes back at you. Dutchmen are like that, Dutchmen are.'

The two fleets were converging very slowly in light winds on the hot, hazy morning of Saint James's Day. With what breeze there was coming from the north, we had the weather gage. With that advantage in our favour, we edged south-east toward the disorganised Dutch line. Whether it was bad ship-handling, which I doubted, or another consequence of their endemic petty jealousies between the provinces, which I very much suspected – in either event, there were great gaps between the Dutch squadrons. Their line, too, was barely worthy of the name, resembling instead a ragged half-moon.

Consequently, our van squadron was engaged long before we were: nearly four hours before. We could see and hear the gunfire as the White Squadron blazed away, but it was as though we were spectators at a bear-baiting.

'Allin will be well content,' I said after two or perhaps three hours. 'He has his own squadron at last, and the Zeelanders give way before him!'

Even through the smoke, which hung over the battle thanks to the negligible breeze, it was apparent that the lighter Dutch ships were struggling to withstand the onslaught from Sir Thomas Allin's more powerful batteries. The likes of the *Royal James*, *Royal Katherine*, *Saint George* and *Unicorn*, some of England's mightiest ships, blazed away to formidable effect. Unlike in the previous battle, the sea was calm enough to ensure that our fleet's lower gunports could be open from the beginning, and our superior weight of shot was literally murderous.

'Now,' said Francis Gale as we finally closed the Dutch in the centre, 'let us pray that God favours those of us under the red banner too.'

Our trumpets sounded, the drums beat, and the King's Prick sailed into battle. Lovell's Marines massed on deck, came to attention, then dispersed to their action stations. The catcalls that had once greeted their appearances on deck were no more. They had been tested in battle, and the seamen knew their worth; the yellow-coated soldiers were Sceptres now.

We were the *Royal Charles*'s second, and there was never any doubt where we were bound. The huge stern of the flagship filled the ocean dead ahead of us, but just to larboard of her, I caught glimpses of a familiar vast Dutch ship flying a huge command flag. It was the *Seven Provinces*, and De Ruyter himself.

There were shouts from our lookouts, and another from a young man over on the larboard side of the quarterdeck.

'One of her seconds is wearing, Sir Matthew! She's coming for us!'

Julian Delacourt, this, the new lieutenant of the *Royal Sceptre*. Son and only heir to an impoverished baron of Munster, he was an eager but impossibly young lad of nineteen, with a mop of jet-black hair. He had lively eyes and a winning smile, so unsurprisingly, the Earl of Rochester swiftly took an unhealthy interest in him. However, Delacourt seemed more than able to look after himself: indeed, he had an easy wit about him that allowed him to hold his own when trading puns with the noble poet. Delacourt even delighted in describing himself as the second lieutenant of the *Sceptre*, Lord Rochester's monkey, naturally, being the first.

'Very well, Mister Delacourt! To your station, and God be with you!'

He went down into the ship's waist, sword in hand, and began to shout encouragement to the gun crews as they rolled their cannon into position.

'He's no Kit Farrell,' said Francis, 'or rather, Captain Farrell. And we sorely needed one, Sir Matthew, what with the new draft of men brought in by the press to make up our numbers – a gaggle of feeble landmen, with not a single seaman among them!'

'He'll do, Francis. God willing, he'll do, and they'll do.'

The oncoming Dutchman was a high-sided Amsterdammer with sixty guns or so.

'Wind's too light for him to try a boarding attack,' I said. 'So there's just one thing he can do.'

Sure enough, the Dutchman opened up with a rolling broadside of his upper deck guns. Bar-shot and chain-shot flew through our rigging, severing sheets and shrouds, punching holes through the Lincoln canvas of the sails. Several shots struck the fore- and mainmasts; Richardson, the carpenter, and his crew attended to them like mother hens, determined that the *Sceptre*'s masts would stand in this battle as they had in the last. Meanwhile the Dutch marines fired down from their tops, although they were close to the limit of their range. I saw several of the new draft cower and shirk, with only the cudgels of some of the petty officers compelling them to their new duties. Directing the petty officers in turn, though, was a familiar frame and voice: Martin Lanherne, the new acting boatswain of the *Royal Sceptre*, who had ridden fast for London with myself, Francis Gale and my small troop, before proceeding directly to the ship while I learned of my impending fatherhood and faced down my King.

'You, there!' Lanherne cried. 'Make fast yonder lanyard, and look lively! That lany – that rope, then, if you prefer! Aye, that rope there, you doltish lubber!'

It was good to hear his familiar Cornish tones again. I regretted that Lanherne's new draft of recruits had not accompanied him from the west, though; travelling as they were by cart or on foot, I doubted if they could be even half way to London yet. So our new men would, indeed, have to do. They would either learn quickly, or they would die: for now, the King's Prick was upon more important business.

Our Amsterdammer was level with us, barely a few hundred yards away.

'Very well then, Mister Burdett!' I cried. 'We know what he's about now, and have his measure! D'you think good English metal can repay him twice over?'

'That it can, Sir Matthew!'

'And Mister Lovell – can our Marines outshoot those butterboxes yonder?'

The young Marine officer nodded eagerly.

'Not in doubt, Sir Matthew!'

'Very well, then, gentlemen! For God and the King –' I raised my sword, then dropped it – 'Give fire!'

The larboard battery on the lower deck of the *Royal Sceptre* opened up. I felt the familiar shock as my entire body shuddered from the blast of the guns and the recoil of the carriages. I caught a glimpse of young Delacourt. He had his hands over his ears, overwhelmed by the shattering experience of his first broadside. In that instant, he looked very young indeed. Meanwhile our own Marines, in the tops and on the forecastle, fired an impressive volley into the enemy.

Our smoke cleared, and I looked out from the larboard rail toward the Hollander.

'She's taken a few hits, low down,' I said to Rochester. 'Look there, My Lord, how the planking is shattered. God willing, we'll have hit her below the waterline too –'

The very sea itself seemed to tremble as the *Seven Provinces*, just across the water, fired her first broadside. I watched as some of the standing rigging on the *Royal Charles* snapped, and great shards of timber from her larboard side flew through the air.

'And seamen call those splinters,' said Rochester. 'I admire the understatement of the nautical realm.'

Our flagship responded at once, the deep roar of the cannon-of-seven unmistakeable as they flung their forty-two pound balls across the water. I focused my telescope on the quarterdeck, and caught a glimpse of Rupert and Albemarle, the former waving his sword toward the enemy as though leading a cavalry charge.

Our own assailant fired again. I felt the impact of her shot in our hull, but instinctively looked up, to see if any of the masts or yards were felled. They stood, but there were shouts from down in the ship's waist. One of the gun carriages had been struck; the demi-culverin leaned impotently to one side, away from its port. Half of the gun crew lay dead. The head was gone from one of them, while another, a tough Tynesman named Robson, had taken a great splinter through the gut, its bloodied ends protruding out of both sides of his body. The blood and gore of the dead men stained the deck around the carriage. Those of the gun crew that remained alive, Massey, Spence and one of the new landmen, were struggling to right the weapon. Burdett had taken command and was pushing against the carriage with all his might, but he was an old man, well into his fifties…

Without thinking, I ran down and joined Burdett at the damaged demi-culverin. Seeing what I was about, Musk, Francis Gale and Lord Rochester ran down and joined me. Lieutenant Delacourt hastened to our side. He stared for a moment at the carnage, especially at the terrible sight of Robson's remains, and turned pale. Then he remembered himself and set to with us as we heaved against the damaged carriage. Small shot hissed all around. Chain and bar shot whistled overhead. Yet none of it mattered. Suddenly that one gun was the most important thing in the whole universe. But the weapon would not move. It was hopeless…

'A prayer, Chaplain, if you please!' I cried to Francis, who was red in the face and breathing heavily.

'My only prayer, Sir Matthew, is for the bodily strength I had twenty years ago!'

'Amen to that,' said Musk.

Despite his willingness to help, the old rogue was of little use, if truth be told; he could only push tentatively at the gun, for fear of reopening his recent wound.

I shifted position, and found myself alongside a landman from the new draft. He may have known nothing of the sea, but he pushed with a will.

'Your name, fellow?' I said, between pushes.

'Loakes, Sir Matthew. Chair maker of Chipping Wycombe.'

'No longer, Loakes. You are a seaman of the *Royal Sceptre* now. On my count, then, seaman Loakes – one, two, three!'

We heaved again. Lord Rochester's monkey jumped up onto the ship's rail and hissed, seemingly in encouragement. The gun carriage toppled back and struck the deck with a great crash, which coincided with another mighty broadside from the *Royal Charles* ahead of us. Now we sprang to the ropes, hauling the demi-culverin back round at an angle to the remnants of the port. Burdett was already acting a part he must have played countless times in his youth, that of captain of one weapon. He gesticulated toward the pile of canvas cartridges on the deck, but the gun crew were still engaged upon the ropes. I had watched my men execute this countless times; why not, then? I took up one of the charges, placed it on a lengthy ladle and pushed it into the bore. As soon as the ladle was clear, Spence rammed home the wad. I picked up a round shot from the small pile next to the gun and pushed it down until I felt it rest upon the wad; Spence rammed in another wad ahead of it.

Now Massey thrust a great pin down the vent to puncture the cartridge, poured powder into the vent, then signalled for the rest of us to haul the carriage round into position. Ship's captain, lieutenant, chaplain, captain's clerk and noble poet alike hauled on the tackles that pulled our weapon round into the port, facing toward the impossibly close hull of the Dutchman. Wait for the downroll – wait – Burdett put the linstock to the touch-hole, there was a spit of flame and our gun thundered forth. Close to, the shock of the blast was extraordinary; I was once kicked in the chest by a horse, and that had nothing like the force. The great demi-culverin recoiled across the deck. At once, we sprang to it and secured it. The whole thing seemed to have taken but a blink of an eye, but in truth it must have been several minutes. I looked out to see what damage we had done, but it was impossible to judge. The side of the Dutchman was full of indentations and jagged holes; any one of them, or none, could have been caused by the first cannon-shot of the most ill-sorted gun crew in the entire Navy Royal.

'At the next firing,' I said to the erstwhile chair maker, 'you load the charge, seaman Loakes!'

The young man looked at me nonplussed, but brought two fingers to forehead in a passable attempt at a salute.

Four men from below came up to make good the complement of the gun's crew. Burdett appointed Spence as captain of it, then saluted me before returning to his wider duties. I, too, suddenly recollected that I had a somewhat more detached role to play, and began my way back toward my proper station, accompanied by the Earl of Rochester.

'Oh, glorious, most glorious!' cried the noble earl. 'I have never known the like. 'Twas very nearly better than buggery, Sir Matthew! That I, Rochester, manned a cannon in a great sea-fight!'

Kellett ran up with bottles of beer, handing one to Rochester and one to myself. Unable to think of any riposte to the poet's remark, I put the bottle to my lips and emptied the entire contents in one long swig. Battle is always thirsty work, but that Saint James's Day felt as hot as the fire that the Saint himself wished to call down upon the Samaritan village. I sent Kellett at once for a second bottle, and tried to wipe some of the sweat from my brow and chest.

All around us, the battle raged. Thousands of great cannon roared. Muskets fired. Men barked orders. Other men screamed in death-agony. Timber broke asunder. And then I had the strangest thought. Could Cornelia, in London, hear the sound of the battle? Would it alarm our unborn child? Would it somehow know that its father risked death at every moment of the day? Was it about to be half-orphaned, long before it was born?

I took another swig of the beer, and resolved to live.

Chapter Twenty-One

Behold that navy, which a while before
Provok'd the tardy English close to fight;
Now draw their beaten vessels close to shore,
As larks lie dar'd to shun the Hobbies flight.

Dryden, *Annus Mirabilis*

We continued to trade blows with our assailant, but neither of us could gain the advantage over the other. Fearful of the power of our larger guns, the Dutchman kept his distance; but his position, and his dogged persistence, meant that we could not advance to assist the *Royal Charles*. And within the hour, it was clear that our flagship was in a terrible condition. Her rigging was in shreds, the foreyard fallen to the deck. The huge Union Flag flying from the maintopmast head was in shreds. Her rate of fire was falling off.

'Allin's advantage in the van will be for nought if the *Charles* surrenders!' I cried.

'Rupert and Albemarle surrendering?' said Musk. 'I think they'll need to have rather less ship beneath them before they contemplate that, Sir Matthew. One plank, maybe, then they'll haul down the colours. Pair of stubborn buggers, one as bad as the other.'

'Perhaps, Musk. But wait –'

'Look, Sir Matthew!' cried Rochester. 'What is happening there?'

'They're manning the ship's boats on the unengaged side,' I said, training my telescope on the *Royal Charles*'s starboard quarter. 'They're going to tow her out of the battle. Get her upwind, and try to effect repairs.'

'But will the Dutch not finish her?'

'If God wills it, My Lord, we can still keep them entertained! Look there – it's the *Black Prince*!'

Kit Farrell's command emerged from the thick, immovable cloud of gunsmoke astern of us and passed our larboard quarter. The Sceptres cheered their old lieutenant, and I raised my sword in salute. Kit responded in kind, the most enormous grin upon his face. The *Black Prince* fired a broadside into our assailant as she passed, but she had other fish to fry. Kit steered directly for the *Seven Provinces.*

'But he's half her size!' said Rochester.

'Two thirds, more like. But Captain Farrell is a good enough seaman to keep clear of De Ruyter's guns, My Lord, and by interposing himself between the Dutchman and the *Royal Charles*, he stops De Ruyter going after her.'

So it proved. As the boats of the *Royal Charles* towed the shattered flagship slowly toward safety, Kit engaged the *Seven Provinces*, skilfully manoeuvring so that he avoided the full force of the Dutch flagship's broadsides while ensuring that his own could bear with maximum effect. Meanwhile, we continued to trade broadsides with our stubborn adversary. But the Dutch had more ships coming up – very soon, they were bound to overwhelm the *Black Prince*, and unless I could disentangle the *Sceptre*, they would have a clear way through to the *Charles*...

To begin with it was almost imperceptible, like the first roll of thunder in the very far distance on an autumn night. But it grew steadily louder, and louder still. The sound of drumbeats, rhythmic and terrifying. The *Royal Sceptre* carried four drummers, but this had to be the beat of at least five times that number. Slowly, all the ordinary sounds on the deck of our ship ceased. Men stopped shouting. Officers stopped blowing their whistles. Even Francis Gale stopped reciting psalms. And over on our opponent, exactly the same thing was happening. The eerie silence was so entire that it was even possible to hear the squawks of a passing gull: entire, but for the frightening beat of the kettledrums, growing ever louder.

'What is it, Sir Matthew?' Rochester demanded. For once, the voluble Earl spoke in the quietest whisper.

'Watch, My Lord,' I said, for now I was certain of the cause. 'Behold one of the wonders of the world.'

A bowsprit emerged from the shroud of gunsmoke, the Union Flag flying proudly from the staff. Then came the beakhead, then a vast, towering forecastle, far higher than that of the *Sceptre* or even of the *Seven Provinces*, across the water. The drumming got louder and louder. More and more of the mighty hull came into view: the mighty, gilded hull. A vast golden ship, with a hundred brass guns protruding from her gunports.

'The *Royal Sovereign*,' I said. 'God willing, she'll teach the Dutch the meaning of the name she was christened with. Truly, My Lord Rochester, she is the very Sovereign of the Seas!'

'Or the Golden Devil, if you prefer,' said Francis. 'That's what the Dutch call her. They shit themselves at the very sight of her.'

'Then why wasn't she with us in the four-day fight?'

'She needs so large a crew, she couldn't be manned in time,' I said. 'But she's manned now, all right. As De Ruyter will find soon enough.'

If the Sceptres had cheered Kit and the *Black Prince*, they shouted themselves hoarse as the *Sovereign* swept past, the terrifying beat of her drums as deafening as a broadside. The giant ship flew a special blood-red pennant from her main-top, as though she had her very own bloody flag, permanently hoisted as a signal of her intent.

'Very well, gentlemen!' I cried. 'This is our moment! This is England's moment! Ready, Mister Burdett?

'Ready, Sir Matthew!'

'Very well! Take your cue from the Golden Devil, Master Gunner!'

'Aye, aye, sir!'

The *Sovereign* sailed majestically onto the larboard quarter as? the Dutchman engaged against us. I saw enemy sailors racing to man the guns on that side of the ship. But it was too late. The *Sovereign*'s lower deck cannon-of-seven roared out, the flames seeming to make the gilded hull glitter even more brightly. A moment later, Burdett gave the command to fire *Royal Sceptre*'s own broadside into the other side of the Dutchman. The smoke from the combined cannonade was so thick that it was impossible to see beyond the quarterdeck. Rochester coughed violently. I rubbed my eyes, and called out to Kellett to bring me another bottle of beer with which to wash away the acrid taste in my throat.

'Look, Sir Matthew!' It was Delacourt. 'The Dutchman's finished!'

Not finished, perhaps, but certainly breaking off the engagement. Her foremast was gone, snapped like a twig and hanging over the side, the topmast under water. There were great holes in her side, where the *Sovereign*'s cannonade had caused havoc. Until she could cut free the useless foremast and rig a jury mast to replace it, she was little better than a hulk. So the Dutchman had his helm over and was beginning to fall away with the wind.

'He's ours!' cried Rochester, rubbing his hands with glee. 'A fat prize, by God!'

'No, My Lord.'

'No?'

'We hold our course and our station. As we are, we can cover both the *Royal Charles* while she repairs, and the *Sovereign* while she tackles De Ruyter. The Dutchman cannot fight – that is the only thing that matters, My Lord.'

The men within earshot bore disappointed looks, and I knew they were with Lord Rochester. (Musk's expression was beyond disappointed; it might be described as homicidal.) A Dutch sixty-gunner taken into

Harwich would earn every one of the Sceptres a tidy sum in prize money. I understood their feelings entirely, for if a common mariner might turn a tidy sum from such a capture, a captain could make enough to buy a small landed estate in some unfashionable county; Surrey, perhaps. But our duty was clear, and the *Royal Sceptre* sailed on.

A thunderous roar signalled the *Sovereign*'s first broadside against the *Seven Provinces*, and the Dutch flagship replied in kind. Kit's *Black Prince* moved astern of the Golden Devil to protect her most vulnerable aspect, but no Dutch ships were able to move against her. Around us, the whole of the Red Squadron was engaged, including some of the biggest and best ships in our fleet. There was Holmes, our Rear-Admiral, in his new flagship, the *Henry*; there Sir Joseph Jordan, our veteran Vice-Admiral, in the *Royal Oak*.

Far astern, ferocious and continuous cannonading told a very different story. The Blue was taking heavy punishment. The squadron had good officers, the likes of Spragge and Kempthorne, but weak ships, for this was where the bulk of the hired merchantmen recruited to make up the fleet's numbers were concentrated. There was a moment during the afternoon when the gunsmoke cleared sufficiently to allow a view back to the rear of the two fleets, and I briefly diverted my telescope from the fight of the *Seven Provinces* and the *Sovereign* to see how the Blue fared. By chance, I saw the foretopmast of one of the Blue's best ships, the stout *Resolution*, came crashing down, and a Dutch fireship moved in for the kill. I watched the flames devour her hull and turn her masts into blazing crucifixes. I learned later that her valiant captain, Will Hannum, managed to escape, but some two-hundred of his men were drowned. The Saint James's Day fight was only my third fleet action, but I was already inured to such things. It will sound harsh to those who have not been in battle, but I felt no more than a pang of regret as I watched the flames destroy the *Resolution*. After all, any amount of carnage in the Blue would not matter if we continued to prevail in the van and the centre.

With no immediate opponent to fight and the *Royal Charles*, our charge, still out of the battle, the Sceptres had a brief respite in which to eat, drink, and rest. Lanherne moved among them easily, exchanging greetings with his old Cornish friends, establishing his authority among the new men. Meanwhile, Delacourt came up onto the quarterdeck, and stood alongside Urquhart, Rochester, Musk and myself to watch the duel between the *Seven Provinces* and the *Sovereign*.

'De Ruyter's fire is falling off,' said Urquhart. 'Their broadsides are becoming ragged.'

'They'd already taken a fearful hammering from the *Charles*,' I said, 'and now they're taking an even worse one from the *Sovereign*. The Dutchman's a smaller ship, with lighter guns. De Ruyter's only chance is to bring her close enough to board, but Cox is too good a captain to let him do that.'

'Cox?' said Rochester. 'I do not know the name.'

'John Cox commands the *Sovereign*,' I said. 'He's a good man, and a veteran seaman.'

I had encountered John Cox when he was Master Attendant of Deptford dockyard, responsible for setting out the *Seraph* when I commanded her to the Gambia River. By rights, the mighty *Sovereign* should have been a flagship, but she had come to the fleet so late that all the flags were already allocated, so Cox had her for his own. And what use he was making of her! The Golden Devil was pouring broadside after broadside into the *Seven Provinces*, the forty-two pound balls from the cannon-of-seven smashing into the Dutchman's hull.

'Look, Sir Matthew,' cried the excited Delacourt, 'they're hoisting a new foreyard into place on the *Royal Charles*!'

I turned and looked out to the west. It was true: her crew had worked wonders. The new rigging was being run into place. The flagship was preparing to get under sail again.

'Once she comes back into the battle,' I said, 'the Dutch won't be able to stand against both the *Charles* and the *Sovereign*! And De Ruyter knows it, by God! Look there – he's putting on sail and hoisting a signal!'

'I don't know the Dutch signal book, Sir Matthew,' said Urquhart, 'but I'll wager it's their equivalent of our blue flag at the mizzen peak. The signal for the fleet to fall into the admiral's wake or grain.'

'Which means what, in the King's English?' demanded Rochester. 'You sea-beasts and your infernal sea-language!'

'Which means, My Lord, that the van and centre squadrons of the Dutch fleet are fleeing. They are running for Holland. Mister Urquhart, stand by to order full sail – aye, studdingsails, every inch of canvas we have! We will fall in a cable's length behind the *Sovereign*, if you please!'

With the scent of victory in their nostrils, the Sceptres set to with a will. The breeze was still light, but a strong ebb was running out of the Thames mouth. Slowly, painfully slowly, we began the pursuit of the Dutch, who were running east toward the safety of their shoals.

'We have trounced them,' said Rochester, a half-hour or so later. 'We have shattered them. Yet still they escape us.'

'That's the thing about this sea-business, My Lord,' said Musk, 'nothing's ever as straightforward as it should be. Isn't that so, Sir Matthew?'

I looked up at our own rigging, then across to the ships around us.

'The one advantage of the Dutchman's way of fighting a battle,' I said. 'If they fire high and shatter our rigging, it makes us more difficult for us to pursue them. A coward's tactic, gentlemen.'

'Sir Matthew,' said Delacourt, lowering his telescope, 'look ahead, sir. Perhaps their coward's tactic will not avail them after all.'

'One of De Ruyter's seconds is in trouble,' I said, peering through my own eyepiece. 'A big one, at least sixty guns – a similar size to the *Sceptre*. Both his fore and mizzen topmasts are down. Looks as though his rudder is damaged, too.'

'The *Sovereign*'s altering course to go for her, Sir Matthew!' cried Urquhart.

'Then we sail with the Golden Devil, gentlemen!'

What a sight we were, bearing down on the crippled Dutchman – the *Gelderland*, as we later learned. With all sail set, ensigns and pennants streaming from our staffs and mastheads, four of England's mightiest men-of-war sailed toward the easiest of victories. The *Royal Sovereign* led the way, a terrifying sight as her huge gilded hull rose and fell on the gentle swell. Then came the *Lion*, the *Triumph* and ourselves, any one of us more than capable of taking the Dutchman on our own. The Dutch saw the danger, but there was little they could do to prevent it. Even De Ruyter himself attempted to come up with the *Seven Provinces*, but his flagship was too shattered. Besides, it was impossible for him to make much headway against the breeze and, more importantly, against the racing ebb.

We were very nearly level with the *Sovereign*, we moving onto the starboard side of the Dutchman, the Golden Devil onto the larboard. The *Lion* and *Triumph* were similarly in parallel behind us, moving to take up position on her quarters.

'He might as well strike his colours now,' I said. 'He's done for.'

'No,' said Delacourt, his telescope fixed on the bows of the Dutchman. 'No, he can't be –'

'Lieutenant?'

'Saw it done once by a sloop in the tiderace at the Shannon's mouth – but surely it can't work –'

'She's dropping anchor!' cried Urquhart.

In that moment, the large anchors on both the starboard and larboard bows of the Dutchman, together with her stern anchor, fell into the sea.

'Jesus,' I swore. 'Jesus, Jesus, *Jesus*! Mister Burdett, there! Larboard battery to engage –'

But it was already too late. The Dutchman came to a dead stop. Carried forward inexorably by the racing ebb, and by the weight of canvas we had aloft, we were past her even before the order to fire could be given. The same was true of the *Sovereign*. The *Lion* and *Triumph*, coming up behind us, managed to fire off a desultory broadside each before they, too, swept past the stationary Dutchman.

'Clever,' said Musk. 'Many-headed, and clever.'

'Surely we can simply turn and capture him!' cried Rochester.

'My Lord,' I snapped, 'ships do not simply *turn*. We cannot sail back directly into the wind, nor into this ebb. That which stopped the Dutch coming up to rescue him now prevents us going back to take him. He has outfoxed us, whoever he is. A brave man, and a skilful one, that captain. A great seaman.'

But that, he was not. When we met at Veere, my good-brother Cornelis told me that the captain of the *Gelderland* was a landsman – a soldier named Van Ghent, a colonel of Marines. It seems that all the old seamen among his officers furrowed their brows and stroked their chins when he ordered the sudden dropping of the anchors, it being a thing beyond the compass of minds that must do things *this way*, because that is how they have always been done. Such is the way of old seamen, and probably always will be.

* * *

We had a new quarry, and this one was not going to elude us: on that, I was determined. It was now well into the evening, and we were much further to the east, where the ebb from the Thames no longer affected either fleet. But it also meant we were much closer to the Dutch coast, which was in sight: a long, low strip of land on the horizon.

'Sixty guns, by my reckoning,' I said, studying the Zeelander ahead. 'A jury mast at the fore, and heeling to starboard. Must be holed beneath the waterline.'

'Might be your wife's brother, then,' said Musk. 'He's a sour-faced killjoy at the best of times, so Christ knows what he'll be like if he has to surrender to you for a second time in a year.'

'While I would not approve of taking Our Lord's name in vain, Musk,' said Francis Gale, 'I think you have the rights of it in this instance. I have met few men more dour than Captain van der Eide.'

'No, wait,' I said, studying the ship ahead intently, 'I recognise this ship. We traded broadsides with her on the fourth day of the last battle.'

'You're right, Sir Matthew,' said Urquhart. 'The Zeeland Vice-Admiral's flagship. Banckert's ship.'

'Not flying his flag now, though,' I said. 'He must have moved to a less damaged command. But it's of no concern. Honour permits us only two courses, gentlemen – take or destroy!'

I pointed my sword at the enemy, like a cavalryman charging his foe. This one would not escape. This one would be the prize that my men deserved. This would be repayment for all that had happened in the last weeks. This would be Sir Matthew Quinton's revenge and apotheosis, all in one.

We moved in toward the starboard quarter of the Zeelander, firing our bow chasers. Part of the quarterdeck rail, and the quarter-gallery, shattered as our iron balls impacted, sending wooden splinters into the air. The Dutchman fired a few of his upper deck guns, but it was little more than a gesture. The heel of the ship meant that he could not open his lower deck gunports, and that most of the guns on the upper deck could not gain enough elevation to bring us within range. Our angle of attack ensured that none of his guns forward of the quarterdeck could bear on us, and the catastrophic damage to his rigging meant that he could barely manoeuvre.

'My French friend, the Comte d'Andelys, would call this moment the *coup de grace*,' I said. 'Let us apply it.'

Although there was hardly any resistance, I was feeling the same rush of blood, the same battle-crazed elation, that I had only experienced previously in hand to hand combat, with my life at stake. I was dimly aware of the likes of Francis, Musk and Rochester speaking to me, but did not properly hear them.

The men aloft adjusted our sails, the helmsman brought over the whipstaff, our yardarms swung, and the *Royal Sceptre* came in astern of the Dutch ship, very nearly at right angles to her stern. I looked forward, along the deck of the King's Prick, and saw the men crouching by the starboard guns, intent on their target. Even the greenest landmen among the pressed drafts had their blood up as much as the Cornish veterans. The gun captains had their eyes on me, and on Burdett.

There was something about the moment. Perhaps it was such a rare thing to have a Dutchman so entirely at one's mercy. Perhaps it was my still-raw grief for Will Berkeley, or my pent-up anger at the duplicity of a King I had once venerated as a demi-god. Perhaps it was the tension of facing down both that King and the Duke of Albemarle. Perhaps it was my anxiety for Cornelia and my unborn child. Whatever the reason, I felt a sudden surge of rage stronger than any I had known in my life. I wanted nothing more than revenge on the Dutch, this nation of bog-born butterbox upstarts. I wanted nothing more than to give the order for our entire battery to open fire, to send in raking broadside after raking broadside, a bombardment that would slaughter every living thing on the ship lying helpless before us –

'Luke Six, Chapter Thirty-Six,' said Francis Gale, by my side. I was suddenly aware of the fact that it was the third or fourth time he had said this.

'What? What do you say, priest?'

'Be ye therefore merciful, as your Father is also merciful. You must summon him to surrender first, Matthew. It is the godly thing to do. It is the honourable thing to do.'

'Be silent, damn you –' But I turned, and saw the face of my friend. The face of a man of God. 'Y-yes, Francis. You are right, of course. We must demand his surrender.'

Young Kellett brought me my voice trumpet, and I called out in Dutch.

'Ho, captain of the Zeelander! I am Sir Matthew Quinton, captain of His Majesty's ship the *Royal Sceptre*! You have fought bravely, but your ship is disabled beyond hope. There is no dishonour if you surrender in such circumstances. And if you do not, I will wreak upon you the full force of England's righteous vengeance! I call upon you to strike your colours, Captain!'

There was silence. Long minutes of silence. We were nearly alone; most of our ships, and all of the Dutch, were already past us, still running for the east, toward the Weilings and the Dutch fleet's harbours. I could see men scurrying about the quarterdeck of the Zeelander, and could imagine the scene. The officers would be in conference. Perhaps her captain, whoever he might be after Admiral Banckert's departure, was a diehard patriot, holding out against sullen warrant officers who wished to surrender; or perhaps the captain was a coward and his subordinates were trying to force him to fight to the death…

'Ho, Matt Quinton!'

The voice coming across the water was a very familiar one, albeit one I had not heard for three years, since the last time that Cornelia and I visited her parents and home town. The voice of a friend. The voice of a friend whom I had very nearly murdered in cold blood.

'Pieter? Pieter de Mauregnault?'

'That it is. Captain Pieter de Mauregnault of the *Tholen*, flag captain to Vice-Admiral Banckert. And you may be a knight of England now, Matt Quinton, but you still owe me a flagon of ale at the Sign of the Ostrich in Veere.'

During the two-and-a-half years when I lived in exile in Veere, before the King's restoration, Pieter de Mauregnault had become a good friend. A big, bluff, bellowing fellow who loved life, he was a rarity in a town thronged with gloomy Calvinists, and a blessed relief from the tedious company of my wife's parents and brother.

He reckoned that his irreverent attitude and love of drink owed much to his French ancestor, a century and a half before.

I tried to be as jovial as I could, given the imperative of the moment and the horror of realising what I had very nearly done. Of what I might yet do.

'I cannot promise you repayment in the same surroundings, Pieter. But you can have your choice of the taverns in London or Bedford, if you will surrender your ship.'

'Surrender my ship, Sir Matthew? Now why would I do that, precisely?'

'You are sinking, man! You cannot manoeuvre. You cannot fire a broadside. You're undermanned – how small a skeleton crew did Banckert leave you, after taking off most of his men?'

Pieter de Mauregnault shrugged.

'We are still Dutch. We are still Zeelanders. So even if we had only one man left, we would not be undermanned. We do not surrender, Sir Matthew.'

I remembered Pieter's stubbornness. When we were young, it had seemed an attractive trait. But now, with the rage still far from gone from my surging blood, it served only to remind me of the power I could unleash with one word of command.

'Look at the position of our ships, man! You know what will happen if you refuse. You are condemning your men to death.'

'Come and try to board us, my friend, and then see what condemned men can do!'

'I don't intend to board you, Pieter, because I know how Zeelanders fight. Even my wife, by God. You'll lose, but you'll kill many of my men before you do. And I've lost enough men, these last two battles. Too many good men. So we do things the English way.'

Friend or not, my fury demanded satisfaction. Friend or not, this was a Dutch flagship, and it would pay. Friend or not, Pieter de Mauregnault would pay.

I raised my sword, then dropped it.

One gun in the forecastle, and one only – a demi-culverin – belched flame. Some of the glass and framing in the *Tholen*'s stern windows shattered.

'What is this?' I cried. 'Who has dared to countermand my orders? *Who has done this?*'

But they all looked at me like a stony-faced bench of judges condemning a man. Francis Gale, Phineas Musk, Julian Delacourt, Urquhart, Burdett, even Lord Rochester. Not one of them gave himself away, nor anyone else. To this day, I do not know who modified my order so that my time-honoured command would unleash only a single warning shot, not the full force of our broadside. A final chance for Pieter de Mauregnault, a man I called my friend, to see sense. Some would call it mutiny. Perhaps some would call it saving the soul of Sir Matthew Quinton. For some reason, though, all I could think of in that moment was my unborn child. My half-Dutch child.

I looked across to the *Tholen*, and saw Pieter despatch a man below. The fellow was back within the minute, and said something to his commander. But Pieter de Mauregnault said nothing. He simply stared at me, across the two-hundred years or so of water that separated us.

'The whole battery is loaded with the same ammunition, Pieter,' I shouted, trying my hardest to recover my composure and authority. 'Canister and grape shot to kill your men. Chain and bar to bring down your remaining rigging. We will sweep your decks relentlessly, until the blood flows from your gunports. We will rake you with impunity, all night if necessary, for your own fleet will be safe behind its sandbanks by then, and no-one will come to save you. We will slaughter every man of your crew, Pieter. We will still have your ship, and you and all of them will have died in vain.'

Still my old friend said nothing. Then, at last, he raised his voice trumpet once again.

'Well, Matt Quinton,' he said, 'if I'd known that the nervous, gangling boy I drank with in the alehouses of Veere would turn into such a vicious, murderous, devilish bastard as you, I'd have drowned you in the harbour there and then.'

He turned, and nodded to one of his men. The fellow went to the staff, and slowly hauled down the Dutch colours.

The cheering began on the gundecks of the *Royal Sceptre.* It echoed from one end of the ship to the other. The shouting followed in short order.

'Glory to England and Saint George!'

'God save the King! God bless Sir Matthew!'

'A fat prize, boys, and riches for all!'

I saw John Tremar and several others of my Cornish following down in the ship's waist, and they were bellowing another cry.

'Glory to Cornwall! Glory to Saint Piran!'

I could not cheer. I had no words; none at all. Countless competing emotions, but no words.

Far forward on the bowsprit, Lord Rochester's monkey, the first lieutenant of the King's Prick, swung upon the jackstaff, where the red, white and blue colours of the Union Flag briefly enveloped it. Then it shat into the sea.

The English are a fickle race.

In the immediate aftermath of the redeeming victory of St James's Day, the calamity of the four-day fight suddenly seemed a distant nightmare, a temporary aberration upon England's divinely ordained road to a victorious, imperial destiny. And very soon, an even greater calamity, one which I witnessed – indeed, one in which I hazarded my life – came upon the kingdom: namely, the destruction of the city of London by fire. No-one, from the king downward, still demanded a scapegoat for the division of the fleet, which was all but forgotten. There was no more talk of traitors, nor of hanging, drawing and quartering. This was a mighty relief to Beau Harris above all, who continued to command the *Jupiter*; and if every seaman in the kingdom mocked him behind his back for not being able to tell the French fleet from the Spanish, Beau had a skin more than thick enough to bear it, especially as he had the love of Bella Mendez to sustain him through it all.

But time passes. Events move from the feverish tempests of the present into the calmer waters of the past. Men have an opportunity to reflect, and that reflection is shaped by the prognostications of the most idle, malicious peddlers of mendacity: that is to say, historians. And the historians, denied the truths that my brother and I discovered in the summer of that fateful year Sixty-Six – the *annus mirabilis*, as that fawning scribbler Dryden called it – these same historians concoct elaborate fantasies to prove how very clever they are. So it has been with the division of the fleet. It is now holy writ that, because of the report of one ignorant gentleman captain, the fleet was fatally divided and Prince Rupert was sent west to attack a non-existent French fleet reputed to be approaching the Channel. Thus George of Albemarle, that pure and virtuous old English hero, was forced to fight against impossible odds. And, of course, this was all the fault of that devious, fornicating mountebank, King Charles the Second.

I could refute the historians. I could write my own history of those events, the true history, in which Albemarle's own arrogance and duplicity would be proved, the Prince's ambition exposed, and the gullibility and bungling of the king's ministers brought into the light. Above all, I would damn the historians for depending on the evidence in the *Gazette*, and warn my fellow Englishmen that whatever they do, they should not believe what they read in those infernal outpourings of rancid untruth, the so-called news-papers.

But I will not write such a history.

For one thing, I doubt if anyone would believe it – 'ah, but he is so very old, his brains must be addled'.

For another, I doubt if anyone would care. It was a very long time ago, and an England ruled by turds like Robert Walpole and George Wettin, while being eaten away from within by gin and Jacobinism alike, is not a place where historical truth is greatly prized.

And for one final thing, to write such a history would force me, at last, to confront that same truth.

I denied that self-same truth when I told young Ned Hawke about the four-day fight. I denied it in the days after I came back from Plymouth, when my thoughts were filled with the prospect of fatherhood. I have denied it to myself for sixty years and more. But this truth niggled away at me over the years, whispering in my ear when I was in a dark mood, sometimes giving me disturbed nights and strange dreams.

For according to this strange, unwelcome truth, I was responsible for the division of the fleet.

Of course, my rational self has no truck with such a perverse notion. How could the young Sir Matthew Quinton, a mere captain who played no direct part in the promulgation or acceptance of the false intelligence, bear such a responsibility? How could he, who was at sea when the orders were given, have played any part at all in bringing on the calamity that followed?

But my less rational self sees it thus.

In the first instance, I told Beau Harris the story of my grandfather and the false ensigns. I planted in his mind the notion that the fleet he saw off Lisbon could only be that of France. True, Beau's intelligence reached Whitehall only after the order to divide our forces had already been given; but his letter reinforced the sense that the approach of the French fleet had to be true, and thus fatally delayed an order to recall Rupert.

That, in itself, would be an insignificant matter.

In one sense, so, too, is the responsibility I must bear for the death of Nathaniel Garrett, the poor creature whom I assumed to have been slaughtered for his knowledge of the French army at La Rochelle. Upon my arrival in Plymouth, I put out the word that I wished to interview him. As he revealed during his interrogation by Francis Gale and myself, Ludovic Conibear convinced himself that I had come to Plymouth, not to investigate the division of the fleet – which, of course, he could not know – but had instead come down from London to investigate *him*. Conibear feared that my public appeal for Garrett to come forward meant that I somehow knew of his dealings with Kranz, and that Garrett might testify to their alliance, and illegal and treacherous partnership in the illicit trade in smuggled French wine. So Garrett had to be killed; and inadvertently, I caused that murder.

Of themselves, these matters would not have been sufficient to give me sleepless nights many times, these last sixty years.

But there is another.

The fact is that I can recall exactly what I said to Prince Rupert of the Rhine, when we were alone in his laboratory at Whitehall on that fateful spring day in 1666, long before the fleet was divided.

'... nought but madness. Englishmen do not like a double-headed monster leading them. I am minded to resign my commission. Let them send out George Monck on his own and see how the fat old turncoat fares. Yes, I am certain I will resign. Now, tell me of your uncle Tristram's experiment with feeding mercury to a monkey –'

'But Your Highness – you must not do that! You must not resign, sir.'

'Quinton? You seem strangely animated in this matter. But no, whatever you say, I am set upon it. If I cannot have the sole command, then I will not go to sea at all. Monck can go alone. He brags constantly of how he beat the Dutch the last time, of how he will do so again. Very well, then, let him go and try to prove it.'

'But Your Highness, think of the greater honour to your name if you were at sea! What if His Grace of Albemarle really were to trounce the Dutch once and for all, and you to have no part of it –'

'Monck will not beat the Dutch, Quinton. Trust me in that. And when he does not, the King will not send his brother – his heir – to sea again, at least for as long as his barren Queen gives him no child. So he will have no choice. Once Monck fails, he will have to turn to me.'

'Perhaps, Highness. But if I may do so with respect, sir, I would repeat the case. What if Albemarle, and Albemarle alone, destroys the Dutch? We nearly did so last year, as Your Highness will recall. And this year, we have more and better ships, while the Dutch letters say that they are even more divided and fractious than ever, with province set against province. Sir, how bitterly would you regret it if you were not there when we ended their pretensions at sea once and for all?'

'You argue a good case, Quinton. You should have been a lawyer. But

then, perhaps your uncle Tristram taught you well.'

'That he did, Highness. And who knows, sir – once the fleets are actually at sea, all sorts of unexpected exigencies may occur. There may be an opportunity for you to revise the King's instructions, and to reorganise the fleet to your own liking – to fly your own flag in your own ship, and to have your own command.'

'Yes, a good case indeed. Very well, Quinton, I will think on it. Yes, indeed. I will think well upon it.'

That he did. So it was I, and I alone, who persuaded Prince Rupert not to resign his commission. In part, this was self-interest of the worst kind: I feared how I might fare under the sole command of the Duke of Albemarle, that ardent opponent of gentleman captains. But at the time, I convinced myself that it was also for the honour of England that the fleet should be at least jointly commanded by a prince of the blood, not solely by a former Commonwealths-man. I did not trust George Monck, who had turned from Royalist to Roundhead, then back again, and obtained a dukedom for himself in the process. I did not trust a man who had effectively ruled England during those frenzied months before the Restoration: who was to say that in the aftermath of a great and final victory over the Dutch, Monck would not use his popularity to seize power, oust the King and make himself Lord Protector? Perhaps thinking such thoughts was a kind of temporary madness on my part. But whatever the cause, it meant I was determined that Rupert should go to sea.

But I also persuaded Prince Rupert to snatch at any opportunity for an independent command of his own – that is, at any opportunity to divide the fleet. When that opportunity came, founded on the false intelligence of the French fleet and the army at La Rochelle, Rupert did indeed snatch at it; for if the prospect of defeating the Dutch was attractive to him, how much more glorious was that of defeating the French, and humbling the mighty Sun King himself! And, of course, the Duke of Albemarle, confident of defeating the Dutch on his own even with a depleted fleet, was only too keen to acquiesce. So by persuading Rupert not to resign, and to go to sea instead, I virtually guaranteed that the fleet would be divided; whereas if Albemarle had gone out alone, who knows what he might have done with an undivided fleet?

As I look into the flames flickering in my fireplace, I see the ghosts of all those who perished in the Four Days' Fight: Sir Christopher Myngs, for instance, that most modest and unlikely of legends, and above all, my poor friend Will Berkeley. I see the men who died aboard the *Royal Sceptre*: Hollister, whose brains Kit Farrell blew out; Lancelot Parks, going mad and jumping over the ship's side; Philemon Hardy, that worthy seaman, his head split open by the whipstaff; young Denton and Scobey, whose hopeful futures were snuffed out by a single cannon ball. I see them all, and when I am in the worst of my cups, or the blackest of moods, I blame myself for their deaths. Yes, others took dubious intelligence at face value, and others made the decisions. Certainly, Albemarle was duplicitous. Rupert was ambitious. The king's ministers were incompetent; although, when are they not?

But I was the one who committed the original sin. I brought about the division of the fleet, the Four Days' Battle, and the slaughter that ensued.

The very few in whom I have confided these thoughts tell me that I am being foolish, that my chance remarks cannot possibly have led directly to all that followed. But I know differently. An oak has to grow from an acorn. When a murder is committed, which is the greater cause: the ready presence to hand of the fatal weapon, or the fact that the murderer was ever born in the first place?

From my desk, I take out a fading yellow paper. *A Satyr Against Mankind*, it says upon the title page: a poem by John Wilmot, Earl of Rochester. The noble lord has been dead for nearly half a century now, killed by the pox that was already eating into his flesh when we fought together in the Four Days' Fight. I read his words again, and I wonder if Rochester somehow managed to look into both my soul and my future, during those days when we stood together on the quarterdeck of the *Royal Sceptre.* For his words describe exactly the nagging doubts that have troubled me for sixty years and more.

Then old age and experience, hand in hand,
Lead him to death, and make him understand,
After a search so painful and so long,
That all his life he has been in the wrong.

THE END

Historical Note

The plot of *The Battle of All The Ages* is centred on the longest, as well as one of the largest and hardest, sea battles in the entire age of sail. Between 1st and 4th June 1666, the British fleet under George Monck, Duke of Albemarle, and Prince Rupert of the Rhine, fought a colossal duel in the North Sea against the Dutch fleet under Michiel Adrianszoon De Ruyter, the Netherlands' greatest admiral. The British were weakened by the fact that Rupert had been detached to confront a French threat believed to be approaching from the west, but when it was clear that this decision had been based on false intelligence, he was recalled and rejoined Albemarle on the third day. The battle featured some remarkable individual events, such as the loss of the huge flagship the *Royal Prince* (her commander, Sir George Ayscue, remains the only British admiral ever to have surrendered in action) and the suicidal attack by Sir William Berkeley and his *Swiftsure*. It is also one of the best illustrated naval battles of all time: the famous Dutch marine artist Willem van de Velde the Elder was present, sketching from a boat throughout the action, and his drawings, now preserved principally at the National Maritime Museum, Greenwich, and the BoymansVan Beuningen Museum, Rotterdam, formed an invaluable research resource for this book. The British fleet was ultimately defeated and forced to retreat into the Thames, having suffered the worst attrition rate among commanding officers in the entire history of the Royal Navy, before or since. But in an astonishing feat by seventeenth-century standards, the dockyards repaired the shattered ships and got the fleet back to sea within seven weeks, where they inflicted a defeat on the Dutch during the St James's Day fight. This book follows the events and timings of the two battles very closely, although certain aspects of the sequence of events during the Four Days' Battle, notably the bewildering series of tacks and passes on several of the days, have been simplified to prevent confusion and ennui.

Incredible as it may seem, the government of King Charles II really did base its decision to divide the fleet in part upon the intelligence from just one seaman, who had been held as a prisoner of war at La Rochelle and disastrously misinterpreted the purpose of the army that he saw being massed there. I have moved the home of this individual from Warwickshire to Plymouth for the purposes of the narrative, and have killed him most gruesomely, a fate which did not befall him in real life! Equally incredible, a gentleman captain – actually Charles Talbot of the *Elizabeth* – really did decide that the fleet he saw off Lisbon could only be that of France, despite the evidence of flags and ship design pointing to it being that of Spain, which is what it was. Again, I have relocated his ship's landfall from Falmouth to Plymouth, but otherwise the sequence of dates of his sighting of the fleet, of despatching his letter to London, and of its appearance in the *Gazette*, complies exactly with the historical record. All in all, the sorry saga of how the fleet came to be divided in 1666 is a salutary reminder that 'dodgy dossiers' and the like have always been with us.

In writing this book, I have drawn above all on the work of Frank Fox. His stunning account of the battle, first published in 1996 as *A Distant Storm* and then in a very different format in 2009 as *The Four Days Battle of 1666*, is an example of naval history at its best. True, it is an account of a battle – now a somewhat unfashionable genre in academic circles, which are notoriously fickle – but its command of the political and logistical realities surrounding that battle is peerless as a demonstration of just how such an account should be written. His reinterpretation of the causes of the division of the fleet, which I have used as the basis of Matthew's adventures in Devon, is a classic piece of historical detective work and revisionism, shattering long-held myths through a painstaking analysis of the evidence. It was Frank who overturned the long-held view that Rupert was sent west to prevent a conjunction of the French and Dutch fleets, and presented incontrovertible evidence that Charles II's ministers were driven more by alarm over the perceived threat of a French invasion of Ireland. It was also Frank who finally laid to rest the old canard about Captain Talbot's responsibility for the division of the fleet. Best of all, though, his book is written as accessibly and dramatically as any novel! I've been fortunate to be able to call on Frank's friendship and expertise for well over two decades, and I know very few experts in their fields who are as unstintingly generous with their time and advice. Frank also commented on early drafts of sections of this book, saving me from a number of errors and infelicities, and demonstrated his customary helpfulness, gentle encouragement, and precise command of the detail. Consequently, there was never any doubt at all about the identity of the dedicatee of this, the fifth journal of Matthew Quinton.

With one exception, the fictional *Royal Sceptre*'s stations and actions during the battle essentially mirror those of the *Fairfax*, a ship of almost identical force; again, I owe Frank Fox a particular debt of gratitude for suggesting to me that she would be the ideal ship for my purposes in this novel. By fictionalising her role, and making Matthew her captain, I have excised from history the valiant part played by her men and especially by her captain, Sir John Chicheley (c.1640-91). I feel a certain degree of guilt for so doing, having written the entry on Chicheley in the *Oxford Dictionary of National Biography*. However, Chicheley has served as one the principal models for Matthew Quinton since I first conceived of the character. Like Matthew, he served in the Mediterranean before the second Anglo-Dutch war; like Matthew, he held several commands in quick succession; like Matthew, he was knighted, aged twenty-five, for his outstanding conduct at the Battle of Lowestoft; like Matthew, he was devoted to the interests of his extended family. Unlike some of the other officers whose real lives I drew upon to create Matthew's 'CV', they were even exactly the same age. Sir William Coventry, secretary to the Lord High Admiral, the Duke of York, called Chicheley 'the best of the young seamen' of the age, which is as fine and appropriate an epitaph for him as any that I could conceive.

The one major exception to the principle of directly substituting the fictitious *Royal Sceptre* for the real *Fairfax* is the night action at the end of the first day of the Four Days' Battle. The ship that actually fought its way through the Dutch fleet in such astonishing fashion, killing Admiral Cornelis Evertsen in the process, was Captain John Harman's *Henry*; the part in saving her that I have assigned to Kit Farrell was played in real life by Lieutenant Thomas Lamming, who was similarly rewarded for his heroism with the command of a Fourth Rate frigate. In fact, the *Henry*'s escape was even more remarkable than the *Royal Sceptre*'s, as she successfully fought off *three* fireships, not two – but if I had faithfully replicated the third attack, it would have taken the ship much too far from the scene of the action to enable her to participate in the rest of the battle! I followed the same principle of directly substituting the *Royal Sceptre* for the *Fairfax* during the Saint James's Day battle, again with just one exception: the *Tholen* was actually taken by the *Warspite* (but the flag captain of the former really was one Pieter de Mauregnault of Veere in Zeeland).

The Royal Marines date their foundation to the establishment of the Lord Admiral's Regiment in 1664, and the force gained its first battle honours during actions like Lowestoft in 1665 and the Four Days' Battle in 1666. Sir Peter Lely's famous double portrait of Sir Frescheville Holles and Sir Robert Holmes, perhaps the most vivid depiction of any of the seamen of the Restoration age, can be seen at the National Maritime Museum, Greenwich, and on the museum's website. Holles is shown in right profile with a cutlass in his remaining hand, Holmes in a characteristically flamboyant turban. Other historical characters to appear in this book include the knighted British sea-officers William Berkeley, Robert Holmes, Christopher Myngs, Edward Spragge, and, of course, the notorious libertine and poet John Wilmot, Earl of Rochester. Wilmot really did serve in the battle, albeit with Spragge, and displayed remarkable – or, as others put it, foolhardy and near-suicidal – courage under fire, although not in the way I have described it in this book. (It is not known whether Lord Rochester had a monkey in 1666, or if he did, whether it accompanied him to sea.) The story of the funeral of Sir Christopher Myngs is taken, nearly verbatim, from Pepys's diary. Perhaps I have wronged Sir William Coventry by suggesting that he forgot about the men's offer to man a fireship; but on the other hand, there is no evidence proving conclusively that the offer was ever taken up. However, there is ample evidence for the Duke of Albemarle's hatred of gentleman captains, and for the reluctance of both the Duke and Prince Rupert to operate in a duel command.

Although I invented Captain Jacob Kranz and his *Duirel*, the depredations of Dutch privateers on the coasts of Britain during 1666, and the previous history of the Dunkirkers, are matters of historical record. For the former, see in particular Gijs Rommelse's excellent account, *The Second Anglo-Dutch War*, published by Uitgeverij Verloren in 2006. Similarly, the character of Ludovic Conibear is fictitious, although he is based loosely on Henry Heaton, the real Navy Agent at Plymouth during the Interregnum, and on an even earlier holder of the same office, the notoriously corrupt James 'Bottomless' Bagge. I wrote the account of Plymouth and the navy during this period, and that on its naval agents, for the *New Maritime History of Devon.* For the history of Sir Bernard De Gomme and the construction of the Royal Citadel at Plymouth, see Andrew Saunders' comprehensive book, *Fortress Builder* (Exeter, 2004).

Finally, Edward Hawke, the unemployed young naval officer who appears in the Prologue, became one of the greatest British naval heroes. He won stunning triumphs at Cape Finisterre in 1747 and Quiberon Bay in 1759, the latter being described as 'one of the supreme acts of seamanship in naval history' (Ruddock Mackay and Michael Duffy, *Hawke, Nelson and British Naval Leadership, 1747-1805:* Woodbridge, 2009). Hawke died in 1781 after serving successfully as First Lord of the Admiralty and being elevated to the peerage as the first Baron Hawke. One of the truly great fighting admirals, his insistence on aggression was encapsulated in his order that no ships were to open fire until they were within pistol shot of the enemy. His example is generally recognised as having been one of the most important influences on a man who, at the time of Hawke's death, was a precocious young post-captain of twenty-three, roughly the same age that my fictionalised Ned Hawke would have been when he presented himself before Matthew Quinton. There can be little doubt that if it really were to look down from the Elysian fields, Matthew's shade would undoubtedly have raised many an invisible glass of nectar to the immortal memory of Horatio Nelson.

J.D. Davies
Bedfordshire
April 2014